D0296893

The
WOMAN
who
DIVED
into the
HEART
of the
WORLD

Sabina Berman was born in Mexico and is her country's most commercially successful and critically acclaimed playwright. She has won the Mexican National Theatre Prize an unprecedented four times and has written film scripts, poetry, prose, and journalism in addition to her work for the stage. This is her first novel.

The WOMAN who DIVED into the HEART of the WORLD

Sabina Berman

Translated by LISA DILLMAN

SIMON &
SCHUSTER

London · New York · Sydney · Toronto · New Delhi

A CBS COMPANY

Originally published in Mexico and Spain in 2010 under
the title *La mujer que buceó dentro del corazón del mundo* by
Editorial Planeta, Mexico, and Ediciones Destino, Spain
First published in Great Britain by Simon & Schuster UK Ltd, 2012
A CBS COMPANY

1 3 5 7 9 10 8 6 4 2

Simon & Schuster UK Ltd
1st Floor
222 Gray's Inn Road
London WC1X 8HB

www.simonandschuster.co.uk

Simon & Schuster Australia, Sydney
Simon & Schuster India, New Delhi

A CIP catalogue record for this book is available
from the British Library

Hardback ISBN 978-0-85720-192-8
Trade Paperback ISBN 978-0-85720-193-5
Ebook ISBN 978-0-85720-194-2

n, CR0 4YY

1

… the sea …
  … and the white sand beach …

The sea flecked with sunlight all the way out to the horizon.

Then the white sand beach, where the waves roll in, dissolve into foam. And, up in the sky, a sun full of white fire.

I'm thirsty.
  I'm going to stop writing and go get a glass of water.

*

And then, suddenly, 1 day, a girl, wearing socks and huaraches, sitting on a red blanket on the white sand, her knees pulled up against her chest. A skinny, gawky girl, rocking back and forth, whispering:

Me.

Over and over:

Me.

Me.

A skinny girl in a big white T-shirt that billows up with wind, her legs bent, her knees drawn up against her chest. A girl whispering into the wind, into the sea:

Me.

Me.

Then a wave rises up and crashes down and the girl loses herself in the din, she disappears from herself, she's not there. What happened to Me? The fragile being made of words has vanished and in its place is only a vast Not-Me: the sea.

I'm going to get another glass of water.

Someone leads her into the wind, takes her by the hand—the skinny, gawky girl, her white T-shirt down to her thighs—and spreads a red blanket on the sand and sits her down and tells her what to say. Repeat:

Me.

Me.

This happens over and over, every afternoon of every day, this sitting on the sand and rocking back and forth and saying Me and this self disappearing in the roar of the wave that crashes and dissolves into foam that skims quickly over the sand.

My aunt Isabelle, as she later told Me, had come from Berkeley, California, to Mazatlán, Sinaloa, to take possession of her inheritance: a tuna cannery called Consuelo, which means Consolation. Consolation Tuna. The most ill-conceived name in the fishing industry on the face of the planet, as a marketing specialist was to inform us many years later.

1 day, my aunt Isabelle stepped off a plane that shimmered in the sun on the runway of the tiny Mazatlán airport, all dressed in white—white linen slacks, white blouse—with a wide-brimmed straw hat and big black sunglasses, and walked across the runway with her right hand clasped to her head so that her wide-brimmed straw hat wouldn't blow away.

She went straight from the airport to the tuna cannery. Her inheritance was valued at several million dollars.

The cannery took up 2 entire blocks—consisting of 2 gigantic cement structures and 1 cylindrical, glass building— and ran from the street all the way down to its private docks: 4 parallel docks where 20 anchored tuna boats sat bobbing in the water.

She hated it. My aunt did. The cannery, I mean. The smell of saltpeter mixed with the rotting stench of dead fish.

Dressed entirely in white linen, wearing giant sunglasses with round lenses, she stepped into the first windowless cement block and stopped at the worktables where, beneath the buzz of a cloud of flies and down the length of 8 tables, women stood mechanically gutting the fish.

She decided to cast her eyes higher, at the cloud of flies, and asked:

Why the hell don't you use insecticide?

Because, señora, her guide replied, the chemicals in the insecticide would contaminate the tuna.

She dared, then, to look down.

At the tables, the women worked methodically. The first would slice open the fish with a machete, as if pulling down a zipper in its side. Then she'd pass the fish to the next woman, who thrust both pink latex-gloved hands in all the way up to her elbows to yank out all the viscera with 1 swift tug and hurl them over the table, into the pile of red, pink, and violet viscera covering the floor. The third woman hacked off the head with a machete blow and heaved it into the bin beside her.

Sickened, my aunt Isabelle covered her mouth and sped on her white, wooden-heeled sandals across the pink foam-covered floor—a mix of seawater and tuna blood—rushed into a bathroom where 100 flies were flitting around and the smell of dead fish blended with that of fresh shit, and before she could make it to a toilet, she vomited into the sink.

The worst was still awaiting elegant Aunt Isabelle.

A taxi took her through a town full of squat, cement houses and potholed asphalt streets—asphalt that glinted like steel in all that sun—and dropped her in front of the house that my great-grandfather—my aunt's grandfather—had bequeathed her.

Behind a courtyard of dried-out yellow grass and giant palm trees with huge, dejected, desiccated fronds, the white, 2-story, French-style mansion with pompous battlements running along the top was in ruins. A mansion with black-and-white checkerboard marble floors where the air got cool, but steel girders hung down from the destroyed ceiling and the windows either had no panes or had cracked glass and broken wooden sills. A French mansion built in the 19th century by my great-grandfather, founder of Consolation Tuna.

In the master bedroom with windows overlooking the sea, the 2 mattresses on the big, king-sized bed had rotted and 1 had a hole in the middle of it, a crater that had become the hub of an ants' nest, red ants that marched single file down each of the 4 legs of the bed and under the gaps beneath the 4 doors, sallying forth down the 4 hallways leading to the 12 bedrooms on the second floor.

So the first night my aunt slept in a hammock she found in the living room, hung between 1 Doric column and another Doric column and close to another large, windowless window that also overlooked the sea.

And when she was half-asleep, as my aunt Isabelle has since told Me, she heard footsteps and then felt someone's breath on her face.

Terrified, she opened her eyes and there stood a creature with a tangled mass of hair covering half her face. She was a dark, naked thing, and Aunt Isabelle could barely make out her large eyes beneath the matted clump of hair, a wild thing staring at her fixedly.

Who are you? Aunt Isabelle whispered.

And the thing took 2 steps back.

Aunt Isabelle got up out of the hammock quickly and the thing took 2 more steps back.

Aunt Isabelle took 2 steps forward and the thing ran away, more afraid of Aunt Isabelle than Aunt Isabelle was of it.

Aunt Isabelle watched it take off down the stairs like a shot in the dark blue air, running for the basement. She heard it bolt the wooden door, heard the tremendous racket made by things being hurled against the basement walls, a tremendous racket that soon increased, accompanied by horrifying howls—like a dog, like a coyote—coming from the thing, and it lasted, Aunt Isabelle said, 2 or 3 hours, making it impossible to concentrate on anything else. She went to her suitcase and took out a bottle of whiskey, threw herself down on the hammock, and drank half the bottle, taking long swigs, but not even that drowned out the terrible racket and let her fall back to sleep, until finally, close to dawn, it ended, after 1 long, final howl.

When she awoke, the marble floor and white walls reflected the noonday sun and she heard a dry rattling coming from the kitchen.

It was Gorda, leaning over the counter, turning the handle

of the coffee mill. Gorda: the fat, dark-skinned house servant, wearing a black fabric belt that bisected her body and made her look like an 8, with huaraches on her chubby-toed feet.

The 2 women greeted each other, Gorda tipped the ground coffee into a pitcher of boiled water, and poured it through a strainer into 1 glass, and then into another, in silence, and although they only knew of each other from third-party references, the 2 women sat down at the table together and immediately began writing in a notebook all the things the house would need.

Provisions and cleaning supplies on 1 list, people they'd have to hire on another. Permanent: a gardener, a butler, and a chauffeur. For 1 week: an ant exterminator. For 1 month: a marble-floor polisher. And for 2 months: 12 construction workers to repair the walls, put glass in the windows, and bring in the furniture, when it arrived in the trailer.

At a certain point, Aunt Isabelle got up from the table, lit a cigarette and, leaning against the stove, told Gorda about her encounter with the thing the night before.

Ah, the girl, said Gorda, laughing softly.

The girl?

She lives here. Nobody told you?

Who do you suppose would have told me?

Your sister, of course.

Gorda was still chuckling.

She actually forgot to tell you about the girl?

I didn't speak to my sister before she died, my aunt said. We weren't close.

Ah, well. There you have it.

And why does the girl live here?

Gorda considered the question before replying.

Charity, I believe.

On the blue-tiled kitchen wall, a machete hung from a nail. My aunt Isabelle snatched it up and headed down the basement stairs, Gorda right behind her. Behind the door, she found a gloomy cellar that reeked. It was littered with broken wood and pieces of furniture and shattered bottles, and after turning a corner she was temporarily blinded by light. In 1 wall, a big, bright, light-filled hole looked onto a turquoise pool of seawater. A pool of seawater contained in a wooden corral, some 50 meters from the hole in the wall, in whose corner stood—water up to her waist, thin as a black line in the turquoise liquid—the thing.

The thing sank down beneath the surface and reemerged with something red and wriggly in her hand, a red fish that slipped from her grasp and slid back into the water. She erupted with laughter.

She seems happy, Aunt Isabelle said.

Oh, yes. She's always either happy, angry or spaced out. Those are the 3 options. Should I call her?

Call her.

Gorda stuck 2 fingers in her mouth and whistled like a mule driver.

The dark girl turned to look at them, wet hair plastered to her face. Very slowly, she walked toward them. But every 3 steps she stopped, fearfully.

She doesn't speak, Gorda said, she just grunts.

The girl was dark skinned, ashy and skeletal—so skinny her rib cage stuck out.

Gorda continued:

She doesn't eat with silverware, she eats with her hands, no matter what you give her, and if she's by herself she eats wet sand.

Aside from the mat of hair on her head, the girl was hairless: not a single hair on her body, not even between her legs.

She spends all day in her cave in the basement or in her little ocean pool, stark naked the whole time. And she's afraid of everyone but me. With me, she's tame as can be.

Gorda smiled and said:

Tame as a doggy.

*

At Aunt Isabelle's insistence, Gorda bathed her in the marble tub in the master bedroom. She scrubbed her with a brush meant for floors and soap meant for dishes, and finally she broke through the crusted-on filth to expose pink skin. Her thick, matted hair was so stiff and tangled that Aunt Isabelle abandoned the idea of cutting it into any predetermined style and ordered Gorda to cut it however she could, lopping it off at the scalp with a scissors, and then Aunt Isabelle herself shaved the head with a razor, while the thing sat, gaga, in the steamy tub, drooling.

They pulled her from the tub, bald and pink and naked, and wiped the drool from her mouth and sat her down on a bench. She was so skinny that her knees were as wide as her thighs, her rib cage so prominent you could count each rib. Her finger- and toenails curled around like snails. They had to use pliers to cut them, the kind builders use to cut copper wire.

My aunt stared at the newly clean, bald thing with faraway eyes, the thing that now smelled like dishwashing liquid, and then she noticed something on her back: a wound. A wound that ran from her right shoulder all the way down to the left side of her waist. And there was another scar on her left thigh. A long scar. And 1 on her right arm and several circular scars on her left.

She was horrified.

Her eyes met the girl's faraway eyes. And they were green. Light green.

Aunt Isabelle lit a cigarette and asked Gorda into the bedroom.

Tell me 1 more time, Gorda, why is it that this creature lives here?

Like I said, charity, señora.

That's just a line. Tell me the truth.

My aunt stood at the open window, a breeze blowing away the smoke from her cigarette, which she held close to her face.

Well, who knows, really. I always say, when people ask, that it's because your sister took pity on her.

And 1 more time, how long has she been living like this?

All her life, as far as I know. When I started here she was already in the house. Or rather, under the house, in her little sea pen in the basement, and when guests came, your sister had me take her out to the woodshed, at the far end of the grounds, so if she got mad nobody would hear the fuss. You saw what a ruckus she kicks up.

Aunt Isabelle slowly exhaled smoke.

And was she beaten?

By who? Your sister?

Or you. Or anyone. How did she get these scars? Tell me.

Well, I didn't do it, Gorda said defensively.

So it was my sister? She demanded.

There were days when señora hit her, Gorda said, looking away. She'd lock her in a room and take a belt to her, the buckle end. I heard the girl scream and I kept cooking. Nothing I could do about it.

Aunt Isabelle kept smoking, staring through the window at the sea.

Gorda recommenced:

She was dim from the crib, you know. That's why, I think.

What does that mean, dim from the crib?

You know. A dimwit. Simple. Born soft.

And that's why, what?

Why your sister lost her temper with her and hit her, why she kept her locked away.

But those right there are burn marks, my aunt said, her voice tight. Christ, beating a girl is bad enough but burning her? Anyone who burns a girl should be locked up.

Gorda kept her lips pressed tightly together. Finally she whispered:

Well, I tell you what. If you sleep on the floor like that, the roaches will get you. A few of the scars might be from that.

Aunt Isabelle snorted. She had another question:

When my sister died, did she call the girl in to say good-bye?

Gorda looked down.

Your sister was very hard, señora, if I may say that. Your sister died alone. After the embolism her body got very stiff. She walked funny, stuck out 1 leg first, then the other 1 a while later. Hands bent up like claws. She even had trouble breathing, in that wheelchair. So she got 2 kids from the cannery to load her into her jeep and she drove off down the mountain road. Later the police said that marks on the pavement showed that on a sharp curve, high up in the hills, she didn't turn, as if the road kept going straight.

Aunt Isabelle said:

Keep going.

There's not much else to say. People said her leg must have gotten stuck on the accelerator. But I knew her and I know that's not what happened. Same way she'd throw away food even if it was just a little off, same way she'd see a plant and say to me, Gorda, blight got its leaves, it's no good anymore, pull it up, and throw it out. Well, I know she said to herself, You're no good anymore, either, and just kept driving straight when the road curved.

A wave broke on the beach, 1 floor below them, and then spread across the sand with a hiss.

Weeks later, Gorda continued, some peasants found the jeep upside down at the bottom of a ravine, among the prickly pear cactus, and her body a little way from it. She was just bones by then, and not even all of them. Her rib cage, skull, arm bones, and the fingers of 1 hand. That's all. The buzzards must have eaten her flesh. And the other bones— who knows?—maybe the coyotes took them.

Runs in the family, Aunt Isabelle said.

What does, señora?

Being hard. Did you bury the bones?

We buried them in the garden, but all the tombstone says is her name. Lorena Nieto. We didn't put a cross or anything. We didn't know what religion she was, or who to ask.

She wasn't, Aunt Isabelle said. The Nieto family has no religion. Gorda, I'm going to ask you something, and please tell me the truth.

Yes, señora.

She's my sister's daughter, isn't she?

The thing?

The thing.

Gorda didn't say anything for a while. Then she said:

No. How could that be? They don't even look alike. Besides, she'd have said something about it at some point, don't you think? And she never said a word.

What about her eyes?

The girl's? Her hair's always in her face, I can't even remember what they look like. Are they green?

Light green.

Your sister's eyes were brown, Gorda said.

Aunt Isabelle turned to stare at her, with her light green eyes.

That was what made her mind up—my aunt's mind. The light green eyes. That's what made her so certain that the thing was her niece, and so she set herself the task of turning it into a human being.

To start, she tried to get her to say her first word:

Me.

Me.

Me.

She'd take her by the hand and lead her to the beach, spread a red blanket on the burning sand, and sit her down, knees drawn up into her chest, and the thing was supposed to say Me, Me, into the wind and the sea.

And that is how, on August 21, 1978, Me came into being, there by the sea, screaming my lungs out, Me, Me, bald and fully formed, wearing knee socks and huaraches.

2

You.

My aunt says it was just as hard to teach Me the second word:

You.

She'd refuse to feed Me, sit Me down at the wooden kitchen table, and sit opposite Me, a plate of shelled walnuts beside her.

Then she'd point to herself and say:

You.

And look at Me and I'd say:

You.

She'd give Me a nut and I'd wolf it down.

Then she'd look at Me and say:

Again. Look carefully.

She'd point to herself and ask:

Me?

And she'd look questioningly at Me and I would protest, pointing to my chest and saying:

No! ME!

Then there would be no nut for Me and my stomach would growl.

You, she'd say, pointing to Me.

Oh, it drove Me crazy. ME! I'd shriek, pounding my chest. ME, ME, ME!

No, for Me, you are You and I am Me, she claimed, and don't throw hissy fits.

But I did. Big ones. Terrible. I'd throw the chair, screaming, and kick the table leg, 1 time, 3 times, 30 times, screaming and screaming, while my aunt sat, shaking, and watched Me, or picked up a newspaper and began reading, until finally she, too, would scream:

SIT DOWN!

And I would sit back down, panting with unspent fury.

Sometimes the fury overpowered Me and when my aunt shouted I would snatch up a glass and hurl it against a window, which shattered into 1,000 pieces while I ran to steal the dish of nuts that my aunt would then confiscate from Me, walnuts falling to the floor as I pounced, trying to grab them. But she'd pull Me up, her arm around my waist, while I howled like a starving dog.

What the hell she wanted from Me, I had no clue.

I'd wriggle free of her grasp and run to the beach, falling to my knees to bring a fistful of sand to my mouth. Hot, salty sand. By the second lick, it would fly from my hand, forced open by my aunt, who was there specifically to keep Me from eating sand.

She'd leave the butler standing guard, watching Me, all set to kick my fist if I filled it with sand and raised it to my mouth again, and I'd wear myself out crying and howling and rocking back and forth, drool dribbling from the corners of my mouth.

Until I evaporated. Until I disappeared and there was nothing left of Me.

Just thinking about our furious You and Me classes is giving Me a headache right this minute.

And I'll concede 2 more things:

1. Even now, 32 years later, I still can't quite accept that anyone, with the exception of Me, could ever be a Me.

2. I still think that glass shattering into 1,000 pieces is the most wonderful sound in the world.

But my aunt wouldn't give up her stubborn idea of turning Me into a human. Or something that could pass for human.

How she came up with the electrical outlet thing, I have no idea. She ordered a long electrical cable, several yards long, with a black plastic plug at 1 end and 3 cables at the other: 1 red, 1 yellow, 1 blue.

She'd tie the wires to my belt and then plug the other end into the outlet in the wall. And that was how we had class. And if I started to run off, or to disappear, she'd shout at Me and tell Me that I was connected, I was plugged in, and she'd tug the cable and I'd come back.

Why it worked, I don't know, but it did. I suppose because I understood that the blender and the vacuum were turned on and made a huge racket as long as they were plugged in and turned on, and to Me, there was no difference between the blender and the vacuum, and Me.

At any rate, the fact is that when I was connected at the waist and plugged in to some wall outlet somewhere, I could venture through the house alone, go from room to room with no fear of getting lost or becoming terrified if I came across something strange, like a construction worker halfway up a ladder whitewashing a wall, and I couldn't lose Me, the way I did the time I followed an ant around on all 4s and forgot all about Me.

I woke up to someone patting Me on the head and was startled when the beam of a flashlight hit my face. It was nighttime and I was sitting on an unfamiliar beach, covered in ants from my tangled hair to my toes, and someone was whispering da da da da da.

Someone who was Me.

In time, if a panic attack was imminent, or if I was about to disappear, I learned to grab the cable with both hands and follow it back until I got to my plug.

And after You and Me came other words. My name (Karen). The name of my aunt (Isabelle) and of figure 8 Gorda (Gorda). Plus: chair, table, window, floor, lamp.

My aunt would stick little pieces of colored paper to things and write the things' names on the little pieces of colored paper so she could remember what she called them. But something mysterious happened.

1 day I said:

Floor, and with my index finger I spelled out f-l-o-o-r in the air.

My aunt stood gaping.

She pointed to the chair and I said:

Chair, and in the air I wrote c-h-a-i-r.

My aunt threw a party that night, with cake and glasses of milk for Gorda, the butler, and Me. And while it's true that learning to speak and read and write when you're over 3 feet tall is not statistically speaking any sort of extraordinary feat, it was fabulous, for my aunt and for Me.

She taught Me to use a pencil on a piece of paper and saw that it was true that I had memorized the letters of the names of the things and I would fill pages and pages with my writing—an oversized, clumsy imitation of my aunt's.

The house was overrun with colored labels. On doors. On hammocks. In the kitchen, each object had a label and when she cooked Gorda had to remove them, wash the things, and then put the colored labels back on. The chauffeur, the gardener, and the butler all wore labels on their chests, which read "chauffeur," "gardener," "butler." And my second-floor room, near my aunt's room, was full of pieces of paper covered with random words.

Soon my aunt switched from little colored pieces of paper to colored plastic and names began appearing on things in the air. 1 afternoon my aunt went out onto the balcony and saw a label at the bottom of the swimming pool, and a label on each of the trunks of ash, avocado and willow trees, and labels on some branches and on some leaves and on a nest, and on the very end of the highest branch of the tallest willow in the garden, she glimpsed a yellow label around the little foot of a brown bird with a red chest, which surely said r-o-b-i-n.

I say it was fabulous, for my aunt and for Me, until I became more confident, and then it was torture. Suddenly, I was talking nonstop. I'd string words together with no rhyme or reason.

Chair rose flesh fridge blender window day. Window night lamp headlight moon butterfly black.

I'd giggle gleefully and applaud myself after each new string of terms.

My aunt bought a radio and left it turned on all the time. Her hunch was right. Soon I was repeating everything. The weather forecast for this winter afternoon, winter afternoon, calls for light rain and sun, sun, followed by clouds, clouds.

The repetition of words brought about by the echolalia I've never managed to overcome: a sort of echo I add to myself, sometimes.

I'd wake myself up talking. The governor has decided to

build a dam, a dam, in the southeastern part of the state for the indigenous communities who live, live there and now a word from our sponsors Coca-Cola relax with the pause that refreshes Coca-Cola.

I'd go into the library to wheedle information from my aunt, who sat at the typewriter typing. What does dam and southeastern and communities and pause mean?

1 day she pointed to a gigantic book that lay open on a wooden lectern.

You can find every single thing in the whole world inside that book, she said.

It was great-grandfather's giant dictionary, a pale-brown leather-bound dictionary with very thin translucent pages full of tiny letters, where, of course, you could not find every single thing in the whole world, just the name of every single thing in the whole world and a lot of colored pictures.

I make note of that because it's been the biggest difference between my aunt and Me: she thinks that words are things in the world, whereas I know that they are simply pieces of sound and that the things of the world exist with no need for words.

At any rate, the lectern with the gigantic dictionary became a place for Me to be quiet. I'd only stop talking when I went—mouth agape—to look up a word on 1 of its pages, or when I disappeared, or when I slept, which is the same as disappearing but horizontally.

But when I returned, boy, I talked nonstop, a walking radio. I'd fall asleep talking and laughing at words that were funny to Me and wake myself up talking. It became torture for Gorda and the butler, who'd see Me coming and ignore Me, while I filled the space with my voice.

Could you at least *sing* the songs? Gorda asked 1 day, emptying a sack of potatoes onto the kitchen counter.

But I didn't sing them. Songs I heard on the radio, I recited in my monotonous, nasal, unmodulated voice. Where oh where can my baby be the lord took her away from me she's gone to heaven so I got to be good so I can see my baby when I leave this world.

Leave this worrrld, I repeated, noting the way my tongue curled back on the r. Worrrld, I repeated. Worrrrrrrrrrrld! And I shrieked with laughter.

Gorda kept peeling a potato into the sink, resigned.

Maybe it's time she started going to school, said my aunt.

I walked into the classroom the first day, saw nothing but dwarfs and weirdos, and went straight to a corner. So I don't

know what my first week of classes was like, because I spent
it staring at the angle where the 2 walls met.

Anyway, it was all very strange. It was as if they'd rounded up
every ignoramus in town (and the vicinity) and brought them
all to the same place. Or should I say, that's exactly what they
did: assemble all the nitwits from Mazatlán and thereabouts,
enroll them, and keep them entertained.

Everybody there was either mentally retarded or crazy, or
crazy and retarded. There were 4 kids who looked Chinese,
who I later found out were Mongoloids, and they laughed at
everything—which really means they laughed at nothing.
There was a tall, skinny nut who would suddenly start jerking and twitching as if he'd been electrocuted and then fall
to the floor and twitch some more until Miss Alegría stuck
a spoon in his mouth, and then he'd spend the next few
hours drooling. There were the wobblies, as they called them:
5 kids who spent all day in wheelchairs with their heads
lolled over to 1 side and a leg jutting out to the other, waving
their hands in the air as if they were trying to fan their faces
but with their hands too low. And there was a retard that

went around with an electrical cord tied to her waist plugging herself into all the wall sockets until she found the best 1 and then, once plugged in, sat and stared out the window at the red tile patio with yellow walls—and the socket freak was Me.

There was also a white cat that often slunk onto the patio and then turned in circles and sprawled out in the sun. Sometimes a flock of seagulls flew overhead. Or a mouse scurried up the only tree trunk on the patio and I watched it scuttle from branch to branch, until it finally took 1 giant leap and vaulted over the patio wall.

That type of thing kept Me enthralled and drooling all day, my forehead pressed to the windowpane.

And suddenly at the hottest part of the day, with no prior warning, lunacy would break out: some kids would start spinning around and around on their axles, screaming; the electrified idiot would have 1 of his jerking attacks; the Mongoloids would hurl themselves to the floor and roll around; the wobblies would be wobbling in their wheelchairs; I would recite the time like the operator used to do, but at the top of my lungs; and Miss Alegría would pull out her knitting and knit very quietly, sitting in her chair.

I didn't like school 1 bit.

Everyone was a lot like Me, but that's irrelevant. I don't like myself very much.

Every morning the chauffeur forcibly pulled Me out of the station wagon and, clasping Me to his waist, carried Me inside while I kicked and flailed, and once inside the classroom he'd deposit Me on a table, tear-streaked and exhausted from the struggle, my hair plastered down with sweat.

Miss Alegría would smile and say:

Good morning, Karen, welcome.

But there were a few appealing things about school. We got to submerge our hands in buckets of paint and paint the walls with our fingers. And they taught us to tie our tennis shoes. And put on our socks. And to put on our socks first and then tie our tennis shoes, which works out better.

They lined us up single file and took us out, each dimwit rubberbanded at the waist to the next as we walked down the street, and we had to read the names of the streets and wait for the light to turn red before we could cross in front of the cars to the other side.

And they took us to museums to learn how to use the restroom in a public place. All the "women" went into the women's room and all the "men" went into the men's room, which is very important to get right, Miss Alegría said. And we had to go pee and poo *in*side the toilet, not *be*side the toilet.

Which is another thing it's very important to get right, said Miss Alegría.

It was always a big mess because the Mongoloids pulled all the toilet paper off of the rolls and strewed it all over the bathroom. Or the electrocutee stuck his penis into any hole he could find in the tiled wall and jerked against the tiles until a sticky white liquid came out and his eyes rolled back in his head. Or a wobbly sitting in his wheelchair would spray the mirrors with urine by aiming his penis—which was 15 centimetres long—like a hose. Or the tireless Mongoloids would pour all of the liquid soap from the dispensers onto the tile floor and call us all, "men" and "women," into the bawdy restroom and we'd all skate from wall to wall as soap-suds bubbled up on the floor.

That was how we got to know all the museums in Mazatlán, which are a grand total of 4.

The Mazatlán Museum of Folklore, where in glass cabinets they keep huaraches and rattles and pots and clay figurines and things like that. The Mazatlán Museum of Archaeology, where in glass cabinets they keep huaraches and rattles and pots, but very old ones. The Mazatlán Museum of Justice, where behind glass they keep old clothes and old papers, and where we never saw anybody except ourselves and 1 little old man, who was the caretaker and who followed us from room to room as if he wanted to be 1 of us dimwits, but every time we got to the exit Miss Alegría would point her finger at him and send him back in. And the Mazatlán Museum of Natural Science, a dark place full of dead animals with their claws out, kept in illuminated glass cases that made the whole gang of nitwits and retards shriek and left Me with my mouth hanging open in fear.

Led by Miss Alegría, we'd march across them all single file, rubberbanded to one another at our waists, headed for the truly attractive feature of the museums as far as Miss Alegría was concerned: the bathrooms. And I remember that seeing all that shiny glass, all those display cases and cabinets, made Me want to shatter a few.

I never broke any glass in those museums, but even now, as an adult, if I visit a museum, the temptation makes Me clench my fist and causes Me to salivate.

But back to Miss Alegría.

With her infinite nunlike patience, Miss Alegría taught us

that everything 1 does from the waist down and the knees up must be done alone, in secret.

How must you do it?

Alone! The crazies shouted in unison.

Because everything you do with that part of your body is ugly. Ugly, she repeated. What is it?

Ugly! We cried.

And whom do we tell about it?

Nobody! We shouted like a chorus of imbeciles, which is, in fact, precisely what we were.

And what are the 2 forbidden parts of the body?

We all clenched ourselves between the legs, first in front, and then pointed to our butts, to indicate the anus.

Very good, Miss Alegría congratulated.

I think the only reason we were in school was to give people at home a break.

Sometimes I'd sneak out of class and go out to the patio to trap the white cat. A cat with lots of fur that was always very clean and very white, with little pink pointy ears and little pink paws. I'd sit on the tiles and stroke her back and her belly, and the cat would meow. And then I'd lie down, face up, and she'd walk on Me with her little pink paws and I'd meow.

Then Miss Alegría called Me back to class and the cat followed, winding in and out between each of my steps without letting Me step on her.

We became friends and when I sat down she sat on my lap and snuck under my shirt to lick the sweat off my skin and then poked her head out the neck hole, emerging to sit on my head like a heavy hat.

1 morning, Mongoloid number 3 decided to drag her around the room by the tail like he was mopping the floor with her, despite the fact that she was yowling like mad. So I smacked the stupid Mongoloid in the head and he fell down, and I dragged him by 1 foot around the room like I was mopping the floor with him, despite the fact that he yowled like mad.

That was the beginning of an inexplicable story.

1 afternoon, after I had come back to my aunt's house, I discovered the white cat sitting on 1 of the black floor tiles of the black-and-white living room floor, cocking her head to 1 side and gazing with her little blue eyes.

Aunt Isabelle asked Me several times:

How did the white cat get here?

I have no idea, I replied several times.

How did she get here, Karen? Concentrate. Did you steal her? Did she follow you?

No idea!

Don't tell Me she walked halfway across Mazatlán and just happened to end up here at the house!

I HAVE NO IDEA! I screamed.

My aunt knows I don't lie. It's not that it doesn't appeal to Me; I just can't. As I found out much later, I simply don't have the neuronal connections required to lie.

So my aunt stopped insisting.

But since that time, sometimes things I really, really like a lot later appear at my house. That's the 1 thing I'm lucky about.

My aunt asked Me what we should name the cat.

You, I said.

Bad name, she said.

Gorda offered another option. Nunutsi, which means "little girl" in Gorda's native language, Huichol. My aunt nodded, and Gorda said to Me:

Now she's the little girl, not you.

I'd spend afternoons at home, reading my great-grandfather's books. I understood almost nothing, but what mattered to Me was learning new words. I would write out each new word in my big, clunky writing and then go stand before the lectern where the dictionary was kept and look it up. Then I'd pin the pages of new words to the walls of my room with colored tacks.

The kind I liked the most, and still like the most, are nouns. Nouns are the things that are most like things. Things that are grabbable, audible, smellable, and sometimes have the added bonus of being alive, like birds, cats, fish, ants, turtles.

I also very much like the names of colors, which are things that are almost not things. I mean, colors are things that just barely exist. Between being and not being, they are like miracles. Green, blue, yellow, black, white, red. It's very funny to Me that there are colors at all, when it would be so easy for there not to be.

But verbs in the future tense I found impossible. How could you talk about a time that doesn't exist and nobody knows what it will be like when it does? Something inside Me was incapable of thinking about the future, the same void that keeps Me from lying.

Every night while I was in bed, I read my new words aloud, reciting the words tacked to the walls so that I could make them a part of Me, until my eyes wouldn't stay open any longer.

*

1 afternoon I was in my great-grandfather's library with my aunt. A library with 4 walls lined high with books and a big table in the middle. At some point I realized that my aunt had stopped typing and was watching Me read.

I traced the lines of letters with my index finger and underlined a word with my pencil; then I went to the lectern and thumbed through the pages of my great-grandfather's dictionary until I found the word, copied it down in my big, slow writing, and went back to the book and placed the sheet of paper with the new word in a stack of sheets of paper with new words.

What are you reading? my aunt asked.

Little Women, by Louisa May Alcott.

That was the first book I read, she said, pleased. Let's have a look.

I gave it to her. She turned it over in her hands. A book with very worn, green binding and yellowed pages. She flipped through it. She stroked 1 page in particular.

Yes, this was my book, she murmured, and kissed a page, which made no sense to Me. Do you like it, Karen?

I don't know.

What do you mean, you don't know? Wait. Tell Me what it's about.

It's about ... a girl named Jo.

Right.

Who has a boyfriend and then Jo cuts off her hair to sell it and buy food for her family because they're hungry and then her sister who is prettier than her marries her boyfriend who is rich. That's what it's about.

But tell Me the story, Karen.

That is the story, I said, tensing up.

But what about all the little things in between?

Those are just little things in between, they don't serve any purpose. You take them away and it's still the same story.

My aunt thought that over for a little while, squinting her eyes. That's how she thinks when she's thinking very hard. And finally, she concluded:

Well, you're right. You know, you have a very special kind of intelligence. But tell Me this: do you like it?

Do I like it? I asked, because I didn't understand the question.

What do you feel when you're reading it?

I feel that I'm reading it, I answered, getting flustered.

Don't you sometimes feel sad, or, I don't know, maybe like you want to cry?

No! And I banged my fist down on the table.

And my aunt's eyes filled with tears.

You feel nothing, she said very quietly.

Well, that was something of an exaggeration. 28 years later, recalling and writing what my aunt said, I know how to reply. I do feel some things. I feel fear, almost all the time. I feel happy, when something happy happens. And I feel pain, if someone hits Me or I hit myself.

And, when it gets late, I feel sleepy and I also feel hunger when I get hungry.

It's true, though, that I seem not to feel all those complicated things and imaginary things that standard humans feel.

Standard: normal, typical.

Standard humans: humans within the norm.

I don't feel those 101 things that are somewhere between pain, fear, and happiness, or between hunger and sleepiness. Which, the way I see it, is to my advantage.

I mean, I know that I am dimwitted, at least compared to standard humans. I know that on standard IQ tests I score somewhere between idiot and imbecile. But I have 3 virtues, and they are big ones.

1. I don't know how to lie.

2. I don't fantasize, so things that don't exist don't worry Me or hurt Me.

3. I know that I only know what I know, and that what I don't know—which is a lot more—I am sure I don't know.

And that, like I said, over the long run has given Me a big advantage over standard humans.

My aunt kept looking at Me. She'd stopped crying but she was kneading her shoulder with her right hand as though someone had punched her.

She said to Me:

Karen, I want you to listen to me and not forget my words. Never let anyone make you feel like you're less than they are. You're not less, you're different. Different from the majority. Atypical would be the precise word. Do you understand that, Karen?

And I said:

I have to poo.

I headed toward the bathroom but on my way out of the library I saw the cat and cried, Nunutsi! and crouched down to bump noses with her. She leaped up onto my shoulder and I could see that my aunt was still squinting and watching Me, taking in the way I scratched the cat's back and she licked my face, and then finally with the cat on my shoulder I went to poo.

When I returned my aunt Isabelle had made up her mind how I'd spend the rest of my life.

I wouldn't go to the retard school anymore; instead, a private teacher would come every afternoon to teach Me only what I wanted to learn, and in the mornings I'd start going with Aunt Isabelle to the cannery.

Do you like that idea? my aunt asked Me.

No idea, I said.

Come here, she said.

She hugged Me, and I stood stiff in her embrace.

3

Mr. Rodrigo Peña, the general manager of Consolation Tuna Ltd., wore thick, coke-bottle glasses with thick plastic frames and a short-sleeved shirt darkened with sweat under each arm, and the whole time he spoke he kept centering 3 pencils on top of the desk, then moving 1 to 1 end of the desk and another to the opposite end, then repositioning all 3 back in the middle, opening a drawer, extracting another 3 pencils, placing 2 inside a jar, and inserting the third into a marvellous contraption from which it emerged sharp and pointy. I looked on in awe the entire time while he, as I said, talked on and on about who knows what.

I think Mr. Peña was even more "atypical" than Me.

Nevertheless, he finally asked Me what I thought about the

grave crisis that the tuna fishery would be facing in the near future.

I twisted my mouth.

He stroked his chin.

He said:

Yes, difficult to know when you're in the dark.

He asked:

Where would you like to begin your investigation?

The dimwit actually didn't appear to realize that in addition to being atypical, I was only 15.

I answered with utter sincerity:

What I really want to know is if the factory uniforms will fit Me.

Peña looked Me over carefully.

I'll be right back, he said.

He walked out of the office, and I watched him through the glass as he made a phone call. When he returned, he said, Alright. Your aunt has agreed so that's the way it's going to be, and he held out a hand.

I don't shake hands, I said. I don't touch people.

Ah. Well, that's fine, too. And he slid his hand into his pants' pocket.

So I spent my first day at work at the cannery trying on all the uniforms.

The drivers': a gray T-shirt with "Consolation Tuna Ltd" in red lettering on the back.

The tuna can box-loaders': identical to the drivers'.

The cleaners' and the tuna gutters' and the canners', which were all white with very elegant accessories, also in white: plastic caps to keep hair out of the way; face masks; stiff plastic aprons; huge pants tucked into plastic boots; and latex gloves in a stylish pink.

The sailors': white T-shirt, denim shirt and pants, and white plastic boots.

The divers': blue neoprene suit with a spectacular gold zipper down the front, green fins, green mask, and a mouthpiece connected via a tube to a great, big orange tank to be worn on the back.

The wetsuit turned out to be a discovery that changed my life. The neoprene compressed my skin, the mask covered my eyes and nose, the mouthpiece barely allowed Me to breathe through my mouth, and the weight of the tank seemed to pin Me to the floor, but the overall effect of it made Me feel—I don't know why—safe. Protected. Out of harm's way. A safe distance from standard humans. With uniform pressure on my body that made Me feel steady.

And everyone else at the factory loved my wetsuit, too.

I'd traipse all over the fishery dressed in the wetsuit, taking huge floppy steps in my green fins, and the women at the gutting tables laughed at Me as they gutted tuna, and the whole billing department would look up from their desks and laugh at Me, and on the docks the stevedores unloading salt-packed tuna from the boats' holds would stop to look and from behind my glass mask I could hear them laughing at Me.

Me and my wetsuit were the joy of Consolation Tuna Ltd.

1 day on the pier I saw something that changed my life. I know that it was only about a page ago that I said that the wetsuit changed my life, and I think that before that I wrote that working at my great-grandfather's fishery changed my life. But at that point in my life, my life was changing on a very regular basis.

3 sailors hauled a swordfish up from a speedboat and dumped it onto the wet concrete dock. The swordfish was still moving: it thrashed its tail, smacking it against the cement; it writhed to 1 side, opening first 1 fin and then the other; and all the while, it drew in air through its mouth, beneath the sword.

And I, from behind my diver's mask, watched the sailors do what they did. With 1 steel hook they skewered the swordfish's tail as it writhed, and with another hook they impaled its mouth, which let out a violent gasp.

At that moment a euphoric Mr. Peña arrived, taking great strides, and over his radio he ordered someone to bring a camera and then kicked the swordfish 3 times with his shoe, kick, kick, kick.

Bastard won't die, I heard him say from behind my mask.

The sailors and Peña laughed.

And Peña kept kicking the fish with the tip of his shoe as they chatted with each other, looking into each other's eyes, grasping each other's forearms, smiling at each other, ensconced in their standard human world, while at our feet the swordfish kept snorting through its open mouth with its gills fluttering quickly.

The standard human world: a bubble where nothing that isn't human is really seen or heard, where only what's human matters and everything else is either background, or merchandise, or food.

I was trembling with rage, or with fear, I wasn't sure which, and my heart was beating forcefully, pounding. I would have given each of them a blow to the head but I understood that they weren't like the Mongoloid I'd knocked down with a single smack to make him stop hurting the cat; there were 4 men here, and every 1 of them was stronger than Me.

Peña saw Me standing apart from them and motioned Me over. When I didn't move, he came and took Me by the elbow and pulled Me into his circle of humans. But standing there in my wetsuit, I was very far away.

And there, standing close to them but far away, I realized that that was how it would always be for Me—close to humans but far away.

Many years later, many words later, many books later, I found a page in an old tome written by a French philosopher: a sentence that expresses in words my distance from humans.

I think, therefore I am.

The sentence astonished Me, because it is, obviously, incredible. All you need is 2 eyes in your head to see that everything that exists, exists first and then does other things.

But here's the most incredible thing about it: the philosopher isn't proposing that as a concept; he's simply articulating what humans believe about themselves. That first they think and therefore *then* they exist.

What follows on from that is even worse: that since humans live that way, thinking that first they think and then they exist, they also think that anything that doesn't think, also doesn't fully exist.

Trees, the sea, the fish in the sea, the sun, the moon, a hill or a whole mountain range. None of that exists all the way; it exists on a second plane of existence, a lesser existence. Therefore, it *deserves* to be merchandise or food or background for humans and nothing more.

And what makes humans so sure that thinking is the most important activity in the universe? Who told them that thought is the 1 activity that distinguishes the superior from the inferior?

Ah, thought.

I, on the contrary, have never forgotten that *first* I existed and *then*, with a lot of difficulty, I learned to think.

And every day that is my reality. First I exist and then, and only sometimes, and with great difficulty, and only when strictly necessary, do I think.

So, that's why I'm far away from humans.

They finally hauled the swordfish up onto a metal harness that was painted black. It was dripping blood and its gills were no longer flapping, except during brief intervals when it seemed to resuscitate, and inflated, and then deflated and grew quiet again.

The camera arrived and Peña called us all to stand with him beneath the dead fish, and we stood with him beneath the dead fish and someone took a picture.

That December the picture arrived in the mail at my aunt's house with the caption:

The Peña Family wishes you a very Merry Christmas.

A few weeks later, I think it was in February, the Mexican secretary of fisheries came to the fishery and they presented her with the silvery cadaver of the swordfish. They'd had it mounted on a long wooden board. Madam Secretary, who had extraordinary teeth that were twice the size of standard human teeth, accepted the cadaver with both arms open wide, and holding it thus, with both arms open wide, she turned to pose for the press photographers, her enormous smile revealing her double-the-standard-size teeth.

Her photo was printed on the front page of the Mazatlán paper beneath the headline:

Tuna Industry on the Verge of Collapse.

But getting back to the swordfish still dripping blood as it was hanging from the metal harness that was painted black. It was already stiff when they pulled it down and 3 stevedores led by a gleeful Mr. Peña took it away, and then I asked some other stevedores to hang Me from the harness.

I wanted to hang there like the swordfish, although it wasn't until after I was hanging that I understood why.

Hanging there in my wetsuit, breathing slowly, I could see the sea, glimmering and golden in the afternoon sun as though it were made of light, a sea of liquid light, and the sky a pale blue, almost white. From time to time a little sailboat would pass by in the distance and then disappear as it crossed the horizon. From time to time a V of black birds flew into the blue of the sky until they vanished.

I hung absolutely still but I didn't disappear, and I felt no fear of dangerous humans.

It became an obsession. I learned to get into the harness myself and I'd hang regularly.

Where is Miss Karen? The chauffeur would ask when he came to pick Me up in the afternoon to take Me to the house where my teacher awaited Me.

They'd call my name over the cannery loudspeaker, and if I didn't appear, the chauffeur would come down to the farthest dock to get Me, knowing that I'd be there at the end of it, hanging in the harness. The chauffeur would sit on a short cement post and smoke a cigarette to wait for Me.

I thought there was nothing better than floating there in

my wetsuit, hanging in the harness. I was wrong. There was something better.

Diving.

I'd sit on the boat's edge with my back to the water and let go, falling in backward so my head entered the water first, and then dive down.

At 5 meters the turquoise water of the Mazatlán sea starts to look green.

At 15 meters it loses its yellow and becomes light blue.

At 30 meters it's blue-blue, blue like ink, navy blue they call it, or deep blue.

It's in the deep blue where I've found the most elegant fish swishing.

The flat-bodied angelfish, shaped like a plate with a pink and green grid pattern and white lips.

The grey ball, 2 metres in diameter, that rotates on its axis and approaches as if it were suddenly going to gobble you up but then just swims by doing nothing more than flicking its 1,000 tails because it's actually 1,000 grey mackerel that are each 1 decimetre long.

The stonefish, that looks like a red stone but suddenly propels itself forward through the water and then drops and sits quietly again like a red stone on the red moss of a big rock.

The seahorse, which is the size of my middle finger and lives and sleeps standing up on the white sand at the bottom of the sea, swaying as it curls and uncurls its tail.

Sea creatures are silent people, which is why I like being among them. They don't speak, and therefore they don't make up things that are not real.

They are what they are and nothing more. And nothing less, either. They think with their fins and their tails and their eyes and their mouths, which open and emit silvery bubble thoughts.

And they're not cruel. A lobster moves on its eight legs and gobbles up a lost mackerel whole, but it doesn't kick it first and doesn't laugh while watching the mackerel that is scared to death die of that very fear. It just swallows it, and that's that.

And jellyfish.

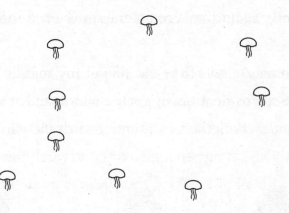

Writing about jellyfish makes Me laugh. There is more black ink in the word jellyfish than there is in a whole jellyfish. They're made of water. Clear water that appears luminous in the navy blue water. With no heart and no skeleton and no brain and no eyes, they descend in groups of 10 or 12 like aquatic skydivers, ribbons of water streaming from their big heads.

Watching them go down in groups enthralls Me and I have to shake my head in order to rouse myself, draw the pistol from my belt, and take aim.

Because my great-grandfather's marine dictionary warns that some jellyfish are very poisonous, and others are deadly: if they rub against you, in 1 second your throat constricts and your lungs pop.

When I shoot my black ink they rush up toward the

surface, expanding and contracting their big heads to propel themselves away.

Sometimes I find a flat rock and rest my head on it and wait for my body to float down onto it and just lay there on the white sand. I check the tank's timer and set the alarm so it goes off when I've got just enough oxygen to reach the surface.

And with all of Me lying there on the ocean floor, I allow myself just to be. To exist.

And the greatest possible happiness: to see.

Mr. Peña showed up at my aunt's house and, sitting at the navy-blue-painted wooden table in the kitchen, they began talking about money as they did every month.

Gorda served them jasmine tea and then stood in a corner in case they needed anything else. I wandered in and out, picking up snippets of conversation. This time their meeting was not short. They seemed to be in a lot of pain, they massaged themselves, Aunt Isabelle squeezing her shoulder or pressing her torso, between her breasts, Peña rubbing his hands together.

Look, Doña Isabelle, Peña said, holding out pudgy, peeling hands. They're excoriated; it's my nerves.

Esssscoriated, I repeated. Or exxxxxcoriated? Or escorrrrriated?

Karen, stop it! My aunt raised her voice. Not now, please.

Come sit with us, she said then. I want you to hear this.

And this is what "this" was: it was all going to hell. The U.S. was going to ban imports on Mexican tuna because a group called Clean Seas was making demands, and for us it would be a disaster. ½ of Consolation Tuna's sales were to the U.S., and if that came to an end then we'd have to think about getting rid of ½ of the workforce.

What would my grandfather have done? my aunt asked. She bit her bottom lip.

He would have fired them before the disaster, Peña said, not after, and he wouldn't have given them any severance pay, either, which by the way is legal in this type of crisis.

Gorda clucked her tongue over in her corner.

We're talking about 1,000 employees, Aunt Isabelle said. We're talking about 1,000 families' food.

I know, said Peña. But 1 minus 1 is 0 and 1 plus 1 is 2.

Which means? asked my aunt.

Which means, replied Peña the moron, that if Consolation Tuna goes under, there will be no work for them, and no work for the other 1,000 employees or us.

Aunt Isabelle spent the afternoon smoking and pacing the house, opening doors as if on the other side she might find someone waiting to give her advice, but in the empty rooms that overlooked the sea from each window or balcony, all she found was Me, her dimwit niece.

That night she spoke on the phone 10 times. And later that night she poured herself a whiskey, and then after a little while another 1 and another 1.

At midnight I found her in the darkened living room, zigzagging between pieces of velvet furniture in her light blue silk nightgown, and I took her by the hand and led her upstairs. She was so surprised that I took her by the hand that she let Me lead her.

She fell into bed. I lay down behind her and stroked her back with a tense hand, unaccustomed to touching anybody. She was cold and still, and I hugged her and whispered to her what I thought:

You always make the right decision. Don't worry.

She sighed. She smelled of rose perfume and whiskey. I scooted closer and wrapped my arms around her, stiffening at the contact.

My aunt said no way. I could not wear jeans and a T-shirt, my usual attire, nor could I leave my hair all tangled, as I did every day.

So after taking a bath, I sat naked on a bench before a

full-length mirror. My aunt stood behind Me with electric clippers and cropped my brown hair close.

Then, using a razor, she shaved the back of my neck.

Let me see, she said.

Nearly bald, I turned to look at her.

Very elegant, she said. Do you remember when the last time I cut your hair like that was?

No idea, I said.

Well, that's a relief, she retorted.

I stood beside her and saw for the first time, in the full-length mirror, that I was taller than my aunt.

Me: skinny and wiry, the taut muscles on my dark skin standing out, flat-chested, and now with 1 centimeter of hair on my scalp. Her: a think mane of blond hair, also skinny beneath her white towel, but with 2 bountiful breasts.

2 pairs of identical green eyes, light green, were the only reason to believe we were aunt and niece.

Or perhaps, I now think as I write this, it was the round, cherry-colored burn marks on my forearms and the vertical scar on my inner thigh and the diagonal 1 across my back that earned Me my alleged aunt's protection.

Your breasts will grow soon enough, she said.

Do they have to? I asked, troubled.

Which made her laugh.

She gave Me 1 of her suits, a white linen pants suit with jacket, but the pants were too short. Gorda let out the hems and then they fit, and I put on a pair of flat white sandals, also belonging to my aunt. She wore white as well: a dress that was like a shirt but without sleeves, also linen, that reached past her knees.

At the door she put a pair of black sunglasses on Me and put a pair of black sunglasses on herself, too. I looked at myself in her lenses and she looked at herself in my lenses and nodded.

She took my arm and we walked through the giant palm garden to the end where the chauffeur was waiting for us beside the black convertible.

The secretary of fisheries, a woman with black hair cut like a helmet, the 1 who had the extralarge teeth I've already mentioned, followed by the mayor of Mazatlán, paced step by step past our 20 ship captains, all wearing white, standing stiffly, their right hands to their sailors' caps, and when she got to Mr. Peña she held out her hand. Next she held it out to Me but my aunt intervened, leaning her head forward to whisper:

She doesn't shake hands; it's a phobia.

And instead she held out her own delicate, long, bony-fingered hand and instantly led her with her marvelous charm up the gangway of the *Chula Bonita*, on whose prow stood the Sinaloa Wind Ensemble playing a lively Heitor Villa-Lobos piece, according to what I have written in my notebook.

On deck stood the owners of the other Mexican tuna fisheries and their chief executives, all dressed in guayaberas, some in Panama hats.

We sat: our company executives and the government officials on a platform, and the owners of the other fisheries and their respective people facing the platform.

The first to step up to the podium's microphone was the mayor—a mustachioed fatso—who spoke at length, saying the same thing in different ways for 10 minutes and getting progressively angrier with each 1. That the Sea of Mexico is Mexico's sea. That Mexican Sea belongs to Mexico and not the gringos. That the gringos had their own damn sea, but it wasn't the beautiful Mexican Sea. Et cetera.

Next Mr. Peña spoke about something he called "national dignity," in his flat, inflectionless, atypical voice that nearly put Me to sleep.

Then the secretary spoke. First, she paid her respects to

many people who were not present. The president of Mexico. The secretary of the interior. The presidents of every country in Latin America—our brothers, according to her. Second, she greeted the tuna fishermen there present. Third, when the midday sun was at its most intense and members of the audience were beginning to pull out their fans, she spoke of the 5 U.S. vessels that the Mexican president had, quite rightly, ordered to be seized because they were fishing our waters, and of the U.S. unjust reaction to this occurrence, namely the banning of imports of Mexican tuna on the pretext that our fishing practices resulted in the unnecessary deaths of dolphins, and that the tuna were killed cruelly.

Ha! Madame Secretary exclaimed into the microphone. Are those not the very tuna that the United States wanted to abscond with for themselves?

And the tuna fishing public responded in unison:

Ha!

Of course dolphins die, Madam Secretary declared. Dolphins migrate with yellowfin tuna and of course some of them end up dying with the catch; that's the way it's been in tuna fishing since the days of our Aztec forefathers. What's more: how else are the tuna going to die, if not cruelly? Is death itself not cruel?

Those present, glistening with sweat, chortled at I don't know what and Madam Secretary continued:

Additionally, they claim that the tuna are "stressed," and standing before you here today, I would like to say to our neighbors to the north that yes, they do die and they die quite "stressed," because death tends to be a fairly stressful activity.

The tuna fishermen chortled again, applauding.

And as for Clean Seas, Madam Secretary went on, jabbing an index finger, this is what I have to say, from the heroic port of Mazatlán: you clean your own seas, because our seas, as the mayor has so rightly and courageously stated, are ours and nobody else's.

Resounding applause, and the fat mayor of Mazatlán stood and pumped a fist in the air.

The secretary held out 2 hands and patted down the air, and the mayor and everyone else fell silent, like dimwits in Miss Alegría's class.

The secretary promised swift resolution to the problem via the courts of justice of an international organization with a very long name that I didn't manage to memorize, and then invited the owner of the world's leading tuna enterprise to come up to the podium.

I'd never seen my aunt cower before. Hunching down in

her chair, she shook her head, looking horrified. My mouth was hanging open, having just realized that it was us, the Nietos, who owned the world's leading tuna fishery, and in order to save my aunt I raised my hand, and before I knew whether or not they were going to call on Me I strode over to the microphone.

Meetings with more than 3 people used to make Me anxious—still make Me anxious. That 1 had 154. Once at the microphone, I froze. The silence, the faces staring at Me, Peña extracting a pen from his shirt pocket only to slip it back in again, only to extract it again, and my aunt lighting a cigarette with trembling hands.

I fixed my gaze on the mike so as not to have to look at anyone and began speaking in my tense, flat voice, which came out too loud because I was scared.

Consolation Tuna Ltd. owns 20 boats, and each boat is worth an average of 17 million dollars, 17 million dollars. On the high seas each 1 has an average of 30 sailors and stays out from 2 to 30 days, setting an average of 100 nets. 5 boats have faulty radios and get lost an average of 18 days per year, and it's always precisely those 5, those 5.

I glanced up for a split second. The tuna fishermen were

listening with enormous interest. I refixed my gaze on the microphone.

The boats return with the tuna already dead, covered in salt from the brine in the ships' holds. The tuna are then transferred into red, blue, green or yellow containers, according to their size categorization—very large, large, medium, or small—and the containers are then stacked, stacked up in a cement warehouse where the rows of containers are hosed down with boiling water, and as it drains the salt water mixes with fresh blood, fresh blood, with fresh blood.

I heard someone in the audience repeat:

Salt water with fresh blood, that's true.

In a second workroom the tuna are then unloaded onto tables where women dressed in white with facemasks and their hair pulled back in plastic caps gut them, chop off their heads, pull out their eyes, and tear out their spines, and then they're transported on dollies to a third chamber, where they pass through a system that uses 5 machines to chop, chop, chop them up, can, can, can them in cans that are injected with olive oil or water, chopped vegetables or finely sliced chilies, pressure-sealed, and labeled with labels that say "Consolation Tuna Fish Made in Mexico," in Mexico, in Mexico.

In Mexico, repeated several isolated voices, made in Mexico, and laughter rang out here and there.

I began to cry, terrified, but when I program myself to do something I go all the way; I simply don't know how to deprogram myself. So I carried on, with a lump in my throat, my voice trembling, tears in my eyes.

70 women, 70 women, 70 women stack the cans in brown cardboard boxes, boxes of 14 cans or 28 cans, or extralarge ones of 56 cans, which in turn are loaded onto 1 of the 39 electric forklifts that transfer the stacks of boxes of cans to the lot where the trailers are filled while an inspector counts the number of boxes of cans of tuna. There are 35 trailers and every hour of the day they leave the lot and head for 1 of the 4 roads in the outskirts of Mazatlán that extend in all directions. 1 goes to the center of the country, another to the southeast, another to the north, and the other to the northeast where it crosses from Ciudad Juárez directly into the United States of America, of America.

That! I cried, losing control. That is what they do! 3 shifts per day! That has been the business of Consolation Tuna since the day my great-grandfather founded the company back in the 19th century, in Mexico, in Mexico, in the 19th century!

I closed my mouth. Engrossed in the microphone, I listened to the sea. It was crashing gently, rhythmically against the boat's metal hull. My linen jacket was drenched with sweat and tears, my black sunglasses were completely wet, and I desperately needed to urinate.

I returned to my seat without seeing, staring through the misty lenses at the platform's wooden floor. But Madam Secretary got up to place a hand on my shoulder, which I shrank from instinctively, frightened, hunching my back, and collapsed into the chair beside my aunt, whom I could hear weeping softly.

I took off my sunglasses and saw that several other people were crying as well, though I can't imagine why, since they hadn't endured the trauma of public speaking. Others sat with blank stares, lips parted, mouths agape like imbeciles.

Standing at the microphone once more, the secretary thanked Me for my emotional (her word) speech.

Young Karen has moved us all, she said, reminding us what it is we must defend. Thank you, again, Karen.

Those present stood and clapped.

The secretary continued:

And standing here before you, Karen, I promise you this: our tuna will enter the United States; whatever it costs, whatever it takes, come what may. Have no doubt about it.

They clapped harder.

Still standing, the tuna fishermen crossed their right hands over their hearts as the trumpets of the Sinaloa Wind

Ensemble blew a hymn that everyone sang at the top of their lungs, and that terrified Me from its first, threatening verse.

Meeeeeexicans, at the cry of war …

… at the resoooooooounding roar of the cannon …

… may the earth tremble at its coooooore …

Then came the swordfish cadaver mounted on the wooden board.

Peña handed it to her, and the secretary accepted it with arms open wide and a big smile with double-standard-sized teeth, and she turned to the photographers who snapped their photos, and the photo came out on the front page of the paper with the headline about us on the verge of ruin, and in the months ahead my aunt auctioned off 10 ships and fired 1,000 workers and employees, ½ our workforce, which was the same percentage fired by other Mexican Pacific coast tuna fisheries, and the stores and warehouses that supplied the fisheries closed down and on every Mazatlán street corner a beggar appeared with a little box of Chiclets to sell or squeegees to clean car windshields for a penny, and my aunt finally gave Me permission to go out fishing on the high seas on the condition that I try to learn English, and we didn't hear from the secretary of fisheries again until years later, when she was again on the front page of the paper.

She'd been elected president of the party that at the time was just concluding its 59th year in government: the Institutional Revolutionary Party, the PRI.

4

It starts on the high seas, the moment the lookout ensconced in the crow's nest sights little vertical spouts of water in his binoculars, approaching.

Those are dolphins, gray and gleaming in the sun, and they always swim close to the surface, breathing through holes in their heads. Much farther below, hidden, are the tuna. Silver, darting.

From the moment of the sighting, all action on board the ship accelerates.

Sailors rush up gangways and rush down other gangways, dressed in yellow windbreakers and white plastic boots. In their rushing up and down and back up, they pass the altar of the Virgin of Tuna in the passageway and go down on bended knee before her: a blue ceramic virgin with a silver tuna in her arms. They cross themselves and pray for luck, the fishermen, and hurry back to their duties.

The seine net is thrown from the deck into the water. A huge net with yellow floats. At that point, 4 outboard motorboats have already been lowered into the sea, and in each boat sailors attach pins to the net.

The boats spread out to set the net: when extended all the way, it forms a circle that measures ½ a kilometer in diameter. That's the trap.

Then the boats move closer to decrease the diameter and lower the trap. The only things visible are the yellow floats. And then comes the wait. The ship and the motorboats and the yellow floats bob silently on the sea's surface. As if nothing were happening.

But it is.

Dolphins begin swimming into the trap and, down below them, so does the school of tuna: a well-ordered gang, first go the mature tuna (those more than 7 years old), then the elderly ones (over 10 years old), and finally the young and the babies.

Once they've all entered the trap, the captain gives the order to begin the slaughter, clanging a bell from the deck.

And on the water's surface the human school springs into action once more.

The motorboats start moving in further to make the trap even smaller, encircling the school. The noise of the motors and the boats' foamy wake alert the fish. The dolphins leap up into the air and the tuna bug out their eyes, panicky. The motorboats stalk them, hounding relentlessly like cowboys herding cattle, 3 fishermen per launch, harpoons raised.

They ram their harpoons into the fish. The pilots, leaving 1 hand on the helm, hurl smoke bombs at the fish with their free hands. And again and again, the harpoons are plunged into the fish, impaling the tuna, who bleed. The water turns pink and frothy.

Then comes the noisy retreat, established as a result of the U.S. embargo.

The seiner reverses and the speedboats advance to form a channel with the net, a sort of chute on an incline from the sea up into the ship. Terrified, the tuna and dolphins react quickly, each species using its own survival tactics: the tuna band together, pressing body to body, and try to escape by sounding—swimming down toward the bottom—to their misfortune, because once in the deep they come up against the pursed net; while up on the surface at the opposite end of the chute the dolphins leap over the net and flee into the open sea, or most of them do, with the few exceptions who are trapped by the inexorable rhythm of the massacre.

The speedboats move quickly to form another circle and begin to trap the fish.

Imagine a drawstring purse. The circular net is drawn up like tightening a drawstring purse 50 meters in diameter and filled with panicking cargo that the speedboats continue to confine in a narrower and narrower space.

On deck is a sort of pail measuring 5 meters in diameter. Using a winch, the fishermen lower it into the net and fill it with silvery fish, now blood-covered. They haul it up full and with a great SPLASH it's upended, dumping the tuna out into a hatch that's been opened on deck for that purpose.

It's pandemonium: fishermen shouting, giving orders; triumphant cries when a large tuna, twice the size of a sailor, emerges from the bucket; the frenzied wheezing, like out-of-tune trumpets, of desperate tuna, their tails thrashing in the giant pail as blood gushes from their wounds, spraying the fishermen red; the boat rocking as the tuna drop from the hatch through a chute into the hold full of whitish brine that turns pink with blood.

The pandemonium doesn't end when the sailors close the hatch on deck and the hold has gone dark. Because that's when the tuna death chamber beneath their boots becomes a frenzied turmoil that goes on, and on, and on.

Until finally, gradually, it dies down and the sound is masked by the motor of the system's freezer.

When the brine freezes, the tuna suffocate to death. The tuna and the odd, unlucky dolphin.

Then the boat slowly changes course, slowly embarks on its next journey to find another shoal, sometimes days away, while the tuna in the brine in the ship's bowels begin to change color.

No longer silver, they start turning pink. Days later, green. And by the time they're unloaded onto the docks and the stevedores hoist them up onto their shoulders, covered in the brine from the hold in the bowels of the ship, they're black.

Fixation: attaching 1 thing to another.

Like the way I became attached to the same haircut—a crew cut—and wore it my whole life. Or the way the iron harness I liked to hang from was linked to my sense of calm. And diving was connected to my joy. In the same way, without initially understanding why or what for, I acquired another fixation.

I became fixated with the blood spilled in the sea.

When the slaughter was over, the sea would remain red and glossy. As if there were red plastic stretched out over it.

It rose and fell, slowly, red, as if it were finally breathing easy beneath the perfect blue sky, so full of light.

3 speedboats would be stowed back on board and I'd stay down in the fourth, whose hull was white, in the sea, that was red. The ship would slowly turn to change course. I would catch up to it later.

I don't know how it was that the same fisherman always ended up with Me in the boat. A dark man with lots of brown hair on his head.

There we'd wait in silence for the sea to slowly turn blue once more. For the blood of the slaughter to become diluted in the water.

The kill: the fisherman was the 1 who told Me that that's the term they use for tuna seine-fishing in Sicily, where he was born. A method that was centuries old, he said. At least 4,000 years, in fact, which was discovered because in a cave in Sicily, on an ochre wall that the sun lit up at noon, they found a drawing from 4,000 years ago that showed men with harpoons raised beside a large oval, which is a lake, in whose center are some diamonds, which are tuna, and 1 diamond has a harpoon jutting out of it.

It was also the fisherman who told Me that Italians call fish and seafood "fruits of the sea." *Frutti di mare*. As if the sea were a tree with foliage made of water and the fish and seafood were its fruit. A metaphor I disliked, for its inaccuracy.

So where's the trunk? I asked.

What trunk?

The water-tree's trunk.

He didn't respond.

1 day out on the red sea, he uncorked a bottle covered in straw.

Chianti, he said.

He sniffed the cork, poured us 2 clear plastic glasses, and taught Me to drink red wine in little sips.

Red wine is the fermented juice of the vine, he explained, as if reciting something he'd learned by heart. But red wine is also the blood of the earth. It has to be drunk slowly, to give it time to enter the heart.

As a young man, in the month of May, he would set off from his town, taking a bus to reach Palermo in time for the bluefin tuna kill. A kill that had not changed in centuries. 4 wooden longboats full of fishermen set a net out in the high seas and lower it. A net with several different chambers, which all lead to 1: the death chamber.

The bluefin would enter the trap without realizing it, the longboats closed in, the nets were closed off, and all that was left was the death chamber, full of desperate tuna, which the fishermen hauled out of the water with their bare arms by sheer brute force, to the rhythm of an ancient fishing song.

The fisherman sang a song in his hoarse voice, a song about a man named Jesú and a woman named Virgin and angels of the sea and things like that, according to what I have noted in my diary.

His eyes shone as he sang and I realized that I was realizing that they shone—Me, who never looked anyone in the eyes except my aunt.

Light brown eyes, I wrote in my diary.

But that's all in the past, the sailor said suddenly, and poured more red wine into his glass.

Every year there are fewer tuna, he said, and now there aren't enough for fishermen from other towns to go out with the fishermen from Palermo. Every year there are fewer, and every year they're smaller.

Besides, I wanted to see the world, he said.

He'd been a sailor on a luxury cruise ship but he hated the tourists.

Why? I asked.

Because I hate them, he said. Bloody tourists.

His words made Me laugh and I repeated them:

Bloody tourists.

In any case, he preferred contract work. He hired himself out as a mercenary on special fishing operations: a whale for a zoo; some whiskered seals in the glaciers for a millionaire; hunting a killer shark in the Bahamas; an arms shipment that had to cross the Panama Canal in a concealed hold on a shrimp boat.

He earned good money and he could spend the rest of the year in his hometown scratching his balls in the sun.

Why would you scratch balls? I asked.

My testicles, I mean, he translated.

These, he added, grabbing himself between the legs.

I asked him:

You spent a whole year scratching your testicles?

A whole year, he nodded.

1 day he was in a seafood bar on the beach in Barcelona eating a sardine omelette, a fork in 1 hand, scratching his balls with the other, when another sailor said to him:

There's contract work on a tuna seiner at the mouth of the Gulf of California. Yellowfin tuna. The catch is, Ricardo, you have to stay all year.

That's how he ended up at Consolation and became captain of a ship.

Look, let me show you something, Captain Ricardo said.

He pulled up his pants leg and instead of a standard ankle, he had only ¾ of an ankle: the ¼ of flesh at the back was missing.

Killer shark bite, he said contentedly. And look at this.

He opened his shirt and I saw, on his dark skin, beneath his brown hair and above his heart, a red cross the size of a hand. But he was pointing to his belly, where 10 centimetres from his belly button was another hole, like a second belly button.

Bullet wound from the United States' police in Panama. Grazed my liver. And wait, look at this, he said.

He unbuttoned his pants and pulled down the waistband of his underpants to show Me another scar, this 1 a straight line 15 centimetres long, running from his hip bone down into his blond pubic hair.

Appendicitis, he said, and burst out laughing. Emergency operation on board a ship at high sea. No anesthaesia. With a fucking kitchen knife.

And the red cross on your chest? I asked.

Don't worry about that, he said, suddenly cold.

Look, I said.

I unbuttoned my denim shirt and took it off. Ricardo's eyes moved down to my breasts, to the nipples of my breasts, which changed color from light brown to dark, and I turned around to show him my back, the scar that ran diagonally from my shoulder to my waist, a scar like a poorly sewn zipper, crooked and discolored at the edges.

I didn't hear him say anything for a long time.

The horizon was dark blue, almost turquoise blue; the red was now a round spot surrounding us, 100 metres in diameter.

I turned back around, swinging my legs to the other side of the bench, and Ricardo's mouth was open.

He said:

How did that happen?

No idea, I said, and put my shirt back on. My aunt says I had it before I learned how to speak.

Ricardo slid his hand into the breast pocket of his shirt and took out a thin wallet. I swore he was going to show Me a picture, but no, he took out 2 very green leaves, and gave Me 1.

Tear it, like this, he said, and we each tore our leaves in ½.

Rub it, he said, rubbing ½ of the leaf between his thumb and index finger. I rubbed.

Now smell it, he said, holding it up to his nose.

I smelled it.

The leaf of a lemon tree, Ricardo said.

I went to button up my denim shirt but he asked Me not to.

This is just between you and me, he said quietly.

I didn't understand what he was talking about but since that happened all the time, Me not understanding what standard humans were talking about, I didn't worry about it; I lay back on the bench, my head resting on the boat's edge, and closed my eyes.

I used to like—I still like—feeling the sun on my face as my head rose and fell with the sea.

I heard a soft sound, opened 1 eye, and saw Captain Ricardo, tan, his dark brown hair bleached blond at the ends, watching Me, breathing slowly and deeply.

Another day, each of us lying on a bench in the motorboat with our faces to the sun, each of us sniffing the leaf of a lemon tree, Ricardo told Me about the mysterious sailors' angel.

What's an angel? I asked.

Haven't you ever been to church?

No, I said.

That's impossible, he replied.

I've never been inside a church, I repeated.

But a few weeks ago I told you about a sea angel and you didn't ask Me any questions.

I didn't answer, which is often the best way to answer if you want to make the other person keep talking.

So he told Me what an angel was:

A winged creature that God sends down to Earth.

When he was done explaining I had another question.

Who's God?

Look, Ricardo said, his head 1 metre from mine over on his bench. Do you want Me to tell you about the sailors' angel, or not?

I didn't answer, and he told Me:

When a sailor drowns, the angel goes down to the bottom of the sea to bless him by touching his forehead and then takes his hand and pulls him off the sea floor as if he didn't weigh anything at all and both of them float up, through the surface of the sea, and they keep floating until they get to Heaven.

That's not true, I said.

Ricardo scrunched up his face.

If it were true, I continued, the angel would have fins, not wings.

Fine, Ricardo snapped, irritated. Whatever the hell you say.

And he stared out at the sea in his direction while I stared out at the sea in mine.

Sometimes, when the catch was plentiful and the weather was good, Ricardo would pull out 1 of the tuna and tell the sailors to bring it out to our boat. The ship would set off and the 3 of us would stay back, Ricardo and Me and the tuna. Me and Ricardo on our benches and the tuna on the floor. Occasionally the tuna would still open its mouth suddenly and flap its tail, and then it was as if a giant whip had lashed down in the center of the red sea.

Ricardo would unbutton his denim shirt, I would look at the blond hair on his dark chest, and he would look at the sun with his light brown eyes.

When our tuna stopped moving, Ricardo would thrust his Swiss Army knife into it and, grunting with the effort, shave off a piece of skin. Then he'd cut off a strip of red flesh. He'd set it on his knees, that hunk, and there he'd fillet it into short, thin strips like little red tongues. He'd extract 2 plastic tooth-picks from his knife and we, each with 1 toothpick, would eat the tuna tongues.

People pay 60,000 dollars for a tuna this fresh, Ricardo said.

That's not true, I said.

He screwed up his face and said:

What do you know? You've never set 1 damn foot out of Mazatlán, a damn sardine port. A restaurant in Japan—Tokyo or Kyoto—pays that much for tuna you can eat before it's been frozen or stored in brine or sprayed. And they eat it just like this, in little bite-size pieces, no condiments. And they give you a little cup of white rice with a few drops of vinegar to clean your palate between bites. 60 dollars for a plate with 3 little pieces of tuna, perfectly fresh.

And there it was, at our feet, in the boat, a treasure worth 60,000 dollars. At least according to Ricardo.

Each bite melted in your mouth like marzipan.

The all-orange sun had almost set, out on the horizon, and Ricardo scratched his beard and I was shocked, because suddenly I realized that his beard had grown, who knew when: a brown beard with golden whiskers.

Now I'm sad, he informed Me.

But the good thing, he said after a pause, is that I'm with you. Nobody listens the way you do.

How do I listen? I wanted to know.

You just listen to me. That's what I mean. You listen to me without judging me. I'm not a man of many words, he added, despite the fact that the truth was the opposite: he talked and talked, with lots of pauses, yes, but he was the 1 who always spoke while we were on the boat, not Me.

That's why I appreciate it when someone listens to me, Ricardo continued, like you. Especially because I've never talked so much with a woman. You know why?

No idea.

Well, you know, because women aren't for talking to, they're, you know, for something else.

No idea, I said.

Yeah. Well, they're for. For screwing, you know. For breeding. You know.

I didn't know, but what did it matter?

Or at least that's what I thought, Ricardo rectified, his eyes moist, seeming quite moved by his own words. That's what I thought before I talked so much to you.

I speared a little piece of tuna with my toothpick and brought it to my mouth.

I want you to know, he said looking at Me very slowly, that you're very special to Me.

I'm different, I corrected.

Thank God, Ricardo replied.

He lit a cigarette sailor-style: unbuttoned his shirt, held it out against the afternoon's soft breeze, lit his lighter behind the shirt, bent his head down with the cigarette in his mouth, and touched the flame to the tip of it.

Then, exhaling smoke, he asked Me:

Can I touch you?

He reached out a big hand to my thigh and, startled, I raised my boot up to place it between his face and Me.

Okay, he said to the sole.

And he pulled his hand back to him and took his wallet
out of his breast pocket and from that took out 2 very green
little leaves and offered Me 1, and only then did I lower my
boot.

We each tore our leaf, rubbed it between 2 fingers, smelled
the fresh-cut lemon scent. In silence on the calm sea.

Then Ricardo said:

Funny. I just realized why I get sad when we're together.
It's because I could be your father.

Hearing that unnerved Me. I began to dig the fingernails of
my right hand into my palm, 1 by 1.

He clarified quickly:

No, no. It's okay. Wait. All I mean is that your father might
be my age. What are you, 17? I'm 34.

Then he murmured:

I'm a sad son of a bitch.

His announcements bewildered Me: first he might be my
father, then his mother was a bitch. My heart was pounding
and I had to take deep breaths to calm down. Ricardo did the
same, breathing slowly and deeply.

Right, he said, as if we were in agreement about something.

So peaceful, he added. Look, the blood's all gone.

He was right. The sea had gone back to blue. Turquoise

once again. All turquoise blue, as if the slaughter had never occurred.

I laughed. I felt happy that nothing, not a drop of blood, was left of the kill.

Can we go now? Ricardo asked. Have you made sure the sea has completely forgotten the kill?

And I asked:

Is that it? That I want to see that the sea has forgotten the kill?

You want to make sure the sea's wound is healed, he replied.

I sat contemplating his words: I want to make sure the sea's wound is healed. I almost understood, but I didn't understand.

And then I said:

Yes. We can go now.

But neither he nor I moved.

The 2 of us, in the little launch, in the big, blue sea.

5

After dinner in the ship's mess hall, the sailors found ways to occupy their free time. They played cards there in the hall. Or read magazines. 1 or 2 read books or went to the radio room to send messages. Me, I put on the headphones of my cassette player and learned English words while walking on deck in my yellow windbreaker. Or in my cabin, lying on my bed. I'd listen through the headphones and repeat the words aloud, and when the tape spelled them out, I wrote them on colored plastic labels and stuck the colored plastic labels on the walls of my cabin.

I'd fall asleep spelling the new words in the new language.

*

1 thing I liked even more than that was nights when after dinner everyone just lingered, talking.

Coffee was served in jars, the sailors lit cigarettes, and bottles of rum would be passed around and poured into clear plastic cups, although Ricardo kept his hand on his bottle of Campari, which he tipped over the ice in his glass.

I loved being there with them while they told sailors' stories.

1 night Ricardo talked about a time when he torpedoed the wrong ship. He trained the sight on a vessel out in the distance that looked like it was the size of a fly ... pressed the launch button ... the torpedo shot out, leaving a straight line of foam in the sea ... and then the captain shouted:

Holy Shit, that's the wrong ship! That's a Red Cross hospital ship!

They stood there staring at the horizon: out where the ship sat on the water they saw a red flash. It had exploded. But it was the wrong ship, and first Ricardo and then the captain whispered:

Holy Shit.

Holy Shit.

And that was it, Ricardo concluded. That was how I came to fuck it up on the Black Sea, too; anything good, I fuck it up.

He stared right at Me for a while, and all the sailors stared at him staring at Me, and 1 sailor asked:

Then what, Captain?

Then nothing, Ricardo replied, still staring at Me. Then I got a tattoo of a red cross over my heart, to remind myself not to fuck up everything good, and that's it.

1 night at midnight when I was walking on deck, pronouncing words in English, I decided to venture down to visit the ship's other occupants. The tuna.

I descended into the belly of the ship, holding the handrail by the stairs with 1 hand, a flashlight in the other. I turned on the lights: 10 spotlights went on, the ice lit up.

The tuna were black stains inside the illuminated block of ice. Some stuck to each other, some on top of each other. Walking on top of them my steps rang out on the ice, puh-*lip*-puh-*lip*-puh-*lip*, echoing on the metallic walls of the hold, puh-*lop* puh-*lop* puh-*lop*.

I don't know how, but suddenly the ice broke and my boot was beside a tuna, a tuna whose black eye moved, and then all the eyes of all the tuna moved at the same time and they all opened their pink mouths.

*

I knocked on Ricardo's cabin door with my knuckles, and he opened it.

He was wearing white boxer shorts, his hairy chest bare, his hair disheveled. He let Me in, and I limped past him since I'd taken my boot and wet sock off, and we sat on 2 chairs, facing the bed, Me still trembling.

In a hoarse voice, he said:

Lack of oxygen, that's all it was. Down in the belly of the ship there's no oxygen. And with no oxygen, you see things.

Things?

You hallucinate. You see things that aren't really there.

I'm, I'm, I'm, I tried to say, my stutter worse from the fear, I'm scared because we kill, kill tuna.

Ricardo was blue in the porthole light of his dark cabin.

Are you afraid the tuna are going to take revenge?

A chill ran through Me and I shivered.

Don't worry, he said. They can't take revenge. I promise you. They're dead.

What about the, the live ones?

Them either. Live tuna have never taken revenge on a tuna boat.

N-never?

Never.

But, I think, I think it's, it's, it's something else.

Something else, he said. Yeah, I know, something bigger. Yeah, that happens when you kill. Something else, something like a hole, opens up in you right here.

He touched the red cross tattoo that was under his chest hair and over his heart.

A hole where fear gets in. Horror, but you don't know what it's horror of. That's the worst part, that you feel so scared and you don't know what you're scared of.

Don't know what, what you're scared of, I repeated.

Listen to me carefully, Ricardo said. In order for humans to live we have to eat and in order to eat we have to kill. God gave us licence to kill other species, as long as it's for food. That's the way it is. Remember that when you feel afraid because it's the only thing that helps.

Can I, can I, can I see it? The, the, the licence? I asked.

Ricardo turned to look at Me carefully.

Of course, he said. I'm going to make you a photocopy. It's on the first page of the Bible, and it goes more or less like this: first God created the light, the seas, and the earth, then the trees and the plants and the animals, and finally he created Adam and Eve, the first humans, and he said to Adam and Eve, I give you the whole planet to rule and to eat.

I said:

The other day I asked my aunt what God was. She told Me

that, that God is everything we can't know. Anything we don't know we put a label on it: God.

I'm not going to contradict my boss, Ricardo replied. But your aunt has no fucking idea what she's talking about. Do you mind if I smoke?

I didn't answer.

He lit a cigarette and smoked half of it in silence. Then he said:

When I was a kid the priest at my church said it like this: God is light.

What else? I wanted to know.

Nothing else, God is light.

I turned to look through the porthole, and ½ of the moon was right in the middle of it.

Not that light, Ricardo said. A different light.

Different how?

Special.

Special how?

Ricardo searched for the words to explain it.

Have you ever seen it? The different light? I asked.

No, but I have every faith that I will.

What does that mean, have every faith?

It means that I know I'll see it 1 day, even if I don't know how I know, or when it's going to happen.

I was about to ask him something else but he held up his hand.

That's enough. You're a damn dynamo when it comes to asking questions.

No, I'm not.

Yes, you are, Ricardo boomed.

But I don't understand. How the hell can you believe in something you've never even seen?

No more questions, Ricardo said angrily. He was breathing quickly, smoking quickly, speaking quickly.

We can't doubt the light of God, because doubt destroys faith, and without faith, you'll never see it. It's that simple. 1 day, suddenly you see it and you feel like everything makes sense, absolutely everything, and that's it. Spend the night with Me, he said slowly, staring at his hairy knees.

He stood what was left of his cigarette up on its filter on the table. Then he added:

Sleep with me. I mean, if you want to.

And a little while later:

I hear you're going off to school, far away.

I said:

Yes. In another country.

Why?

Because my aunt wants Me to.

And what do you want?

He stared into my eyes so hard I had to move mine to the wall.

I don't know, I said. And I really didn't.

Ricardo lay down on the bed and I considered it and then went and lay down beside him on the bed, stiff.

And at some point before I fell asleep, I thought: I'm going to sleep with Ricardo. And then I fell asleep.

In the middle of the night, ½ awake and ½ asleep, I felt Ricardo under my shirt, kissing my back. The scar on my back. He kissed all the way down, 1, 3, 5 kisses.

And that was it. He didn't kiss Me anymore, or move, or anything. And then I heard the Me within Me say inside my head:

2 killers.

6

I took colored plastic labels with English words written on them in my big, clumsy handwriting and started sticking them up from my dorm room all the way to the rooms where classes would be held.

Door, hallway, stairs, trees (numbered 1 to 67), animal husbandry building, hallway, classrooms (numbered 1 to 35).

I'd make the trip whimpering at the fear of getting lost. And sometimes getting sidetracked to stare at some light that seemed to Me to be special for some reason, thinking about what Ricardo had said.

God is a special light.

In fact there were 2 times when I got so absorbed in 2 very special lights that I disappeared from myself. 1 of them I saw through a small square window in a door, coming through the darkness from the other side of the door: a ray of light that hit the floor and produced its own square of light. The other was a very long cylindrical beam in which I could see dust floating.

My aunt found Me the first time in a darkened closet, my forehead pressed against the glass of the small square window full of light, standing among brooms and buckets and boxes of detergent. The second time she found Me in an enormous, empty auditorium directly in the beam of light shining in through a skylight, rocking back and forth on a bench, staring up at the dust suspended in the light, drooling, disappeared from myself.

We had arrived 1 month before classes began. In addition to slowly mastering the route from my dorm room to the classrooms and back, I was taking classes in faces on a computer, with my aunt Isabelle.

I had only 4 faces: panic, joy, neutral, and disappeared from myself. If I was going to relate to other people at the university, I had to increase the number of my faces.

Look at the computer, my aunt said:

You turn it on and you hear music, as if it were saying, I'm

ready! You open a file and it goes: ping! If you ask it something and it takes a little while, a tiny hourglass full of sand
appears to say, Give Me time, I'm thinking. The computer
doesn't actually need to make sounds or show symbols but
nobody would use computers if they didn't show signs of
communicating with the users. What I'm trying to say is that
you have to give people more signals, Karen, use more faces.

My aunt had uploaded 1-minute videos onto the computer, clips showing standard humans wearing different
expressions. The idea was for Me to imitate them and thereby
learn to show: anger, rage, hostility, sadness, disgust, happiness,
surprise, embarrassment, jealousy, envy, scorn, desperation,
boredom, distrust. But more important: pleasure, friendship,
curiosity, desire, adoration, pride.

And all of that was to be achieved just by moving the
muscles of my eyelids, eyebrows and lips in certain specific
combinations.

It was an exhausting undertaking that left my T-shirt
drenched in sweat.

We finally agreed that it would be up to Me to decide
when to turn on my Relating Mode (and thus be alert and
ready to employ 1 of 20 human faces) and when to turn it off
so I could just be Me, that is, in Non-Relating Mode (with my
same 4 faces as always), because if all of my effort went in

relating to others, when was I going to learn anything else at college?

On computers back then there used to be an "office assistant," a caricature of Einstein that would pop up on the screen and walk around happily nodding his head, then he'd take a picture or open a book and leaf through it. Every time that cute little Einstein appeared I'd burst out laughing, then quickly jump up and imitate him, taking little baby steps as I laughed, nodding my head, and my aunt would get angry.

No, no, no! She raised her voice. You can't laugh so loud! Close your mouth, press your lips together; laugh, but with your lips closed, make all of your emotions smaller.

Resembling a standard human would turn out to be a tremendous effort that took many years of practice and much discipline. In fact, now at 41 I'm still struggling.

Anyway, I'd end up sweaty and infuriated at the attempt to make my emotions small and to express so many things that were uncertain for Me, all just by contracting the muscles of my eyelids, eyebrows and lips. And at night I'd dream of free, red fish and grey balls that in an instant dissolved into 1,000 darting mackerels and 3 shiny dolphins leaping through the air.

*

SABINA BERMAN

My aunt told Me about Albert Einstein, the mathematician. Like Me, Einstein had fixations. He'd spent years and years sitting in a patent office in Berne, Switzerland, thinking about just 1 thing: the Universe. And he'd come up with a very elegant and very simple theory about the Universe that I didn't understand, and that my aunt, after attempting to explain it to Me 3 times, confessed that she didn't understand either.

Like Me, Einstein was incapable of saying anything he didn't think was true, and he did things slowly and with great concentration, and he also solved problems in new and unique ways. And he won the Nobel Prize, the most prestigious prize on Earth.

He was probably autistic, my aunt said, spearing a little round potato with her fork.

We were at a restaurant, having dinner.

Another man who was probably autistic was Charles Darwin, who as a young man spent 5 years sailing the coast of South America, southern Africa, and Australia, and in each place, he walked around or rode a horse, collecting plants and animals that he later dissected in his cabin, until 1 day the captain said, That's enough, kid, the ship's going to sink with all those dead animals, and then he spent 3 decades carefully studying all of his specimens, until 1 day a friend said, That's enough, Charles, you've already gone gray and half-blind, and it turns out that another biologist from Malaysia is about to publish what you should have written 25 years ago. And it was only then that Charles sat down to quickly compose the theory that explains why there are so many different species living on Earth simultaneously, and why they resemble each other and yet are distinct.

And Beethoven, the musician who was sometimes volatile and obstreperous, like you, my aunt went on, and was the bane of his neighbors, and from the door of his apartment shouted at them, demanding they give him silence so he could compose, silence so he could hear the sound of the stars:

Give Me silence for pity's sake, Beethoven shouted again and again, until 1 day he went deaf.

What I'm trying to say, my aunt concluded, is that all of these geniuses probably had some degree of autism, like I suspect you do. Even though back then the term *autistic* wasn't used.

She deposited another little round potato in her mouth, chewed it, took a sip of red wine, and said:

People with different abilities are the ones who make different contributions to humanity.

What if you're just crazy? I asked Aunt Isabelle.

That's 1 thing I'm not, she said with unexplainable joy, wiping her lips with a napkin.

And I felt a shiver run down my spine.

I noticed, as we stood from the table and walked through the restaurant on our way out, that people turned to stare at her. In her gray tailored suit, so slim, her blonde hair like a yellow helmet that stopped halfway down her neck, my elegant aunt Isabelle, followed by her lanky niece with a crew cut, jeans, and stevedore's boots, avoiding eye contact as she walked, electing to stare at the walls instead, and walking like a sailor. Stamping the soles down on the floor completely with each step so as not to lose balance.

The next morning my aunt left and, lying in my dorm room alone, I stared at the ceiling. Fear was the only thing that reminded Me I was there, alive.

I took out my tools—an electric drill and screws—stood on my bed, and proceeded to attach my harness to the ceiling, then put on my wetsuit and hung from my harness above my bed, in my wetsuit.

Through the window I could see the university's enormous grounds. Students began to appear on the paths and walkways.

For Me, each 1 made my heart skip a beat, produced a moment of panic.

Suddenly the door opened and there was a girl, holding a suitcase in each hand. She looked at Me in my blue neoprene wetsuit hanging in my harness. I suppose she was my room-mate.

I'm not certain, because she turned and left and never came back.

Hours later, another student walked in, this 1 blonde and freckled, also holding 2 suitcases, 1 in each hand. She put them on the bed. From the bathtub, where I was floating in hot water in my wetsuit, I saw her open the suitcases and begin to unpack her clothes. She was coming and going from the suitcase to the closet, where she hung up her things.

I got out of the tub and walked into the bedroom taking great big steps because of my fins, and she began walking backward until she bumped up against the wall.

She asked Me to pardon her, I'm not sure for what, while grasping her head.

She asked Me if I wouldn't please mind taking off my mask, so I took it off and looked the other way.

She told Me I probably played basketball, because I was tall and strong, or actually, she rectified, I must be on the swim team, or no, she knew, probably on the diving team, if indeed the university had a diving team, and then without so much as pausing she asked Me what I studied.

Animal husbandry, I replied.

Thrilled, she responded, That's wonderful! I have a Labrador retriever at home!

And still without pausing she asked Me if I wanted to know her name and what she studied.

That's not necessary, I answered.

She quickly repacked her things and left, and she didn't come back either.

And that was how I ended up with a room with 2 beds all to myself.

Before going to classes, I put a yellow label on my chest that had 2 words: Different Abilities.

That was 1 of my survival tactics.

Another tactic: in class, in order not to have to look directly at my professors, I placed a video recorder on the desk and watched them through its little screen.

Another tactic: in the hallways, if someone spoke to Me, I looked out the nearest window or wound my watch, in order not to have to look the unknown speaker in the eyes.

It unfortunately became apparent that students' main

activity was talking and talking and talking, standing in the hallways or on the lawn or in the stairwells, creating fields of sound between themselves, and staring at each other's pupils. Absorbed in their world of standard humans. So it often happened that someone insisted on crowding my face with their voice and seeking my pupils. In turn, I'd grab their shoulder with 1 hand, push them out of my field of vision, and wear an expression of Extreme Surprise (lips and eyes wide open: ☺), as if I'd just seen something unbelievable that required Me to run off.

What's more, students were always saying idiotic things. 1 time a student said to Me, when I asked where New York City was:

You know the train station? New York City is 5 minutes south of there.

So I went to the train station and walked south, consulting my wristwatch on several occasions. And what was 5 minutes south was still the platform of the train station. And after the platform ended I walked another 15 minutes. Nothing. Rails, trees: nothing.

How much better the world would be if people didn't use metaphors.

Or euphemisms.

*

Metaphor: saying 1 thing to say another.

Euphemism: disguising a big thing as a little thing; or disguising a terrible thing as a good thing.

Example. My methods class on how to murder different animal species was called Meat Industry: Early Notions.

Example. The class where you learned how to make money by killing animals or by selling them whole or in pieces—skin, viscera, corneas, hooves, hair, teeth, glands—was called Animal Industry Economy.

Example. The classes where they taught you to torture live animals (poisoning them or giving them electric shocks or crucifying them by cutting them open while still alive) was called Scientific Experimentation I, II and III.

Example. The class that justified our license to kill animals was called Human Intelligence.

Professor Huntington was the best professor on the faculty, or that's what everyone said, and they called him the Killer, because:

1. He was the top expert in all of America on slaughterhouses.

2. He was the professor who failed the most students.

He was an emaciated man, about 60 years old, with a pale

face that looked like it was made of wax, and he always wore white, short-sleeved shirts and a tie, always black and always narrow. Perhaps he even wore that to bed, or at least that's how I imagined him: asleep in his bed in his white shirt and his narrow black tie, his tapered grey pants with the perfectly ironed crease.

He wore glasses with plastic frames.

Yes, he was the star of the faculty. It was he who'd been responsible for nothing less than the famous stun gun used on cattle.

A compressed-air pistol that when fired into an animal's forehead stuns it for 1 minute.

A bull, let's say. The bull is led into a metal restraining pen and then an electric mechanism contracts and the bars of the pen move in until they squeeze the animal's ribs, immobilizing it. And a bull that's being squeezed doesn't become stressed; on the contrary, it becomes calm.

Then the gun is positioned at the point exactly halfway between its eyes, fired, and the bull loses consciousness. At that point the slaughterman has 1 minute, no more and no less, to slit its throat with a big knife and hang it from a meat hook to bleed out.

Which is less painful than slaughtering it live. Or slitting its throat after banging it on the head with a hammer or firing

a lance or a bolt into its head or electrocuting it with 2 elec-
trodes—1 on each temple—as used to be done before
Huntington's invention.

Huntington invented his compressed-air stun gun expres-
sly for the purpose of killing cattle with a minimum of
stress, as stress releases toxins into their blood and poisons the
meat. But it outstripped all expectations when he demon-
strated at a cattle fair attended by 5,000 ranchers from all
over the world that it worked just as well for cows as it
did for horses, sheep, pigs, and just about any other
quadruped mammal you wanted to kill, and that the restraining pen with movable bars wasn't indispensable in order to
use it.

The gun could just as easily be used in open air simply by
firing it directly into the quadruped's forehead, as long as it
was fired quickly. That is, before the animal realized that
something strange was happening. The gun was put to its
forehead, fired with a tzzzzup sound, and that was it.

150 steer were tethered to a rubber conveyor belt, and
Huntington himself personally went along firing against their
foreheads at a rate of 4 per minute (tzzzzup, tzzzzup, tzzzzup,
tzzzzup); the cattle collapsed onto the moving rubber belt as
5,000 ranchers looked on, nodding, then 1 metre later 2
workers bound their 2 front legs together, 2 chains hoisted

them up, and 1 throat slitter went from steer to steer with his knife, slicing open their throats in 1 go.

That's why Huntington's invention can be found in every slaughterhouse claiming sensitivity to animal stress and to the palate of human carnivores.

They said the patent for the marvelous quadruped stun gun had earned Huntington the Committee for More Humane Animal Slaughter medal, the most prestigious award there was in the humanitarian murder trade, as well as hundreds of thousands of dollars. Which explained, they also said, his disdain for students.

Sometimes Huntington didn't show up for class and in his place sent his assistant, Gabriel Short, a short man—as his name well illustrated—and bald, and he read from his boss's notes without adding a single word, making mention of each period and comma. Huntington had instead chosen to give a paper or do an appraisal of 1 of the slaughterhouses he'd designed or simply hadn't deigned to come to class.

It was said that university officials were less than pleased with those absences. Huntington didn't care. He lived off the royalties he got from the sale of each cattle stun gun.

He was very serious when he asked questions, but he listened to the answers with a little smirk, because as he himself explained during 1 class, other people's stupidity never ceased to amuse him.

He took questions with the same little smirk, but answered them with seriousness and a fluency and precision that struck Me as inconceivable; it was as if everything he said was already printed in a book.

And he often spoke gazing right into the lens of my video camera.

1 day he suddenly spoke directly into the lens:

Miss Different Abilities. For your information. My words enjoy the status of intellectual property. Any public use of them will incur honoraria.

This is what we did in our Human Intelligence class: Professor Stern—whom students nicknamed the Walrus because he was big and fat and moved slowly and had a scruffy mustache like a walrus—gave us texts to read that stressed the difference between humans and other animals, and we had to write compositions about them.

Why it was so important to stress the difference between humans and other animals I did not at first understand, but I did understand that it was very important to humans, given that they'd written about it for centuries.

About a text written by a Mr. Aristotle that claimed that humans are unique because they have souls, feelings and intelligence, while other animals are complex robots with no souls, minds, reasoning or ability to suffer or feel, I wrote 1 word:

Idiotic.

The Walrus held my paper up in front of all the students in his usual slow fashion and exclaimed:

Concise, resounding, adamant! Excellent!

And the rats in the cages flanking the right and left sides of the laboratory scuttled, terrified.

About a study undertaken by a certain Mr. Giscard from the 18th century that locates the difference in the human ability to use tools while other animals don't, I wrote 1 word.

Idiotic.

The Walrus again held my paper up and exclaimed:

Excellent!

And the rats scurried around in the little cages some more.

But then the Walrus added:

But you should have built up your case better. Mentioned the exceptions that disprove the universality of the rule. In this case, for example, mention the animals we've discovered that do use tools, like chimpanzees and bonobos and dolphins and elephants.

Then he set us to read a series of other famous theses from the 20th century about why humans are unique.

1. They can solve problems in their heads before implementing the solutions.

2. They possess awareness of their own past and future.

3. They have language.

4. They understand the concept of number.

5. They recognize themselves in the mirror.

6. They kill members of their own species.

Again I wrote the word *Idiotic* about each thesis, followed by the example or examples that contradicted the theses according to my evidence.

1. My cat and squirrels and seagulls and ants.

2. Squirrels and my cat and dolphins and ants.

3. Dolphins and my cat.

4. My cat.

5. My cat.

6. Chimpanzees and mad dogs.

And back in class the Walrus terrified the rats by banging his fist down on the desk, shouting like a madman after each blow.

No! No! No! Give me more words, Karen! More grammar! More bibliography! Develop your argument! We know you already have ample experience with animals, but your

arrogance is unacceptable! I'm giving you an F on each com-
position!

His last sentence terrified Me, too.

I raised my hand, trembling, then stood up and asked:

Is it that I'm wrong?

The Walrus responded very quietly:

No, but I've already told you, you need to be more persuasive.

And he changed the subject and that afternoon I looked up
the word *persuasive* in the dictionary and that's where I began
to lose my confidence: aside from not understanding why it
was even necessary to locate the difference between humans
and other animals, I didn't understand why we read so many
texts that were incorrect.

Finally we read a certain René Descartes from the 17th
century and then I wrote, very carefully:

*Descartes writes, I think, therefore I am. That is, definitively
and obviously, idiotic. Anyone with 2 eyes in their head knows
that any creature exists first and then does other things, like move
its fins or breathe or spread pollen or think. Human beings, like
every other being that exists, exist first and then at times think.
Proof of that is that I have seen many human beings exist when
they are asleep and I have heard of others who existed when they
were already dead.*

You didn't understand a thing, the Walrus said curtly in the following class.

He leaned over the desk and gripped it with his giant hands, big as a walrus's fins, and said from beneath his walrus's mustache:

My entire course is structured to lead logically to the only unarguable difference between humans and animals: the 1 Descartes formulates, and the 1 that you, Miss Nieto, didn't understand for shit.

23 years later, I walked into a white room to meet a parakeet that didn't only think but also talked—a lot. Max.

Measuring 30 centimetres from beak to tail, with pearl grey feathers, a white face and red tail, Max stood on a little trapeze and followed Me with his eyes as I went to sit in a chair. The floor was lined with sheets of that day's newspaper. I opened a bag and took out 2 chocolate glazed donuts and showed them to him, 1 in each hand, and Max, flapping his wings, came down to perch on a donut and to make the following comment in his raspy little voice that sounded like a poorly tuned radio:

Yyyyyyummy!

And then:

Yyyyyummy donut!

And then after pecking at a piece of donut between his feet:

Ketchup!

Because Max, who has mastered 50 nouns, plus the names of 7 colors and 11 numbers—from 1 to 10, and the most mysterious number: 0—likes everything with ketchup on it.

No ketchup, I said.

Flapping a wing, he hopped up onto my head. Then he dropped down to my shoulder, where he perched and gave his donut another peck, and I recalled Descartes and the Fs I got on the Walrus's compositions, and ultimately in Human Intelligence.

But let Me clarify. Parakeet Max doesn't disprove philosopher Descartes, though he does think. If you take him out to the garden, perched on your shoulder, and ask him, pointing to the grass:

Max, what color is the grass?

And then show him a cookie, Max will think about it for a bit, about 30 seconds, maybe ask himself why the hell it matters what color the grass is, but since Max wants the cookie, he'll say:

Grrrrrrreen!

What I'm absolutely sure of, however, is that Max has never thought:

I think about green, therefore I am.

Therefore, Descartes is right in asserting that the only being that thinks that sort of idiocy is the human being.

And all these years later, I do feel confident enough to talk at length about what I think about it. I believe that to sustain, on a daily basis, the fantasy that first someone thinks and then "is" is what makes it so tiring to be a human being—or in my case to attempt it.

I believe that's the reason human beings always feel uncomfortable wherever they are; and I believe their discomfort leads to them always thinking about other things, objects that aren't right there in front of their eyes.

Other things: the human body is always uncomfortable and fantasizing about stuff that would make it happy.

Other things that either already exist or that human beings feel they should invent in order to finally be comfortable. Beds, tables, chairs, houses. Streets, buildings, cities. Trains, ships, planes, rockets that will take them to other planets. Books that will make them think they're someplace else, libraries, universities.

Other things that for centuries have filled the space around human beings, that have accumulated to such a degree that they now form an exclusively human world that blinds human beings to the nonhuman world.

A human world that is so complicated that their young must be trained anywhere from 10 to 19 years just to be able to move around in it without tripping.

So, by the time their young have become adults well trained enough to live in the human world, 2 things have happened.

1. They are completely trapped in the idea that they think first and then they are.

2. They are blind to anything that is nonhuman.

Now, is a human being superior to parakeet Max?

That is a question that must be asked seriously. I say that because from my college days until writing this right now, I've heard this type of question often: is a human being superior to X or Y animal? And it always provokes much laughter among the humans.

So I ask whoever might be reading this not to laugh, because you can't laugh and think at the same time.

As I was saying, in order to respond, you have to ask the question seriously, and preferably make it more concrete, for example: is parakeet Max capable of inventing a telephone?

Of course not. Even to use a telephone would take him 2 years of training. So a human is superior to Max.

But you also have to ask: is the human world superior to the world where parakeet Max lives, the natural world?

And in order to respond, I would first ask: can a human use a phone without the existence of the planet Earth?

I think not. Therefore the Earth is superior to the human world.

And finally, if the question is who is happier, parakeet Max or a human being, the answer is most definitely: parakeet Max. And that is simply because standard humans live isolated from nature by their thoughts, even isolated from their own bodies, and since nothing can be happy if it is not in its own body, human beings are not happy.

Huntington approached my desk and stood beside Me and I kept watching the screen of the video recorder where Huntington no longer was. His hand crossed in front of my face to grab the Different Abilities label on my denim shirt. He tore it off.

He walked down the aisle's steps and returned to the front of the classroom to face the students and spoke of Me, Miss Different Abilities, holding up my yellow tag.

I don't know everything he said because I only managed to catch a few sentences, as anguish encircled Me and the pounding of my heart rose to fill my ears.

This won't save anyone in my class, was 1 of his sentences.

He rolled the label into a little circle between his thumb and ring finger, aimed at the trash can, and flicked the little yellow ball in with a piiiing.

Another sentence I managed to catch:

9 and ½ seconds is the world's record for the 100 metres. And anyone who can't run it in that time isn't the world's champion and can piss off somewhere else with that Different Abilities shit.

I fixed my gaze on my desk, on a mark in the wood that might have been carved with a penknife.

What's more, Huntington said, his voice sounding very far off, in the meat industry we don't have a special category for women, who in track can win an Olympic gold medal by running the 100 meters in 15 minutes, nor do we have a Retarded Olympics or a Queer Olympics. In the meat industry we play fair; nobody hires an animal husbandry engineer out of pity, not even to build an egg-processing facility. Fire it up, Short.

Short turned on a projector and there, on the screen that was pulled down over the chalkboard, was the technical

drawing I had made for the course, the draft of a swallow trap:
a net that covered the foliage of an ash tree.

The students giggled. My body began to rock at my desk
and my Me began to evaporate.

Observe, Huntington declaimed, and I heard him as if from
another world. Admire the awkwardness of the strokes. And
especially admire the stupidity, by following the arrows of this
alleged swallow trap. I repeat, trap, trap, trap. What is a trap?

All hands raised and Huntington pointed to 1 student. A
redhead who stood and said:

A device used to capture an animal.

My arrows indicated the movement of the swallows from
branch to branch. Their alighting on a branch was noted along
with the time they would perch there. Their flitting onto a
lower branch and flapping up to a higher branch, and again
pausing, with the number of seconds and the word *Song*. And
finally, another long red arrow indicated their flight out
through an opening in the trap that led up to the sky.

You forgot the vital component, Miss Different! Huntington
exclaimed. Capturing the little birdie!

Now the students were rocking, laughing so hard that their
desks were shaking, and my legs were trembling, but the
laughter was hardly audible to Me because I had retreated so
far into myself; nevertheless, the last thing Huntington said,

although I heard it so softly it had almost no sound, stayed with Me, and to this day it still makes my heart pound in panic:

Have mercy. When you find a little bird with a broken wing, break the other 1.

I need a glass of water.

7

1 morning my dorm-room door opened and a dark-skinned young woman with a black braid walked in with a suitcase in each hand. She saw Me sitting at my desk, absorbed in the screen of the video recorder where Huntington's hand was making a technical drawing.

The dark-skinned young woman said:

I was hoping to see you hanging in the harness dressed in your wetsuit.

She smiled.

I made no reply. Now Huntington was sharpening his HB graphite pencil in a steel pencil sharpener. I rewound the tape and prepared my pencil sharpener and my pencil, identical to his. I turned the video recorder back on. I imitated the way

Huntington sharpened without stopping as the wooden shaving flowered from the sharpener, the way he then brought the tip of the pencil to his lips, blew on it 2 times to dislodge any specks of graphite.

In the meantime the young woman had placed her suitcases on 1 bed and begun to unpack, and as she strode from the suitcases to the closet and back, she informed Me that she studied psychology and that she knew all about my case, which she found fa-sci-na-ting, and in fact she already knew that we were both going to be in the same Quantitative Psychology class, the class taught by Professor Paulina Glickman, who was Chilean—Hispanic like us, she said— because she was Mexican, too; her name was Selma, it was a pleasure to meet Me.

I got up from my chair and left, slamming the door behind Me.

No, I wasn't at all happy about losing the room to myself.

Sociable: inclined to engage with humans.

Selma was the most sociable person I had ever met. Correction: *have* ever met. Looking into someone's pupils was her idea of living. If it was Sunday and there were no classes and no Student Mixer and she didn't have a date with anyone—a girlfriend or, preferably, a boyfriend—she turned on the television or read a magazine in order to keep looking at people's pupils and find out about lives that weren't hers.

If she was desperate, she went to the movies and paid 5 dollars to see 3-by-4 metre faces on a large screen.

And if those thousands of faces on the screens or printed on paper left her "empty" (her word), she'd talk on the telephone to someone who made her feel "fulfilled" (her word).

And if that still wasn't enough, she'd start pestering Me and force Me to phone someone, which in my case could only be my aunt.

She would sit on the edge of 1 bed to make sure that I, sitting on the edge of the other bed, kept in "close contact" with my aunt via the telephone. Listening, she smiled, she became sad, she went through a sequence of 15 faces expressing different emotions.

1 day she went so far as to take the phone from Me and tell Aunt Isabelle that I received letters with 2 lemon-tree leaves in them and that I spent days and days sniffing them, but refused to write back to whoever was sending them to Me.

My aunt explained to her that I didn't do that, respond to letters.

Well, there began a close relationship between Selma and my aunt, and the relationship, whose basis was Me, revolved around making decisions about my life.

1 example: that I simply had to go to 1 of the Mixers. Another example: that I had to stop thinking the Killer was a genius and realize that spending all night copying the way he held his pencil when he sketched was ludicrous.

It wasn't ludicrous. If I didn't learn to draw like Huntington, I wouldn't pass Technical Drawing I, II and III and I wouldn't graduate. But Selma and my aunt couldn't understand that.

There were 2 bookshelves in our dorm room: 1 against a wall next to the window, which was my bookshelf, and another 1 next to Selma's bed, which was Selma's bookshelf.

My bookshelf slowly filled with books on animals and hers slowly filled with books on relationships between human beings. Now it was my turn not to understand: how was it possible that not 1 of her books was about anything outside of the interminable circle of faces? About the sea, for example, or the arid desert or the snow on the planet's poles.

A Mixer was a nighttime meeting in a dimly lit backyard where they cooked hamburgers and played music and students in shorts and T-shirts stood in groups of 2s or 3s to talk and laugh and talk more and sweat in the summer heat, staring into each other's pupils and drinking glasses of alcohol disguised with artificially flavored refreshments, essentially in the attempt to form a stable 2, that is, in the attempt to find someone to mate with.

At a certain point in the evening, when several couples had already formed, the music became slow and the lyrics gave mating instructions, and there began phase 2 of the coupling:

The pairs embraced and took 1 step that way, 1 step this way, the pubic area of 1 person's genitals pressed into the pubic area of the other person's genitals, albeit separated by a few layers of intermediary fabric.

Those who were still pairless kept talking among themselves, louder now, and drinking faster, distressed that the night was moving on without them having found anyone to mate with. Suddenly 1 would stumble drunkenly and fall onto the grass. Suddenly 5 would leave the Mixer Indian file, downcast and defeated. Suddenly in a dark corner 4 or 5 would pass around a marijuana cigarette and then also collapse onto the grass, defeated.

All the while those who'd already found a mate kept embracing in the dance area, 1 step that way, 1 step this way, their genital regions pressed against the intermediary fabric, the songs giving mating instructions.

Then came phase 3.

A few hand-holding couples would enter the house where the party was taking place and go upstairs to the bedrooms and close the door, and this is what they did: take off their clothes and mate, this time for real.

Technically: their genitalia finally united with no interceding fabric.

In 89% of instances, the process involved a penis and a body cavity: the male introduced his erect penis into the female's vaginal cavity (65%) or anus (12%) and the 2 of them thrashed energetically, as is the case in copulation with all quadruped mammals. On fewer occasions the penis was introduced into and sucked by the female's oral orifice (12%), as occurs only in a few mammals, most notably erect primates.

In only 11% of cases did the process involve female genitalia and the male oral orifice. The females separated their legs, and the males licked between them diligently, raising their heads at, on average, 20-second intervals, to take air, as occurs in bonobos, meerkats and other female-dominant species.

All of this activity was accompanied by sound (screaming, wailing, moaning, swearing, etc.).

(The statistics are approximate, as they come from a sample taken by a single observer [Me, looking through keyholes and making notes] over the course of 3 Mixers.)

Meanwhile, as the copulation phase was going on in the bedrooms, below on the grass, the defeated, still clothed, were taken ill. Some cried, others stumbled from tree to tree, searching for solitude so as to vomit alone, 1 might embrace a tree trunk, arguing that he missed a certain human being that was his true mating partner and who lived very far away, or some other absurd nonsense.

Selma was number 1 at the university when it came to mating. She rarely repeated partners and was never lacking 1. This is how it worked out: she was in "close contact," as she called speaking about personal things, with 30% of the university (again, these percentages are approximate), and of that 30% there was always someone new to meet at a Mixer to enter into genital contact with. So by the time I stopped seeing her, Selma had already exchanged sexual fluids from various orifices with 10% of the university's student body.

It's important to note that it was a large university.

But here is what still makes Me laugh: Selma didn't even

realize she was good at it. Some nights, when the 2 of us were lying in bed in the dark, she would say:

Oh, Karen, I'm so alone. I just can't find a mate.

But as I said before, this is common with humans. In addition to wandering around thinking that they think before they exist, they are usually thinking about something besides whatever is right in front of their faces.

Other times she said something even odder:

Oh Karen, I really have to find myself.

Which, to Me, was just the limit. Where did she expect to find herself if it wasn't right there where she was, lying in bed talking about it?

Nevertheless, Selma went out 3 times a week at 6 o'clock in the evening with the express intention of finding herself.

She'd put on a kilt and white knee-high socks and braid her hair in 2 braids and walk over to the Faculty of Psychology, where on the 4th floor she would enter the office of a 75-year-old therapist and lie on the couch in order to try to find herself for precisely 50 minutes.

Inconceivable: in a room that measured only 4 by 4 metres, she had 50 minutes and still couldn't find herself.

Why she dressed that way, like a high school girl, I don't know, but she would come back crying because she hadn't managed to find herself that time, either.

Oh Karen, she said 1 night lying in bed, every day I'm a little more lost.

At 1 of those Mixers, at approximately 1 in the morning, Selma dismounted her partner, put on her tailored jeans and her shirt, and came looking for Me.

She found Me deep inside a pine forest, standing facing a string of colored lights hanging from the pines; the mating songs were barely audible in the distance.

I sensed her standing beside Me.

What are you doing? she asked cheerfully, which is how she always was, with the exception of those hours when she was desperately in search of herself.

What are you doing? she repeated cheerfully. I mean, besides looking at the lights.

I'm also looking at the flies, I answered.

There were flies buzzing in the air, painted with colored lights. I explained:

I'm watching the way the flies are attracted to the light and some of them land on the bulbs.

Ah, Selma replied.

I kept explaining. They were energy-saving lightbulbs, so they radiated cold light and the glass didn't get hot, which is why the flies, attracted to the light, could land without getting burned by the red, blue and yellow lights.

If the cold light conducted electricity too, I continued, it would electrocute the flies and they'd fall to the ground dead.

Oh Karen. Selma laughed. The things you think of. That's why I love you so much.

Then she went up on tiptoes and gave Me a kiss on the neck and I jumped back, startled. Nobody but my aunt and Ricardo had kissed Me, and Ricardo only on my back and while I was sleeping.

I'll be back for you in half an hour, Selma said happily, and I heard her retrace her steps.

I didn't go to many Mixers. Once I'd recorded the pattern of the mating process I lost interest and preferred to keep learning to make technical drawings of the slaughterhouses of the meat and fish industry.

My Theory of Evolution professor was a tall, skinny man who wore black jeans and black short-sleeved shirts, had hairy arms and a big wide mouth; the students called him the Primate.

During the Primate's first class, he walked through the

aisles of desks passing out a thin booklet while he said and then repeated:

Go read this. Go read this. If you have any questions, come see me in my cubicle. Go read this.

The book was *On the Origin of Species* by Charles Darwin, and I never got over reading it. That is, reading it and rereading it. And rereading it.

Selma would often walk into our bedroom, close her eyes, and exclaim:

Don't tell Me what you're doing, let Me guess. You're either trying to imitate the Killer's sketching technique or you're reading Darwin.

And of course she was right.

Well, now that I'm writing about it, decades later, the first thing I should say about Darwin is that I now understand *On the Origin of Species*, or almost, and that's why I'm convinced that we should burn all of Descartes's books given that Darwin disproves Descartes entirely.

I'll try to explain.

I don't know how to explain.

My language gets all mixed up every time I try to talk about this topic, my favorite topic: the difference between Descartes and Darwin.

I'm going to go for a walk to loosen up my body and

prepare to write about the difference between Darwin and that wretched fool Descartes.

So. The wretched fool Descartes wore a black cape that went down to his ankles. When he wanted to think, he wrapped himself in his cape so that the world couldn't distract him from his thoughts.

He said:

I'm going to think, then I'll return to the world.

Which explains his idiotic sentence: I think, therefore I am.

And it also explains why his thoughts, which were thought beneath his black cape, are such dark thoughts.

Darwin, on the other hand, liked being out in the fresh air, going for walks. He walked for miles. When he was a young man wearing explorer boots he hiked the length and width of the Galápagos Islands in the South Pacific, and when he was hiking he stopped to make sketches in his notebook of every animal he saw.

And that's why what Darwin thinks about life is full of sun and movement and all sorts of animals.

Deranged Descartes said under his black cape:

There is a line between human beings and animals.

He opened his cape and added:

No human can ever cross that line.

But Darwin never saw any such line. On the contrary, what he saw everywhere he looked were similarities, the similarities that exist between all living beings.

He saw that the different birds on the different islands of the Galápagos resembled each other so much that they might actually have been a single species that had evolved over the course of time, due to being in places with different climates and different flora and fauna, into 10 different species.

He also saw that birds were so similar to reptiles that they might be reptiles whose scales had in time turned into feathers and, in a moment of joy, taken flight.

And he saw that the same could have happened to other reptiles but in a different way: that they might have evolved over millions of years into hairy, warm-blooded animals, that is, mammals.

He saw that quadruped mammals might at some point in the remote past have stood up on 2 feet and turned into biped primates.

And then, many years later, when his explorer's boots had been sitting in a box in a closet in his house in England for 30 years, he saw something that made him very quiet: he saw that it was likely that out of all the biped primates, the chimpanzees had changed over time until they turned into him, a scientist, a thinking primate smoking a pipe in the sun in his English garden.

A thinking, talking primate who said:

There is nothing bizarre about that. That is, there is nothing bizarre about thinking that I am a descendant of a very intelligent monkey. All species live together on the planet Earth, interacting and evolving.

Which seems obvious now, but until he articulated it nobody had seen it so clearly.

I don't know if I wrote this before: Darwin published this in 1859, and since then it's been taught in all universities as a fact. And yet I don't know a single human being who truly believes it.

What I mean is, I know lots of people that, if you ask them what Darwin said about life, can recite it with greater or lesser accuracy, but I don't know 1 single person whose daily life proves that he or she really believes that there is no impossible-to-cross line between him or her and all of the other beings who don't think in words.

Here is the curious thing: Descartes lived in the 17th century, and Darwin lived in the 19th century, and yet humans keep being educated by Descartes. They keep being trained during the first 2 decades of their lives to think that they are their thoughts and that thinking is the highest act of all and what undeniably sets them apart from other species.

It's true that thinking sets them apart from everything, but that's because they've been educated by Descartes and not by Darwin.

Professor Paulina Glickman rode into class on a yellow bicycle, dismounted, and left it against a wall. Big square-framed glasses, gray bangs, children's lace-up shoes, a beaver smile: her 2 front teeth showed when she laughed.

She made Me come up to the dais where she was, beside the blackboard, and introduced Me to the Quantitative Psychology students like this:

Before you today: Karen Nieto, hypothetically, a highly functioning autistic.

Based on the enthusiasm of her introduction I thought they were going to applaud Me, but that wasn't the case. But from her desk, Selma turned to her fellow students and whispered, That's my friend that's my friend, as if I were her gift to the class.

The professor continued:

That's what we'll be doing on Mondays, nailing down Karen's diagnosis. And now, let's get to know her a little.

Karen knows the names of all of the Nobel Prize winners in science. Karen, please take a seat at the table and give us their names.

I took a seat at the table and gave their names. The Nobel laureates in physics, the Nobel laureates in chemistry, the Nobel laureates in medicine, the Nobel laureates in economics, from 1901 to 1994, which was the year we were living in.

When I finished the very long list of names I received a standing ovation from the students.

I asked for a glass of water and a minute later there it was before Me.

I drank the whole glass in 1 long, slow swallow.

When I put the glass back on the table, a student raised his hand and then stood and asked Me very respectfully:

Now could you tell us all the kings of the French dynasties, please?

I don't know them, I replied.

You could hear an ahhhhhhhh of disappointment in the audience, but what could I do? I didn't know them.

I said:

But I can recite 3 chapters of *On the Origin of Species* by Charles Darwin.

Not today, the professor said, and ended class.

*

I had to go to Quantitative Psychology every Monday, and on other days the students studied other cases. Seated at a table on the dais, I took all of the tests the professor, who sat before Me, administered.

I remember the inkblot test very well. The professor showed Me sheets of paper 1 by 1 and I told her what they were:

Inkblot. Bigger inkblot. 2 inkblots, 1 black and 1 red. Several black inkblots.

When it was over I asked what my grade was and the professor said cheerily:

Don't worry, you performed perfectly.

And I was sure that she was also a highly functioning autistic, but much more adept than Me at getting rid of inconvenient people.

I recall especially the triangle test.

She gave Me some colored wooden triangles, and using them I had to replicate the designs she showed Me on different pieces of cardboard. But then she took out a stopwatch and held it close to my face and gave Me only 1 minute to recreate the design.

In several instances I was unable to replicate it before she called:

Time!

And she'd stop the stopwatch with her thumb. Which frustrated Me very much and in the end I became furious.

So the following week I arrived having studied and asked her to give Me the triangle test again.

No, thank you, the professor said, today we'll do a different test.

I want to do the triangle test again, I insisted.

No, Karen, she said with a Hostile Face ☹.

I, in turn, put on my Hostile Face ☹.

Karen, she threatened, don't be obstinate.

But obstinate is what I am: I opened my backpack and took out the box of triangles that I'd bought at the university bookstore, right in the Quantitative Psychology section, opened it up, and spilled the colored triangles out on the table with a Blam!

Then I sat and slowly, carefully replicated the designs 1 by 1 until I had completed the 35 of them that Doctor Glickman had showed Me in the previous class session.

The professor had gone to sit at a desk and she and the students let Me work in silence. It's true that rather than 35 minutes it had taken Me 7 days, but I've never denied that I'm slow.

Then Doctor Glickman sent Me to a hospital.

They put Me in a white metal tube. And in the following

class session, all of the people in the class, including Me, held color photos of my brain in their hands.

The professor said:

Note the white matter between the 2 hemispheres of the brain. As you know, white matter transmits information between brain regions. Note that Karen's white matter is narrower than that of a neurotypical person's brain. Why is that? Is it simply genetically programmed that way or is it because during the critical developmental period the necessary stimuli were not received?

I thought she was asking Me so I said:

I don't know, Doctor.

And nobody will ever know, Karen, she replied, taking 3 steps toward the students.

That's why her brain has fewer connections between regions than a normal brain. But it's also why Karen possesses certain enviable abnormal traits. A superior memory, for example, as we've seen. Or, for example, she also . . .

She began the sentence but then instead of finishing it she bit her lower lip with her big beaver teeth and scratched her head and announced that class was over.

There came more tests. Tests on paper. Tests with photos. Tests and more tests.

They went on all semester.

At the end of the last class, the professor promised Me I'd get an A+ and I asked her for the results of the psychometric tests she'd given Me.

That's neither useful nor recommendable, she said. Let me stress: you're perfect.

Give Me my diagnosis, I demanded.

The doctor squinted from behind her square-rimmed glasses, leaned over the desk, picked up a pen, wrote something on a blank piece of paper, and held it out to Me.

She had written:

Karen Nieto, highly functioning autistic

Paulina Glickman, Ph.D.

That was the first diploma I'd ever received in my life, the certification of my highly functioning autism, and it made Me happy. I was about to thank the doctor, but she got on her yellow bike and Selma and I watched her pedal down the hall, and then we saw her through the window riding down a path among the pine trees and Selma invited Me to lunch.

In the cafeteria she told Me she was proud to be my best friend, that she'd do anything for her best friend, that I should tell her what I wanted most, and suddenly, that very night, Selma and I were by the side of a road in another state of the United States—Pennsylvania—in a run-down station wagon, drinking black coffee from a silver thermos and waiting for the sun to come up.

Light began to extend across the sky from the horizon and then we saw the most humane pig-slaughtering complex in the whole of the American continent.

Actually, that's an imprecise way of speaking. From the run-down station wagon we really couldn't see anything except for a gray cement wall silhouetted against the yellow mountains that stood out against the green grass.

It's huge, Selma said.

Once out of the station wagon, over my wetsuit—minus the mask and fins—I put on the blue overalls and white hard-hat and rubber boots that I'd bought in the next town over. Selma held my backpack so I could get it on, and with 1 hand I picked up from the grass my video recorder and with the other the mountain climber's rope and hook, and I began walking.

But then I turned back and retraced my steps to ask Selma:

What if the Killer doesn't like Me doing my final project on his complex?

He'll feel flattered, she said. Isn't this plant his pride and joy?

She thought about it some more and said:

Listen, Karen, I want to ask you a favor. Don't tell me what you see in there.

She stood on her tiptoes to press her lips to my cheek but I sidestepped her so she couldn't.

Okay, I said.

I retraced my steps again. It smelled of chlorophyll and I could hear the crickets and the chirping of birds.

It turned out the wall wasn't that high. I hooked the rope over the top, climbed up, and stood on top of it.

Yes, the complex was huge.

To my left, looking like toys, were long pens where the pigs probably spent the night. Before Me lay some 2 kilometres of pasture and a few apple trees, where hundreds of pigs, looking microscopic—like fat pink ants—grazed placidly, chomping on green grass. A few bipeds in blue overalls and white hard-hats herded off a group of pigs, guiding them into a high-walled red-brick chute that led to the abattoir: a windowless white concrete mass, approximately ½ a kilometre in length. And finally, to the right of the cement mass, the pigs reappeared in the parking lot. That is, they reappeared converted into stacks of chopped meat, packaged and refrigerated, that other tiny employees transported on forklifts and lifted into 55 red trucks, each with nearly microscopic writing on the side:

Happy Pig, Co., stress-free meat

My boots stomped firmly into the mud.

Other students' technical drawings were 1.5 metres by .70 metres, each rolled up and placed in a .8-metre document tube. Mine was 5 by 7 metres, rolled up and stored in a 5-metre document tube.

When Gabriel Short called my name and I walked down with a 5-metre-long tube, the room filled with silence. Short simply gestured with his hand for Me to leave it on the desk with the other drawings.

I watched Short leave with all of the drawings in something that looked like a leather pail, strapped onto his back. Mine he held beneath his arm. When he got to the corner where he was supposed to turn, he had to maneuver for a while with my drawing before he could finally turn.

A week later I went to room 27 for my grade. I walked up to the grade sheet posted on the chalkboard. ½ the students had failed, but by my name there was no grade listed. There was, however, a note in pencil.

Come to my house Saturday at noon.

I went to the desk where Short was handing technical drawings back to downcast students.

My drawing, I said.

Short replied:

Come to Professor Huntington's house Saturday at noon.

A 2-story glass house made of enormous windows that joined at sharp angles with black iron arrises, surrounded by green pines. A house that I'd heard someone somewhere say had been built by a famous architect named Frank Lloyd Wright.

Finally, Short opened the door. I looked up at the ceiling and he looked down at my yellow leather boots.

Come in, he said, and opened the door wide enough to let Me pass.

On the stairs I stopped to look at the famous Committee for More Humane Animal Slaughter medal, which was framed and hung from a blue ribbon: a large gold coin with the profile of a man in bas relief and the inscription *Nihil consensui tam contrarium est, quam vis atque metus: quem comprobare contra bonos mores est,* which is Latin, and since I didn't speak Latin (and still don't) I didn't know what it means (and still don't).

Don't keep him waiting, Short whispered from 4 steps up.

8

Huntington was standing in his second-floor study, my map spread out on the ground, as big as a rug.

He said:

You've either got some serious balls or you're a complete idiot. Excuse Me: ovaries. Ovaries the size of balls. Making a blueprint of my meat-processing facility and handing it in as your final project.

He adjusted his spectacles, thick as magnifying glasses.

The detail of your drawing is ... how can I put it? ... maddening. You drew each 1 of the bricks in the chute the pigs go through.

It's made of bricks, bricks, I said.

Yes, he replied, red bricks.

Red, I concurred. But I drew them gray because the lead in my pencil was gray.

Thank you for that explanation, Huntington said.

You're welcome, I replied.

He continued:

You drew the water pump outside the entrance to the chute leading to the slaughterhouse. You drew the water pipes on the roof of the pigs' bathing chamber. You drew the signs and company logos, which are everywhere. Each and every 1 of the 33 fucking brass logos with its 2-millimetre HP. You drew the grates on the floor in the death chamber.

I smiled complacently.

Huntington, though, did not smile.

Did you not attend my course, Karen?

I attended your 3 courses and never missed a single class. And I drafted blueprints for close to 1,000 hours to practise.

Huntington snorted, his nostrils fluttering quickly, and I didn't understand why he was now angry.

A blueprint is an abstraction, he raised his voice. It should only contain useful information. Why didn't you just go ahead and make yours 30 square metres?

I couldn't find paper that size.

Concentrate! he shouted. A useful map ignores minute details in order to capture the general design!

This, the Killer said lowering his voice slightly, lifting the edge of my drawing with his shoe, this shit is useless.

It's useful to the pigs, pigs, I whispered.

What's that? Repeat yourself, I can't hear you.

It's useful to—I raised my voice—to the pigs!

Huntington raised his eyebrows behind his glasses, surprised.

Pigs don't know how to read blueprints!

I swallowed, tense, and kept shouting.

What I mean is, it shows everything the pigs see and hear!

How the fuck do you know what the damn pigs see and hear??!!

I walked with them through the facility to the death chamber!

You walked with them …!!??

Huntington pressed his lips together. He scratched his head.

Then he spoke in a normal tone of voice:

And who let you in? It's restricted access.

I climbed over the wall.

And nobody stopped you once you were in?

I was wearing a worker's uniform. Blue overalls and white hard-hat.

And how the hell did you get that?

I bought it in the shop in the town where they all live.

That's a crime, Huntington said, threatening Me with his index finger, you trespassed on private property. I can demand that the authorities lock you up.

I didn't know, I whispered, both hands in the pockets of my white jeans.

I didn't know, Huntington said, imitating my nasal voice.

But then he put on a Friendly Face ☺.

Well, what now, Miss Different Abilities? The pigs don't pay the slaughterer, you know.

Oh, I said.

Irony! he exclaimed. And he hissed between his teeth, I believe it was a laugh. If so it was a furious laugh. Finally he tugged on his black tie.

That was irony, he repeated. Don't you know what irony is? Christ, nevermind. You're a robot. A fucking extraterrestrial android. Forget it.

But then he lowered his voice and said:

Okay then. Tell me what you saw.

The pigs, I began, the pigs react with fear to the red bricks because they're unfamiliar, they've never been in a redbrick tunnel, and they feel trapped and don't know where they're going in the dark. So they cry.

They squeal, Huntington corrected Me.

They squeal, I said. They squeal very, very loudly, I added. Then, since they are already terrified, when the tunnel roof ends and suddenly they're out in the bright light, the pigs squeal like crazy and bump into each other, and some of them turn around and try to go back, and then the ones behind them crash into them, and then every company brass plate reflects the sun, dazzling them and making them even more agitated, and they squeal louder and louder.

Huntington said:

We can amend that. We can extend the tunnel all the way to the death chamber.

Yes, I said. That would be nice. But. The real terror happens in, in the death chamber.

Not true, said Huntington. What happens in the death chamber is death, and that we cannot amend, this is a slaughtering facility. Death, not terror, is what happens in the death chamber.

Terror, I repeated. Terror. When they reach the death chamber, they see, while they wait their turn they must see, how the stun gun is applied to the other pigs, other pigs who are their brothers, their cousins, their friends, who they've spent the last few days with, they see how they get shot, shot, and fall down, and they watch in terror, in terror, the way the chain shackles their hooves and jerks them up toward the ceiling and how, once they're hanging, the slaughterman slits them open beneath their snouts and they watch them bleed out, and the ones hanging also keep watching and they kick and watch sadly, hanging their heads and looking at each other sadly, and, and, and.

Stop stuttering! Huntington interrupted forcefully. For the love of God, can you please stop stuttering?

No!! I shouted. I can't!! Not, not, not now!!

I apologized, staring down at my boots:

I'm very, I'm very stressed.

Huntington began to walk around the edge of the map, nervously, saying:

Fine, stutter all you want, but take pity on me and stop with the asinine comments like: the pigs feel this or that, the pigs are terrified, the pigs see their brothers and their cousins, the pigs look at each other sadly. Stop all of that if you want to sound like a livestock engineer and not an imbecile. Nobody can feel like a pig except a pig. You're simply giving an anthropomorphized interpretation. They were squealing and you translate that into panic. Maybe they were hungry. Maybe they were singing to the god of pigs, the Pig God.

He hissed, that is, I believe he laughed.

At any rate, he said, stopping short, this—your blueprint— is fucking idiotic.

Fucking: the gerund of the verb to fuck—here used adver-
bially—which Huntington went on to use many times and in
several derivations that afternoon.

Behind him I saw a glass case with a double-barrel shotgun
and lowered my eyes, anxious.

He carried on:

To begin with, in order to really see what the pigs were
seeing, you'd have to have walked at their height. How far up
on you did they come?

To my thigh.

That's right. And you'd have to have eyes on the side of
your head, like pigs. Isn't that right?

I thought about it for 30 seconds. And I answered:

Maybe.

No, not fucking maybe! he exclaimed. It's absolutely fucking true! Having eyes on the side of your head is totally
different from having them in front, like you. It means seeing
at a wide angle but having no depth of vision, whereas you
see at a narrow angle with great depth of vision! And as far as
them looking at each other after their throats were slit, that's
nonsense.

I saw it, I whispered.

Well, it's fucking nonsense. The stun gun had already
dazed them.

I saw them looking, looking at each other very sadly, I insisted.

You saw it, yes, but again, you misinterpreted what you saw. It's that simple.

I shook my head.

Don't be a fool! Have you ever been shot with a stun gun?

No.

What a shame!

What a shame? I don't understand.

For your information, the pigs had already lost consciousness! The kicking, the expressions, those are conditioned responses! Automatic reflexes from the vegetative system! Look at me and tell me if you understand me or not!!

I looked at him. His bespectacled face wore an expression of extreme hostility, and I glanced over at a shotgun in his display cabinet.

Fine! I heard him exclaim, and then inhale. Fine! he exclaimed again, inhaled again. Fine, and I heard him calm down, now oxygenated. Stay for lunch.

Lunch? I asked, still staring at the shotgun.

Yes, lunch, he replied, still somewhat tense. I have a proposal for you, Miss Porcine. But first we'll have a whiskey.

*

He and Short had whiskey on the first floor, because I don't drink, and finally, whiskeys in hand, they flanked Me and we went to sit at the dining room table.

A servant appeared out of I don't know where and served us soup. I looked down at the soup; it was tomato. I heard Huntington say:

You will recall that 1 day I spoke in class about a little bird with a broken wing. I said that the merciful thing to do is break its other wing, so that it doesn't try to fly in vain. Well, you have managed to attain, there's no denying it, a skill for drawing like none I have ever seen.

Photographic, Short murmured.

Photographic, Huntington confirmed. That's your good wing. But your intelligence is inferior. That's your broken wing. Nobody's eating the soup, let's move on to the meat.

The servant, who took tiny panicked steps, rushed to exchange soup for meat.

Huntington used his knife to cut off a bite of meat. He brought it to his mouth and chewed. Still chewing, he pointed with his knife to my plate:

Eat, he ordered.

I don't eat meat, I said.

He said:

A vegetarian livestock engineer, for fuck's sake. How twee.

Well, Huntington finally said, after a silence in which you could hear silverware on porcelain, here's the dilemma facing the professor—that's me. I either discourage you from continuing your studies; that is, I prohibit you; that is, I fail you and I strongly recommend to the university administration that you be expelled. Or ...

He cut off another hunk of meat, put it in his mouth, and chewed over the idea.

... or I give you wings, Karen. Do you know that expression: I give you wings?

You give Me wings? I asked, trying to think quickly which wings he might be referring to.

I give you a marvelous opportunity, he said, and swallowed his meat.

What opportunity?

I give you the opportunity to replace the broken wing with another 1. I lend you a wing, as it were. Do you see?

I don't know, I said.

Short reached for the pepper mill.

What I mean, Huntington said, is that I'll give you a way in, a way to become an important person in our field. In short, I'm offering you the chance to work with me.

I couldn't believe it so I said:

I can't believe it, Doctor Huntington.

Believe it. Your being able to draw something that already exists to the centimeter is no good to you. With that sort of talent, you could become a landscape artist, exhibit your work at small-town art fairs, but you can't become a real live-stock engineer. But what you can do is make Charles Huntington's blueprints.

I smoothed the tablecloth in front of Me with my finger-tips, intent on pressing down the air bubbles that had formed.

I'll come up with the designs, Huntington explained, describe them to you, make a general sketch, and you fill in all the details on 1 of your enormous drawings. You make it realistic for the buyer.

I heard him take a sip of something.

We could even publish a large-format book together, I heard him say. Short, show her our book, Huntington said.

I kept my gaze fixed on the tablecloth.

Beneath my eyes Short slid a large book and on the white cover was written in red letters:

KILLING WITH COMPASSION

By

Charles Huntington

What do you think of our book? I heard Huntington ask.

Without looking up I responded:

Short's name isn't on it.

Out of the corner of my eye I watched Huntington move his empty plate 10 centimeters to the center of the table and heard his exasperated voice:

Short's name is *inside* the book.

I heard Short justify:

It wasn't in our interest for my name to be on the cover. Publishing strategies.

So, there you have it, I heard Huntington say. I want to employ you as my right hand. My draughtsman. With a considerable salary, to boot. 3,000 dollars a month just for working ½ days. Plus ½ the course credit you need to graduate. You'll work here, and you won't have to take my courses, which are the most difficult and important ones, because I'll give you the credits so you can get your degree—otherwise I fear you'd never graduate. What do you say?

Short's hand removed the book from my field of vision.

Karen? Huntington asked. Answer, he ordered. Well, what do you think? Are you happy?

I looked up and asked, staring at the wall but keeping Huntington in 1 corner of my field of vision:

154

What about my grade in Technical Drawing?

Always distracted by the fucking details, he muttered, nostrils flaring in agitation once more. Nobody gives a shit about the Technical Drawing course, Karen.

I need an A in that course, I replied.

What is it that you're not getting, Karen? he said, leaning into the table, his face tense, eyes froglike behind his glasses' lenses. I'm offering you the chance to be Doctor Charles Huntington's draughtsperson. Tell Me this instant what the fuck it is that you're not getting here.

I need an A, I repeated.

Fine, the Killer murmured. I'll give you an A if you accept my offer. And an F if you don't accept it.

If I don't accept the A? I inquired, my gaze fixed on the ceiling.

A tinkling sound startled Me: Huntington, with a little spoon, rapping on his glass. The servant came scurrying out with her tiny steps of terror to clear the plates.

I asked again:

Are you going to give Me an A? I need an A.

Gabriel Short intervened:

Let her think about it over vacation, Professor.

With this idea, everyone relaxed.

But then I was again startled, this time by dongs. A grave,

sonorous, mysterious donging that nobody at the table was producing.

The living room clock, Short explained.

Huntington said:

All right, Karen. Think about it over vacation. But the first day of classes I'll expect a yes.

He laughed between his teeth, hissing, and out of the corner of my eye I saw him smooth his gray hair with both hands. He added:

I'll tell you what. In the meantime, I'll give you an A. As a sign of good faith. Happy now, Karen?

I nodded vigorously several times.

He held his right hand out to Me at the door, using a Friendly Face ☺.

I don't do that, I said, also using a Friendly Face ☺. Shake hands.

So he reached instead for the doorknob and opened the front door.

Enjoy your vacation, he said.

Can I have my drawing back now? I asked.

Ah, your drawing. I wonder where I left it?

Upstairs in your study, I replied.

Ah, yes, upstairs. I'll give it back after vacation. Good afternoon.

But, I began, but he interrupted Me forcefully:

I don't want to go upstairs now, Karen. You tired me out. You can be very tiring. Did you know that?

Short could, I began, but he interrupted Me again:

Short is not my errand boy, Karen! I'll return it when we see each other in December. Now, have a nice vacation.

And after I had taken 3 steps and was already out to the front yard I heard him say something very odd:

Yes, I'll have a nice vacation, too, thank you.

I never fantasize. Except when I do. Fantasizing is so unusual for Me that whatever I imagine I take to be almost solid, factual.

As soon as I opened the door and saw Selma sitting with her legs crossed in bed watching television, I was convinced: Huntington had stolen my drawing. I'd never see my drawing again. My floor plan that proved that his humane slaughter facility was in fact a house of horrors.

Huntington would take a blade to it and cut it into 5 pieces, put all 5 pieces in his fireplace and light them on fire, warm his palms with the bonfire of my drawing, and my drawing would turn to ash in his fireplace.

I leaped down the dorm stairs 3 by 3. I rang the doorbell

at Huntington's house. Short opened the door, I grabbed him by the shoulder, pushed him to 1 side, ran up the stairs past the award hanging on its pale blue ribbon. My floor plan was no longer on the floor of the study, it was probably in its red cardboard document tube, which was in Huntington's hand, and I rushed straight toward him to take it from him but he scooted to 1 side, saying:

Calm down, Karen. Let me have it. What do you care? Besides, it's more mine than yours, anyway.

Why? I asked.

Think about it—carefully. This is a drawing of my pig-processing facility.

I shouted, enunciating each word:

I! WANT! MY! DRAWING! HUNTINGTON!

And my hand gripped the wrist of the hand in which Huntington held the document tube. I squeezed until he let it fall to the floor and then I crouched down to pick it up but Huntington kicked it and it rolled over to the wall, which he reached before Me, and then picked it up, opened a window, and hurled it out.

Short, he said to Short, who had appeared in the doorway, go down and get that drawing from the yard. And you, Karen, just go.

So much training to control the size of my emotions, make

them smaller, make them civilized as my aunt Isabelle called it, just to lose it all in an instant. All of my rage exploded. I rushed at Huntington and grabbed his neck with my right hand, forcing him to back up until he hit the wall, and then I kneed him, hard, in the testicles, that is, in technically the softest part of the male human body.

Huntington went entirely limp, but I held him up by the neck, pinning him to the wall, and with my other hand I punched him in the glasses.

And then I let go.

He fell to the floor as if he were a sack of potatoes, his face against the floorboards, his shattered glasses to 1 side, and he didn't move.

He didn't move and a small pool of blood began to form beneath his head, spreading to touch the soles of my boots.

I took a step back so as not to stain the soles of my boots with his blood.

And the blood continued to spread across the floorboards.

I took another step back.

And that was when Huntington moved, quickly: suddenly he got up on his hands and knees and with his face all bloody and his tie dragging across the floor he began to crawl toward the corner of the study where his double-barrel shotgun sat in the glass case.

He stood, grabbing onto the wall and leaving bloody hand-
prints, and he was taking the shotgun from the display case by
the time I finally reacted: when I snatched it from him, the
gun went off. In an instant, the glass window shattered into a
marvelous design of irregular triangles whose vertices met at
the bullet hole.

I pulled the trigger: another window shattered into irregular triangles.

There was 1 window left, and I took full advantage: I fired,
laughing as it shattered into even smaller triangles and then
fell into the yard in 1 block.

Down in the yard Short was shorter than he had been a
few minutes earlier, standing among the shards, holding my
red document tube. He handed it to Me quite amicably, and
I in turn handed him the shotgun.

Tell him I don't want to be his fucking draughtswoman,
I said.

And that's how I was expelled from college.

2 days later I was walking down the stairs of the Mazatlán
mansion in my wetsuit, fins over my shoulder, Nunutsi
snaking in and out around my feet with the precise grace
required to keep from being stepped on as I moved, while

several men in the living room were hanging my enormous drawing, which Aunt Isabelle had had framed in a black wood frame. I walked out onto the veranda, where a bald man was having breakfast with Aunt Isabelle—her new partner, she'd informed Me—whom I kissed on the cheek (my aunt Isabelle, not the bald man). I crossed the patio, passed the pool, and reached the beach where 2 lemon trees had been planted by Ricardo, a token he'd left Me so I wouldn't forget him before he sailed off to who knows where, and from the wooden dock I stepped down into a little boat, started the motor, and set off for the horizon, sailing out to the high sea, where I cut the motor and—finally—returned to the landscape of my tranquillity.

No people and nothing human in sight.

Sea and sky.

All of a sudden a Y of small black birds.

The sun, a ball of white fire.

Perching on the boat's edge, I fell backward into the sea so as to enter the water tuna mask first.

Tuna mask: I'd blocked the mask's frontal vision with 2 slanted mirrors that allowed Me to see sideways as if I were a tuna, and thus descended seeing the turquoise water out at my sides.

*

Descartes didn't write only about human thought. He also wrote, at the end of his life, a very short book on happiness, which I did read and which, unfortunately, is less famous than the others.

After many words and 24 pages, Descartes wrote that happiness is a matter of the senses. Seeing, hearing, touching, smelling, tasting: that is happiness. Then Descartes wrote many other pages full of words, which is a shame because he'd reached the truth on page 25.

Yes, the most basic, most happy form of happiness is simply feeling with your senses. Thinking with your eyes and skin and tongue and nose and ears.

In the turquoise layer of water I stretched out on my side so I could descend while looking through the tuna mask and through the lucid water's surface to the white clouds.

And watching 6 red fish swim from cloud to cloud, it once again seemed so unclear to Me why humans need to fantasize.

Oops. A yellow fish covered the sun.

For a moment.

Then in the deep blue a grey ball came swirling at Me and then, after delicately bumping Me in 1,000 places—plip plip plip plip plip plip plip—dissolved into 1,000 steel-colored mackerel that darted toward the dark blue.

Again, why is fantasy necessary? Fantasy: philosophy and religion and the history of imaginary things.

Why, when there is reality and we have our senses?

In order to be happy all you need to do is to listen to your senses and not to Descartes. Feel with your senses and without words. All you need is to be in your body in the real world.

And to be even happier you have to treat the real world as if the real world were the things you think.

Think with the fins of a barracuda darting diagonally upward and leaving a line of bubbles in its wake.

Among the red strips of the red forest of algae, I came upon a sandy clearing with a flat green rock at 1 end, and I lay my head on the flat green rock and waited for the rest of my body to drift down onto the sand.

A white triangle: a white manta ray. As its shadow slid across the length of my body, I set my tank's alarm to go off when I had just enough oxygen left to reach the surface, and I left my Me behind; my Me dissolved into the slow, heavy, blue water—the enormous, joyous Not-Me: the sea.

Here's something strange. 1 sunny morning I happened to find, hanging from a nail on the wall in my room, shining like a small, flat, round light, the Committee for More Humane Animal Slaughter medal.

As I said earlier, living in the human world has required a huge effort from Me as well as a tremendous amount of perseverance, but I do possess that lucky trait: things that I really like unexpectedly turn up later in my house.

9

Yellowfin tuna are in constant motion. They never sleep.

Truly, they never stop to sleep or even rest. If they stopped, they'd sink, so they spend their entire lives migrating.

Their entire lives: 7 to 11 years.

They migrate through warm water in schools that hug the coastline of the American continent, all the way from the United States down to Chile and back again. They have no calendar like other tuna. They follow no fixed annual route. They don't return to the same place to spawn. But what they *do* do is never stop migrating.

Some biologists think they migrate in search of food, because they consume ⅓ of their body weight in food every day due to all that movement. Which is like saying they move in order to feed themselves so that they can keep moving.

At some point in their journey, which is thousands of kilometers long, dolphins join them, swimming above the tuna. Breathing above them through the holes in their heads. Guiding them from above. Looking out from above for the approach of a fearsome shark or tuna-eating whale.

Metres below, the school of tuna catch smaller fish. As they chew them, pieces float up to the dolphins, who feed off of these leftovers.

At the halfway point on their journey lies the coast of Mexico. And the tuna boats of Mexico, which lie in wait.

And high above the boats, 35 kilometres above the sea's surface, in outer space, floats a silent polyhedral satellite with the ability to photograph cities, ports, islands off the Mexican Pacific, and even discrete movements in the ocean, such as a procession of fins and columns of mist, that is, a procession of dolphins, that is, the sign of a school of tuna down below.

Out on the high seas, at the latitude of Mazatlán, the 360-degree skyline had red rays to the right and the round white moon to the left, floating in the night. That was when I saw them, the first fins drawing closer.

I let myself drop backward into the water and swam down to the school of tuna, who immediately became agitated.

1 of them sideswiped Me, another pushed Me, a third swished Me with its tail, launching Me all the way to the back of the school.

I let all the tuna pass Me and then beneath the shadows of the last of the dolphins I turned on the cylindrical motor beside the oxygen tank on my back so that I could follow them.

2 big tuna stayed behind to swim on either side of Me. Without touching Me, they kept Me at ½ a metre's distance. For an hour I did nothing to stand out, aside from existing in a form different from them, which I hope did not stress or offend them.

After an hour of swimming beside Me, they forgot about Me and the 2 tuna went back to take their places in the middle of the school.

I looked at my wristwatch.

If the captains of the 2 ships anchored at sea had followed the satellite images closely, they would right now be lowering the outboard motorboats into the water, and those in turn would move out to set the net measuring ½ a kilometre in diameter. This time, however, there would be no yellow floats, only blue ones—the colour of the sea.

Once the net was submerged, they'd turn off the motors, and then the most nerve-wracking part of the catch would begin: the wait.

I could imagine the fishermen on deck leaning over the edge of the hull, 1 or 2 lighting cigarettes, preparing for the slowest catch they'd ever taken part in. A catch that had been the idea of the slowest woman they knew: the dim-witted niece of the owner of Consolation Tuna's.

The dolphins, the tuna, and I all swam into the net. I could see beneath Me that the net was beginning to be hauled up.

Using the 10 pulleys on both of the 2 ships, the net was being raised. The motorboats slowed, circling the enclosure, and the fishermen harpooned only those tuna intent on escape. The dolphins, though, were not bothered by anyone, and with plenty of time given how slow this catch was, they jumped over the net 1 by 1.

3 divers—4 including Me—wrapped our arms around the few disoriented dolphins and hauled them out of the trap. A tremendous full-body struggle to force any defiant dolphins to escape.

The dolphins are out, a captain called over the loud-speaker.

The net was raised on ship 1 and a sluicegate was opened in ship 2. The net became a slide forcing the silvery tuna to fall into ship 2, 1 after the other, into a huge tank of seawater lit by skylights.

The tuna dived down looking for a way out, thumping into the ship's bottom; on deck we felt their pounding gradually become slower and less intense.

Until it stopped.

The experience had been unexpected for them, but it had been fast and there had been little blood spilled.

The pink stain on the surface of the sea was approximately 400 metres in diameter.

½ an hour later, the pink had dissolved.

Okay.

That's what I said to Peña and my aunt over the radio; they were awaiting news in the tower on the dock.

I like that word very much: okay. It's from the 19th century, the American Civil War. Generals used to write it in their war reports when nobody had died that day.

Zero killed = 0 killed = OK = Okay.

Okay, over and out, my aunt responded.

Outside the radio cabin on deck, the man from

2

Greenpeace tugged off the hood of his wetsuit. He had brown hair with blond tips like Ricardo.

The most stress-free tuna catch on the planet, he said. Congratulations.

I corrected him.

Except for those in Palermo, where they still use pre-industrial methods.

No, he smiled. More stress-free than those.

And then he added:

And 100% dolphin-safe.

We'd submerged a spacious metal enclosure for the tuna beside dock 4. Why confine them in tiny spaces?

Because it costs less, Mr. Peña had said when I gave him the cage's dimensions. He removed his glasses and immediately put them back on.

Because it costs less, he insisted to my aunt Isabelle several times. Why use that much metal if the tuna can be kept in a small enclosure?

But my aunt said:

Don't be a penny-pincher, Peña.

A stream of tuna, 80 in total, entered the enclosure, and before they reached the grates at the far end, we dumped in a load of sardines from above. They began feeding on them immediately, the grates forgotten.

I swam into the enclosure in my wetsuit, wearing my tuna mask, to make sure they were all okay, a basket of shrimp on my back. The tuna turned to look at Me. They began to surround Me. Their round black eyes, pupils enlarged, turned hard, fixed on Me.

The technical term for that is a *predatory look*. When large animals surround a smaller animal, which in this case was Me, the predatory look precedes their devouring it.

Did they recognize Me? I wondered. Did they understand that I had led them to this prison?

I stared at 1 tuna in particular, 1 whose black eye palpitated almost imperceptibly; the eye had a yellow spot that suddenly seemed threatening to Me. I turned slowly, tossing handfuls of shrimp, and to my relief the tuna opened their mouths to gobble them up.

What happened next was totally unexpected.

The tuna with the yellow spot in its black eye swam up to Me and nudged Me with its nose, as if waiting to see how I'd react.

So I leaned my head forward and butted the damn tuna, although not forcefully, just to make sure it knew that I could push, too.

Then the other tuna swam over and another 1 nudged Me with its nose, slowly, and I butted it with my head as well.

We played like that for a while, head butting like good friends, the catch of a few days ago forgotten.

We'd installed a conveyor belt that ran the whole length of dock 4, all the way from where the tuna enclosure was to the walkway in front of the cannery, where benches had been erected for the public.

Our 10 captains, our employees, Rabbi Chelminsky from Maine and his butcher, whose name I can't recall, the new secretary of fisheries, and the new mayor of Mazatlán.

3 fishermen pulled the first tuna from the enclosure and secured it to the conveyor belt, a fourth dazzled it using a neon light, and then they turned the machine on and the belt brought it to Me, where I stood waiting in my white gutters' uniform and white boots, a compressed air gun in my hand.

I placed my other hand on the tuna's side, which beat rapidly as if it had a little drum inside it. I exerted pressure, my firm hold calming it although the fish did keep opening and closing its mouth because it was asphyxiating, and its eyes kept darting anxiously, because it was probably freaking out from the asphyxiation, and then I quickly held the gun next to the spot beside its black eye, which suddenly turned to stare at Me, watery.

THE WOMAN WHO DIVED INTO THE HEART OF THE WORLD

I fired.

The tuna arched and then suddenly slackened.

2 sailors hauled it into a long, orange plastic container full of crushed ice.

The next tuna arrived. I pressed into it firmly to calm it.

I fired.

They placed it in another refrigerated coffin.

As the third tuna approached on the conveyor belt, the rabbi and the butcher walked over. They wore white butchers' aprons and white gloves, and both had beards down to their chests; the rabbi also wore an elegant wide-brimmed hat. They unfolded a plastic tarp and knelt on it.

Following my instructions the butcher calmed the tuna using long, firm strokes.

I said, in English:

Fire.

1 moment, the rabbi replied, also in English.

The butcher said I don't know what, in Hebrew, his white gloved hand on the asphyxiating tuna, his eyes looking up at the perfect morning sky; it seemed an eternity while he chanted in that strange language, and I looked up at the benches, where our guests looked down at the ground or over at the cannery, that is, anywhere besides the place where the murder was occurring, and in fact even my aunt Isabelle, seated beside her bald new partner and wearing big dark glasses and a white linen hat, stared off at the farthest place possible: the horizon out above the silvery sea.

The butcher finally finished his prayer with an Amen.

And fired the air gun into the tuna's brain.

And on it went until all 80 tuna were killed. The rabbi, the butcher, and I killing, the guests on the benches, looking away, chatting among themselves as if they were in a different place for a different reason.

Only the penultimate tuna was hard to kill, because I recognized the yellow spot in its black eye, and, startled, I let go at exactly the same time as the rabbi fired the air gun. The gun exploded the tuna's eye and a gush of blood spurted out, soaking the rabbi, the butcher and Me.

At the end of the ceremony, Rabbi Chelminsky stood before the bleachers, his face, hat and beard covered in blood. A microphone was placed before him, and he dripped blood and sweat onto the cement.

He spoke, in English, into the microphone:

These tuna are certified kosher. *Kosher*, that is, properly killed according to Jewish law, and they can now be eaten by Jews all over the world.

At this Peña suddenly perked up. He took a calculator from the breast pocket of his shirt. He'd finally understood why the hell my aunt had paid the rabbi's and butcher's high fees.

The Greenpeace representative also took a turn at the microphone, saying:

Greenpeace also certifies that these tuna are dolphin-safe and stress-free, and can be eaten by eco-conscious people the world over.

Peña frenetically keyed numbers into his calculator while the entire audience, drenched with sweat and lightheaded from the sun, stood to applaud. Then the secretary of fisheries, who nobody had invited to speak, climbed down from the benches and headed for the microphone, and the people on the benches reluctantly sat back down, baking in the sun.

Tall and silver-haired, dressed in a pearl-colored suit and red tie as though he were at some elegant city reception hall, the minister leaned into the microphone and said:

I'll be brief.

We knew, then, that we had a long speech ahead of us, the kind fashioned by secretaries of fisheries.

I'm afraid I'm not a fisherman but an economist.

Long pause.

1 person clapped tentatively, hopefully, but unfortunately the minister had more to say.

Nevertheless, I am honored to be with you here today to officially declare broken the embargo that the United States placed on Mexican tuna. At least unilaterally, on the Mexican side, the embargo is broken.

Click! went Aunt Isabelle's red parasol, which she opened there on the benches, a sign we all decided to interpret as the conclusion to the secretary of fisheries' speech, and we applauded to stop him from talking anymore and rushed to the cylindrical glass tower on the dock where on the 4th floor they were serving frosty mugs of beer and tamarind martinis and empanadas filled with marinated tuna.

I almost couldn't hear him. In 1 corner, Peña was whispering to 1 of the captains of our fleet:

3 million dollars, including salaries, new facilities, air transport for those refrigerated coffins. Fucking waste of money if you ask me.

The captain removed his sailors' cap, wedged it under his arm, and said:

But we broke the embargo.

Peña:

Unilaterally? What bullshit. The gringos were the ones who

imposed the embargo, not us. There's no reason to assume they'll let us sell our tuna. And if we can't sell them, we're going under and the fishery closes regardless.

Captain:

Does the boss understand that?

The boss only listens to her idiot niece. I'll tell you something else ...

Peña opened his mouth to tell him something else, but the secretary of fisheries walked up to him and they changed the subject.

Mugs of beer in hand, weaving as they walked, the specially invited guests followed my aunt on a guided tour of the cannery. They walked through the gutting room and she pointed to the ceiling, where my fly-killing light hung. A spiral neon tube 1 metre in diameter at the base.

The flies were attracted by the bluish light and not driven off by the heat, as would have been the case with other lamps. They landed happily on the blue light and were instantly electrocuted with a zzzzzt, then dropped dead into a long plastic tray of water on the floor.

The secretary of fisheries and the rabbi stood agog, staring at my invention.

Okay, Rabbi, the secretary of fisheries challenged, let's have a prayer for the flies.

The rabbi took a swig of beer and said, foam in his beard:

There aren't any, secretary, because we don't eat flies. But I can tell you what the great Maimonides wrote about killing in legitimate defence.

Here we go, said my aunt.

The rabbi cleared his throat.

Just a moment, said my aunt, and asked the gutters to be quiet. The women stood motionless in their masks and latex gloves over ½-cut tuna.

And the rabbi, with his deep, melodious voice, began to intone a series of things in Hebrew that we all supposed referred to killing in legitimate defence.

The party continued on the beach among the lemon trees that Ricardo had planted in order to be remembered by. At a long table beneath the trees' leaves.

Waiters brought out enormous oval trays of food. Baby tuna wrapped in Mexican pepper leaves with a thin lemon and *morita chile* sauce, mounds of wild rice, smoked sardines, and roasted crickets in an egg-white batter. Then came plates garnished with lemon quarters, bottles of rosé wine poured into crystal goblets, bottles of Oaxaca *mezcal* poured into little glasses.

At 1 end of the long table, I sat sipping wine and carefully watched our guests bring the tender tuna to their mouths, tuna that they'd been unable to look at when it was still whole, still alive, with an air gun pressed to 1 eye.

The rabbi stood, glass in hand.

Not in Hebrew this time, the secretary of fisheries requested, still wearing his tie but now without his jacket, his sweaty shirt sticking to his body.

Translate for us, my aunt said from the other head of the table.

Today, the rabbi said in English, and I said in Spanish, I have learned how precious life is. How fragile and how precious.

A wave could be heard crashing in the distance, and then a tock-tock among the trees just beyond the lemon trees.

Killing 80 tuna, 1 after the other, the rabbi continued, I felt how close death was, felt it in my hands, in fact, in the compressed air gun I held in my hand. And I also felt how close God was. I felt, forgive my presumption, the angel standing guard at the gates of Heaven, a flaming sword in his hand.

My aunt lowered her glass, disheartened. Every time God is mentioned she loses interest. Through the leaves of the lemon trees the sky turned orange and then, like every evening, night began to overtake day, a surge of energy flowing out, letting Nature run free.

The cicadas began to buzz, the birds sang louder, and the rabbi raised his voice to be heard above them:

God has given us dominion over animals, to use them and to eat them, but animals are part of his creation as well, and it's our human obligation to treat them with dignity. To kill them without torturing them. With no unnecessary suffering.

It occurred to me, he continued, in competition with the uproar of the ocean's waves, the cicadas, the bird whistles, the tock-tock-tock in the trees, that Consolation Tuna should be a destination for those who want to make peace with death and with animals. Who want to respect animals. Kill them with respect. Eat them with gratitude and compassion.

I finally figured it out: the tock-tock still coming from the branches of a royal poinciana was a woodpecker hammering the trunk.

I'm a Jew, the rabbi sang at the top of his lungs, and it was as if he were about to sing like all the other birds, this 1 almost 6 feet tall and with a beard, striving to be heard above Nature with his booming voice. I'm a Jew, and the Jews were systematically massacred by the Nazis like animals. My congregation is made up of Holocaust survivors, and the children and grandchildren and great-grandchildren of those survivors. I'd like to propose to those Jews that they visit Consolation Tuna this summer, to witness the beautiful execution of the tuna—no gunpowder, no bullets, no knives—so they can learn what I learned here today, that is, if you'll allow me.

Enthused, Peña stood to reply that of course we'd allow it and what's more, we could organize a tour for visiting Jews, they could go out in sailboats, learn to scuba dive! And so as not to be left seated, the mayor of Mazatlán also stood, although it was only after the crash of an enormous wave that we managed to make out that he was offering the Jews a special rate for lodging, at Mazatlán's extraordinary hotels, which provoked much laughter among the diners, 1 of whom asked what hotel in Mazatlán wasn't a dump; and finally the secretary of fisheries stood to add his voice to the competition of human voices, voices all battling it out with the sea, the birds, and the tock-tock-tock of the woodpecker.

There stood the 4 men getting breathless, shouting, and there was Nature, obliterating them with its whistling and buzzing and general uproar. I poured myself another glass of *mezcal*. I drank it. I poured another 1. And then I saw it.

A squirrel leaped from the bough of 1 royal poinciana to the bough of another royal poinciana, and there among the orange flowers it seized the woodpecker between its teeth, leaped into the air, dropped to the sand, and ran off with the bird in its mouth, rushing down the beach that had turned blue like the night sky, in which I could make out 3 points of light very high up: 2 white, 1 blue.

I looked at my wristwatch: 8:23.

It was the plane transporting the 80 refrigerated coffins, and my future.

I quickly downed a third glass of *mezcal*.

Suddenly, there were 2 moons in the sky.

10

The white dawn slowly poured itself out over the black night. I poured steaming hot milk into steaming hot black coffee in a jar and handed it to the rabbi, while outside the kitchen door, the sea receded, wave by wave, enveloped in a white breeze.

We'd stayed up talking all night at the blue wooden table, he asking about the details of good tuna murder practices, Me asking him about good fish murder practices in general, according to Jewish law.

It turned out that according to Jewish law, any fish can be killed just about any old way, and in general they just let them suffocate in the air, but only fish that have scales and fins can be eaten. Which meant that the butcher's work at Consolation

Tuna would be very simple. He'd come each month to ensure that the tuna weren't mixed with other fish with no scales and no fins, and to make sure that once the tuna were chopped up and canned we weren't adding any nonkosher oil or other forbidden substances.

It will be like a vacation for him, the rabbi said, accepting the jar of milky coffee. Just supervising the process and then signing the papers that certify everything was kosher.

Oh, I said. So then why did we go through all that on the dock? Why did I teach you to kill the tuna, and why the blessing?

Miss Isabelle requested that, said the rabbi, stroking his beard. Perhaps so people would know we'd come from Maine.

Off in the distance, dogs were waking up and barking, birds chirped, trying to outsing each other, a rooster cock-a-doodle-dooed at a ranch on a hill somewhere.

Why does Nature make such a racket at dawn? he asked.

For the same reason it does at dusk, I responded.

Which is?

An excess of energy that gets released when night turns to day and when day turns to night.

The rabbi, barefoot, bags under his eyes, in his black pants and wrinkled white shirt, took a sip of coffee and suddenly said:

Let me confide something in you, Karen. Just between you and me. Adam and Eve were vegetarians. As far as we know, according to the Bible, they ate apples. In paradise, I mean, before they fell from grace and were expelled from paradise.

I asked for more particulars. Against my aunt Isabelle's express advice, I found myself intensely interested in religion that morning. Or perhaps, I think now as I write this, I was simply interested in the rabbi, who reminded Me—with his thick beard, long legs, higher-primate feet, and talk of angels—of Ricardo.

You really don't know what paradise is? the rabbi asked.

No idea, I replied.

He laughed, shaking his head.

Well, I'll send you a Bible. A real Bible, not a Bible that's been corrupted by 2,000 years of Christian interpretation. The Bible of Jerusalem. If you promise to read it.

I promised, and then he told Me about paradise anyway.

The mountains and the hills will burst into song, he said in his deep voice, his eyes ½ closed, and it seemed he was speaking from memory. The sea and the clouds in the sky will travel their peaceful cycle, from dawn to dawn. There will be no dangerous thorn bushes, only gentle cypress trees will grow, and instead of nettles there will be myrrh. The wolf shall dwell with the lamb, and the leopard will lie down with the goat, and ferocity will vanish from the Earth.

I liked the sentence and repeated it:

Ferocity will vanish from the Earth.

And nobody, said the rabbi, nobody will ever go hungry or thirsty, because food and water and wine will be given freely.

After a brief pause he said:

Amen.

That's wonderful, I nodded. When will it happen?

Nobody knows, he replied.

Oh. And where?

Everywhere.

Who's organizing it?

The rabbi looked at Me for a long time and didn't reply.

Is it just a story? I asked. A fantasy?

It will be a miracle, he said.

What's a miracle?

Something that happens without cause. May I have some more coffee? he asked.

And then I knew it was a story, a fantasy. I served him another jar of milky coffee and as I handed it to him, steaming, I asked him another question:

Are you mated, rabbi?

Married, you mean? He sighed. Yes. I'm very mated, he said quietly.

Then, in almost a whisper:

3 children bind me to my wife with 3 very thick ropes.

The idea of 3 children binding him with ropes to his wife seemed to Me a very cruel Jewish custom, so I said:

That seems very cruel.

And the rabbi replied:

Life's not easy.

He drummed his fingers on the table and then after a while he stopped drumming his fingers on the table and said:

You're all quiet now. What are you thinking about?

Right now?

Right now.

The fate of my 80 tuna.

In short, it was a disaster. A week later the refrigerated coffins had been returned with a note.

The most expensive tuna on the planet, ha ha ha.

And the embargo wasn't even lifted. The ecological organization Clean Seas alleged that the dolphins we'd saved in our fishing expedition had been so stressed by the experience that they would never be able to reproduce.

How did they ascertain so quickly that for the rest of their entire lives those dolphins would be sterile? No idea, but they held a march on Washington and although there were only 54 people in dolphin masks at the march, they passed in front of the White House and their photo was in newspapers all over the world—including in Mazatlán, where I stared at it, transfixed—and their claim was universally accepted: that we'd ruined the sex lives and reproductive capabilities of those dolphins.

What's more, as if by chance, Clean Seas announced in those same newspapers that they would be the ones to label whole tuna and canned tuna as dolphin-safe and that the label would be required in order to be sold in U.S. supermarkets and that the label would only be given to tuna fished from boats that hadn't used nets to fish anywhere near dolphins, all of which led Peña to ask 1 day:

And how the hell are we supposed to convince yellowfin tuna to swim far away from dolphins?

I thought about it for months without coming up with an answer, and then cans of U.S. tuna—Chicken of the Sea— began appearing stamped with the phrase "100% dolphin safe 100%" and it was all over. Chicken of the Sea flooded the shelves of all of the supermarkets north of the Mexican border and Peña subjected us to an emergency company meeting that in fact consisted of us listening to him curse Chicken of the Sea for 3 hours:

Liars, he said. Giving the people tuna instead of chicken. Liars. Giving the people cheap albacore instead of our golden yellowfin. Liars. They're in cahoots with Clean Seas. What a coincidence: they're so concerned about dolphins, and albacore don't migrate with dolphins and only migrate far from Mexico.

The only thing that was clear to Me was that despite its name Chicken of the Sea sold white tuna—albacore tuna—but called it chicken, and for some reason that I couldn't comprehend, ecologists were more concerned about dolphins than they were about the tuna themselves, or the sea turtles, or the tiny little anchovies that dolphins swallow by the kilo each day.

My aunt auctioned off 5 more ships, ½ of the 10 we had left, and fired ½ of our sailors and workers and cancelled the contracts she'd made with the eco-friendly net weavers, and on every third corner in Mazatlán there appeared 1 more person selling little boxes of Chiclets or 1 more person wanting to clean your windshield with a sponge and a bottle of soapy water, and Consolation Tuna opened a soup kitchen that served powdered soup made of tuna bones and the lines of people with bowls in their hands waiting to get in grew longer week by week.

Back at the mansion Aunt Isabelle began to drink sugarcane rum in the mid-afternoons and long into the night and

1 very red morning she dragged out to the giant palm-tree garden the 3 suitcases and the Panama hat that belonged to her bald boyfriend and she called a taxi to take it all away, the suitcases, the hat and the bald boyfriend, but my aunt wouldn't fire Mr. Peña from his post as general manager of Consolation Tuna even though I begged her.

So we went back to the old business of tuna canned with herbs for the limited domestic market.

1 afternoon when I had too much free time out on the gray rocks on the beach, I began reading the Jerusalem Bible that the rabbi had sent Me in the mail.

But I was disillusioned right after the first page, where God creates light and the sky and the earth and the seas and the stars and the animals and man and woman. Specifically: I was disappointed in line 28, when God names the 2 humans—suddenly and with no reason—"masters of the world" and asks them, or orders them, I'm not sure which, to "be fertile and increase, fill the earth and master it; and rule the fish of the sea, the birds of the sky, and all the living things that creep on earth."

Which, apparently, is what they do the rest of the very long book, where (as far as I can tell) all of the other stories are about God and humans, and humans and God, and all of the other living creatures make appearances only in the form of food or clothing or transport or to be sacrificed or—moronically—as metaphors for human or divine things.

2 things I learned from the Bible:

1. God is very strange. He creates the world and the stars first, but then sequesters himself in the human bubble.

2. Human insanity didn't start with Descartes; it started long before him, at least 3 millennia ago when the Bible was written, if not earlier.

Anyway, who knows where I lost the old book, the Bible. But a few days later, maybe a few weeks, I went down to the beach 1 morning and saw before Me on the sand a line of tiny letters walking by.

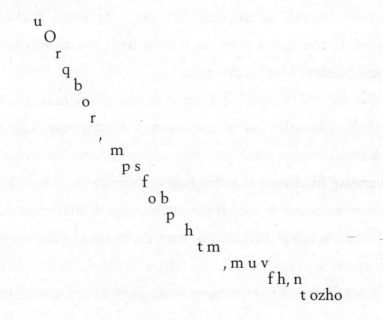

Carpenter ants had shredded the Jerusalem Bible with their sharp teeth and were transporting it letter by letter to the crater of the anthill, where they joined the whirl of 7 other lines of ants who were transporting little pieces of very green leaves, before disappearing into the sand.

Some of the only happy things that happened during those years, which my aunt Isabelle referred to as the Years of No and Never: Nunutsi made the acquaintance of a tabby cat but rather than get pregnant she ran off to who knows where. The Jews who survived the Holocaust never showed up on dock 4 to see the black tuna corpses. And we never saw the secretary of fisheries again, until 5 years later when Mazatlán awoke to the photo of his coiffed white hair and his perfect smile plastered on every lamppost.

He was the PRI candidate running for president of Mexico, and the Mazatlán paper came out the same day with the headline:

Failing Mazatlán: Assured Political Victory

In those days in which everything failed, that prediction failed as well. The PRI lost the presidency for the first time in 70 years.

Luckily, long before then we found out why the sale of our

stress-free, dolphin-safe tuna had failed. That happened 2 years after we caught them, when Mr. Gould stuck out his index finger and rang the doorbell of my aunt's mansion.

Gorda took her standard 5 minutes to go answer the door.

Mr. Gould said he had come looking for Miss Different Abilities, and Gorda thought long and hard, squinting, before responding that yes, she lived there, but no, she wasn't home right then.

Then I'll wait for her inside, Mr. Gould said with such authority that it didn't even occur to Gorda to argue, and she stood aside to let him in.

Mr. Gould took off his red baseball cap in the middle of the living room with the marble checkerboard floor, and, holding it in his hands, he approached a drawing in a black wood frame, my pencil sketch of Huntington's slaughter-house. He looked at it from up close, his nose right up against it, then stepped back to take it in in its entirety, and then examined it from up close again.

Next he stopped before another, equally large, framed piece—an oil painting of a nude woman surrounded by penises, done in different shades of orange—and leaned in to read the little plaque on the frame that read: *Woman*

Threatened by Red Snappers, and Gorda blushed and told him that Señora Isabelle's new boyfriend—a Zapotec Indian—had painted it.

Finally Gould went and made himself comfortable on the best sofa—the red velvet 1—and sat staring at the fly-killing lamp, which I had hung from the ceiling.

3 flies alighted on the bluish spiral tube, fried themselves to a crisp with a buzzing sound, and fell straight down into the nickel-plated tray of cool water awaiting them on the floor.

Gould said:

Excellent.

He was about 70 years old, his oval head perfectly bald like an egg, and his strong, blond-haired legs stuck out from his white Bermuda shorts that had at least 1,000 wrinkles and ended in his black huaraches with soles made from trailer tyres.

Bring me a shot of tequila with salt and a slice of lemon, he told Gorda in his oddly accented Spanish, already in full possession of the house.

11

As Gould would later inform Me, there are 2 ways to see the world. Like a clock where things happen in their own time, beyond your control. Or like a surface with innumerable dots that you can connect however you wish.

Gould was a dot connector.

As a child his mother gave him 1 of those dot-to-dot books that were sold for 10 cents in stationery stores in Scotland, books whose pages each have 100 numbered dots, all out of order. Children are supposed to use a pencil to draw a line from dot to dot, in order, and a tree or a castle or a rocket headed to the moon appears.

What Boy Gould did was forget about the numbers and connect the dots however he pleased. Maybe the tree he drew wasn't the best tree, but it was his tree. Maybe his rocket headed to the moon looked more like a hose with a drop of water leaking from it, but it was his hose. Maybe his castle more resembled a cinder-block house, 1 of those boxes with little glass windows, but that's what Gould wanted: to work in a modern cement-and-glass skyscraper.

When he was 35 years old he summoned the man who was his boss at a household appliance company and told him to go down the drain.

Go down the drain, that is, down the sewer's duct system that carries the city's water away once it's been contaminated with shit.

Go down the drain! Gould the 30-something told his boss: he was going to start his own business because he was sick of wasting his energy on a company that was already going down the drain itself.

I should clarify that what I'm reporting here is what Gould told Me and as he told it to Me and I faithfully took it down in my diary, translating from the English without adding my doubts—those that I had then and those that I have now—when I wrote it.

At any rate, his boss promoted him, made him second in command in the Scottish office, and a few years later he was running the household appliance company from its global headquarters in Seattle, but decided he was tired of selling irons and toasters and televisions; they were minor players in the field anyway, so it would be better to move headquarters to London and instead make television programs and clothes and bread, and each year they'd divide their companies into 3 categories.

Those that yielded considerable profits, they'd invest more money and enthusiasm in; those that showed mediocre earnings, they'd invest with ideas and enthusiasm but no money; and those that weren't yielding a profit, they'd send down the drain.

Gould, you see, hated failure and loved success.

He made a lot of enemies: the thousands of employees that he unemployed cursed his name, journalists and politicians cursed him, and his favorite phrase just about turned into part of his last name—he became Gould-the-down-the-drain-bastard.

But Gould told them all to go down the drain, and for 20 years the shareholders adored him and 3 times they approved the doubling of his salary, because like him, they too loved success and hated failure.

And when he turned 63, the shareholders held a general assembly and voted for him to retire.

Bastards, Gould called them, leaving the general assembly and telling them all to go down the infamous drain.

But after 3 years of fighting not to go down the drain himself, on a golf course 1 day as he prepared to take a little swing to sink a little ball into a little hole 30 centimetres away, he had a heart attack that felled him right on the green, and lying there staring up at the sky, seeing the white clouds float by, slowly changing shape, he decided that what he needed to do was to change his body.

Or else have several replacement bodies.

He managed to achieve it, but not without some difficulty. This is what he did.

He had an operation on his heart. He had an operation on his prostate. He had an operation for the bags under his eyes. He had a monkey's gland implanted in his neck to make him young again. And he decided to dedicate his new unemployed life to seeing the wonders of the world and spending more time with his family, because he'd realized he didn't even know them.

To begin with, he bought a yacht in which to ply the seas up close with his family. It turned out that from up close he didn't actually like his family. His 2 sons had 2 wives and 8 children in total. They all went around with their noses in the air and tiptoed around in Italian shoes and spoke about almost everything with scorn, and what they didn't speak about with scorn they spoke about with envy.

So and So has Such and Such a private jet, and So and So has Such and Such a castle, and the president of Such and Such a country is an idiot.

They never said anything original, even by accident; they brought nothing to the world nor did they desire to. There were 2 emotions that consumed every hour of their days: the aforementioned envy and scorn.

Finally, after dinner 1 night on the yacht, somewhere between Cuba and Spain, his children informed him—in front of his grandchildren—that they were the way they were, bitter, they said, because he, Gould, their father, had been the way he'd been: an absent father, a father who chose his business over his children, a father who traumatized them with his nonpresence.

Sitting in his chair, surrounded by his complaining family, Gould hung his head at the accusations and thought:

With all my heart, I wish I were not here with these horrid people.

The worst was yet to come.

Halfway between Japan and Fiji, Gould got into bed and when his hand touched the pelvis of the woman who had been his wife for 37 years, she confessed to him that she loved another man.

Since when? Gould asked.

For the past 10 years, she confessed.

How is that possible? he cried angrily. You've had a lover for 10 years and I didn't even know?

Or maybe I got that wrong; I might be misreading my handwriting since I wrote it in my diary quickly. It might have been Mrs. Gould who said that, and probably also angrily:

How is it possible? I've had a lover for the past 10 years and you didn't even know!

Gould left the yacht in a motorboat and gave the captain instructions to take them all down the drain.

And that's how, at 67 years of age, he found himself un-employed, with no family, and his days filled with idleness.

There's nothing harder for an active man than being idle, Gould told Me (?). Inevitably, so much free time depressed him (???).

(The question marks are mine; they're in my diary. Even now I don't have a clue what he meant.)

Luckily, men and women from all over the world began to call to invite him to go on dates with other women, which gave him something to do: fly his new jet to his dates.

Being a multimillionaire at age 67 is like being a blue-eyed blond-haired movie star, Gould explained (?????). Highly unlikely, but he seemed to believe it when he told Me the story on the 132nd floor of a skyscraper in Shanghai, China, 1 idle afternoon.

So at age 67 he began his life as a blue-eyed blond-haired movie star, despite the fact that he was a rather short, stocky, entirely bald man.

And that was how he got not 1 but 3 new bodies: those of his new mating partners.

He began to go out with 1 and then another 1 and another 1, and on his outings he met very rich people who devoted themselves to the difficult task of not doing anything (?), like him, and he learned of the activities they engaged in to combat the stress of not doing anything. Like them, he bought very expensive paintings. He bought a castle to store his paintings. He bought 5 different apartments in 5 different cities to relieve himself of the boredom of the castle full of paintings.

Deep down, Gould told Me, it all bored me to pieces (???).

At an auction, he bought a pistol that had belonged to a very famous pirate whose name I didn't record in my diary. The gun barrel was made of iron and the handle of gold. 1 night in his castle lying beside mating partner 2 he found himself thinking about sticking the barrel of the pirate's gun into his mouth like a straw and pulling the trigger, but then he said to himself:

I was the kid who connected the dots as I saw fit. What the hell happened to my mojo, my drive? Who did such a terrible job of connecting these dots (the castle, mating partner 2, the pirate's pistol in my mouth)? This isn't what I wanted, that's for sure. I've become a conformist who draws from dot 3 to 4 to 5, without even trying. I have to get my drive back!

He pulled off the sheets and uncovered himself.

In the castle's tower, he shouted to the heavens:

My drive, my drive, my drive! I've got to find my drive!

Whiskey? Gould offered at the windowed balcony on the 132nd floor of the glass skyscraper in Shanghai.

I don't drink, I told him.

Gould asked the young Chinese woman sitting beside us for a whiskey.

1 afternoon he was on the beach of who knows what island, lying on a plastic chaise, when an old woman with almond-shaped eyes and bare feet approached him and tried to sell him a necklace made of seeds.

Any other time he'd have told her to go down the drain. But this time Gould didn't know what the hell to do with his time, so he decided to learn how the old woman had made the necklace, where she'd got the red seeds, the small ochre-colored acorns, the oval sunflower seeds. He watched those little beads of color moving between the woman's dark, creased, old fingers, moving like a rosary, Gould said, and he discovered that he was actually quite touched and asked her how much the necklace cost.

1 dollar is what it cost.

Gould paid her for 10 necklaces in advance and sent to her home some gold-plated baubles he'd bought for 10 dollars a dozen at some market in Tunisia.

He sent the 10 necklaces to a friend who sold them in the accessories department of his New York department store for 100 dollars each.

Thus began Gould Trading Co.

In a park in Shanghai he saw a little Chinese boy playing with a toy: a string with steel balls on either end. The string hung from the boy's index finger with the balls hanging down on either side, and as he moved his finger up and down, the metal balls knocked against each other, separating a little farther apart with each clack. Gould bought the toy from him for 10 dollars and replaced the metal balls with solid, semi-transparent plastic, which cost less and rebounded more. He had the balls and string manufactured and assembled in the Philippines, and sold the item in toy stores all over the Western world at an 81% profit.

2 balls and a string, Gould said, shaking his head. For 2 years it was the top-selling toy on the planet.

Gould Trading Co. was ready to expand.

He diversified his line of toys and fashion accessories and took an interest in softer things, low-cost clothing lines, and he opened an Internet portal to receive tenders for patents for things that had just been invented.

The material for his apparel was made and cut in China, assembled in the Philippines (because Filipino women have the nimblest and cheapest hands in the world), packaged in Milan (because the Italians are masters at making cheap trinkets look stylish), publicized in London (where they have marketing geniuses who can sell a sheep in a tank of formaldehyde as avant-garde art [???]), and sold internationally: to ½ a million department stores around the world.

What Gould was not going to do was repeat his mistakes. No more wearing a stupid tie every day, no more desks bolted to the floor in rented offices, no more ungrateful shareholders, and above all no more workers or employees who were resentful that they weren't as rich as Gould.

None of that.

Just a team of 10 captains of industry, each managing 10 very young school graduates from decent business schools, each with 2 cell phones and 1 laptop so they could be well connected.

Of course, Gould explained, after 3 years of selling a product at a 50% profit margin, there are always going to be competitors. Copycats, envious conformists.

What he did was sell those greedy, worthless fools his production chain and customers at a 250% profit over and above original investment.

And once again, I'm the best, he confided. The best. The best.

Come, he said then. I'll show you my 1 and only personal office.

We stood up, but looking out the windows of the 132nd floor made Me dizzy, with the cars below looking like ants and the people looking millimetric, so Gould had to wait while I advanced slowly, grabbing on to a sofa and then making my way to a chair, which I'd hold on to in order to dare walking to the next sofa.

From his office, through the 2 floor-to-ceiling windows, you could see the 132nd floor of the building next door, which was under construction. 102 Chinese construction workers moved quickly and wordlessly among the black metal girders, caked in whitewash, pushing wheelbarrows and emptying sacks of cement that fell to the ground raising clouds of white smoke.

It's going to have 150 stories, Gould informed Me. And it'll be ready next year. They finish 1 floor a week and each worker gets a dollar a day. Isn't China wonderful?

I didn't respond, engrossed in trying to count the workers 1 by 1 to confirm my first impression that there were 102 of them.

What I mean, Gould said, is that China is the most admirable capitalist power in history. Some people say the workers are slaves, but I'll tell you what. That's what they were under the Communists. Now, in the 21st-century mixed regime, they get paid for their work.

Gould didn't say anything else for a while. We stood watching the workers scurry around the same floor in the next building over.

What did you say you wanted to drink? he asked suddenly, moving over to the desk, which was actually a green marble slab on wooden columns.

Water is fine, I replied.

What about food? Sandwich okay? Ham and cheese?

And I said:

A sandwich with no ham and no cheese and with lettuce and tomato.

Gould spoke into the phone:

1 ham and cheese sandwich and 1 no-ham and no-cheese sandwich with lettuce and tomato and 1 glass of water and

1 whiskey. Sit, he said, pointing to 2 black leather sofas.

And we went back to sit and to his story.

1 night Gould was out to dinner in Rome with mating partner 3 and he was twirling spaghetti around his fork when he overheard a guy laughing at the next table over, slapping his thigh and saying:

The most expensive tuna on the planet, ha ha ha.

Gould lit a cigar, leaned back, and stretched so he could listen in.

Then the man told the story of some poor woman with different abilities who had sent the most expensive yellowfin tuna on the planet from some port called Mazatlán to the New York market in luxury coffins.

A woman sitting at the table chided him, saying that it wasn't a very funny story.

Quite the contrary, she said, it's actually very sad.

Then the man apologized, saying he'd heard a VIP tell the story at a meat and fish industry conference.

And who was this asshole VIP? she asked.

Professor Charles Huntington, the man responded very seriously.

Gould wrote the name down on an Egyptian cotton

napkin, which he stole from the restaurant.

And that's how Mr. Gould came to land his white jet on the Mazatlán runway shimmering gray in the sun.

When he reached customs he answered the official's question about whether he had anything to declare with a No, nothing, I don't even have luggage, and in turn asked the official casually where he might find a young lady with different abilities who owned a tuna fishery.

15 minutes later, he stuck out his index finger and rang the doorbell of my aunt's mansion.

12

Let's cut the shit, Gould said.

(I assume it was a metaphor.)

Consolation Tuna's location is all wrong.

Gould said this in his astonishingly wrinkled white Bermuda shorts, hands in his pockets, pacing around the living room in his black huaraches, Me staring at their trailer-tyre soles.

In the 19th century, when the company was founded, maybe the location was adequate, but in the 21st century it's all fucking wrong, Gould insisted.

My aunt lit a cigarette.

Now then: the product, yellowfin tuna, that's another fucking mistake. A depreciated product with no future. And finally, the market: the great USA is of course the biggest fucking mistake of all, a market hostile to foreign food products.

But. What you have, he said, stopping, what you have here is the most valuable thing you can have: an idea. A simple, original idea, an idea so brilliant it's dazzling. Look me in the eyes, Miss Different Abilities.

My aunt intervened:

She doesn't do that. At least not until she trusts people.

Aha, said Gould.

And his stubby toes disappeared from my field of vision.

And that idea, I heard him say, the idea of killing fish without cruelty so they don't release the toxins that spoil their flesh, without freezing them and thereby deadening the flavor, that's worth executing.

My aunt:

So …?

Gould:

So, it's very simple. You need a different ocean, a different product, and a different market.

My aunt raised her eyebrows.

Gould explained himself:

You have to move your fleet to an island in the Atlantic, an African island, say. You have to catch a different kind of tuna, bluefin, which lives much longer—up to 30 years—and grows much larger, and doesn't migrate with dolphins, which are the ecologists' pet species. And you have to sell to Japan, where bluefin tuna belly is considered the caviar of the oceans.

He formulated the entire plan in under a minute. He warned, though, that implementing it would take a little longer for the fishermen in our fleet and the cadre of business graduates in his company.

Are you sure this will work? my aunt wanted to know.

Sweetheart, the only sure thing in this life is death, Gould replied.

And he smiled and showed all of his teeth.

But we'll split the losses down the middle, if there are any, and if there are profits, we'll split those down the middle, too.

He took a cigar out of his breast pocket. He bit the tip. He chewed on it and then put the cigar back in his breast pocket again.

Then he told my aunt:

Do like me, my friend. I divide my businesses into 2. The ½ that are moderate successes or obvious failures, I flush down the drain. And I only hold on to the ½ that are a resounding success. That's how come I'm 100% successful.

Out of the corner of my eye I saw my aunt suck on her cigarette and exhale a stream of smoke. Aunt Isabelle's only business was Consolation Tuna. What's more, what was left of her inheritance was only 5 of Consolation Tuna's original 20 ships. And here was a complete stranger telling her to gamble the rest on 1 bet.

Oh, and I'm interested in that, too, Gould said.

I looked up and saw him standing in the middle of the checkerboard living room floor staring at my fly-killing light.

The tray, though, he said stretching his right hand over the top of his head to scratch his left ear. That should be integrated into the lamp, all part of the same unit. And as for the tube …

What about the tube? I asked.

I don't know, I've got something against tubes, he said. First question: why is it a spiral?

So that was the topic of our first conversation, and we had it in the dining room over dinner. The spiral tube of the fly-killing light.

At dawn Gould quickly scribbled on 2 pieces of paper in crooked handwriting that sloped to the right:

1. The contract in which I sold him the patent for my electric fly killer.

2. A cheque for 100,000 dollars.

*

At the bank I asked them to cash the check in the smallest Mexican bills they had, which turned out to be very pretty, blue 20-peso notes. The blue paper bills filled a black plastic trash bag, and I walked with the black plastic trash bag over my shoulder down Mazatlán's main street in the midday sun so white that parked cars seemed to disappear for a moment in its glare.

I don't know why I remember that so well, the image of the cars disappearing in the glare.

I emptied the trash bag onto my bed and wads of bills covered it completely and it was then that I understood that Gould was as real as the pretty blue bills.

I returned the trash bag to the bank and of course from that moment on I believed everything Mr. Gould said.

Not so Aunt Isabelle and Peña.

Peña showed up 1 morning with 3 giant ledgers under his arm.

Sitting at the kitchen table, he read out Consolation Tuna's declining numbers, his coke-bottle glasses perched on his nose, making him look as moronic as he in fact was, his index finger pointing to each number as he read it aloud.

After ½ an hour my aunt interrupted him:

Okay, Peña, enough. You've made your point. In short, in your opinion we should do nothing and just keep lurching closer to hell.

Well, yes, doña Isabelle, but gradually, not risking it all at once, Peña replied. That way we can try new strategies here in the domestic market. For instance, doña Isabelle, allow me to show you the plan I developed with a PR firm.

He placed some pamphlets on the table and explained:

We can give out free recipe booklets, all over Mexico, so people can learn lots of new ways to use canned tuna.

My aunt took a long swallow of rum and Peña unfolded 1 of the booklets and began to read aloud:

Tuna ravioli. Tuna tacos. Tuna and bean soup. Tuna and apple salad. Oven-baked tuna melts.

In total, there were 33 new ways to eat canned tuna, the last of which was tuna with chickpeas sprinkled with powdered sugar, as a dessert.

And here's the best thing, Peña informed us, holding up an index finger. We've discovered that tuna has a very promising property. It provides lots of energy without being fattening. So we'll launch another campaign, nationwide, also using pamphlets, so people trying to lose weight will also eat tuna—without the rice or spaghetti, just plain tuna on its own.

Peña grinned inexplicably and my aunt took another long

swallow and finished her rum and then refilled her glass halfway.

What do you think? she asked, looking to Me with watery eyes.

Excuse me, madam, I don't want to be rude, but.

But what? Aunt Isabelle wanted to know.

But who cares what someone with the intelligence of a second-grade girl thinks?

Even I understood that he meant Me.

You yourself showed me the results of those psychometric tests, Peña went on, and correct me if I'm wrong but that's what they say.

Aunt Isabelle showed Peña to the door and told Gorda to take Me to the library.

I had disappeared. Suddenly finding out the elegant-sounding diagnosis that Professor Glickman had given Me at college (highly functional autistic) actually meant that I had the intelligence of a little girl erased Me from the planet, so Gorda took Me by the hand and pulled Me through the living room and up the stairs and then pushed Me into the library and over to a chair by my aunt, who sat at the head of the mahogany table.

My aunt turned on the computer. She typed for a little while and the screen filled with words and numbers.

In overall terms you are simple, she said.

She slapped my cheeks.

Karen. Karen. You have to listen.

She repeated:

In overall terms you are simple.

I said nothing.

Now, let's take a look at where your low scores are.

She typed some more and the words and numbers rearranged themselves and turned into red and blue diagrams. My abilities and disabilities translated into incomprehensible numbers.

My aunt continued:

Look, in every 1 of the timed tests, you are, indeed, ranked at the level of a second-grade girl.

I said nothing.

But in everything related to matching pictures or concepts by similarity, you tested at the level of a first-grade girl.

Why are you doing this to Me? I asked.

My aunt ignored the question.

Now let's look at this category: in everything related to projecting your own subjectivity onto objects, you're at kindergarten level.

I hate you, I sobbed.

And I began to rock softly in the chair. But my aunt wouldn't stop.

Although personally, I think not projecting your subjectivity onto objects is a virtue, not a disability. Now then, your memory is in the top 2% of the world population. Did you hear that, Karen?

The top 2%? I asked, still hypnotized.

Now let's look at your spatial awareness. It's so high that the test can't fully measure it; all it says is that you are probably in the top 0.1% of the world's population.

I laughed.

Your attention span, too, is through the roof: the test can't measure it.

Through the roof? I asked.

It surpasses the uppermost limit that the test can measure, she translated. And then she said, Doctor Glickman notes that as far as your attention span is concerned, when you concentrate on an object, you do more than concentrate, you seem to become part of it.

I slapped at the table, gleeful, recognizing myself in those words, and continued slapping at the table while I listened, over the slapping sound, to the next result.

Your organizational abilities are in the top 3% of the world.

I pumped my arms in the air to accompany my cry of joy.

You're a genius when it comes to spatial organization, my aunt repeated, and I echoed her:

I'm a genius!

And finally, your ability to grasp the subtleties of complex situations is that of a child.

I sat back down, sombre once more.

In short, my aunt said then, in 90% of standard measures of intelligence you are somewhere between imbecile and idiot, but in 10% you are on top of the world. So we're going to follow Gould's doctrine and here's what we're going to do. Come, come here and watch me do it.

I leaned in to see the computer screen. My aunt tapped a key and only the blue results remained.

We'll forget the 90% red, the disabilities, and we'll bet on the blue 10%, the outstanding abilities. What do you think?

She called Gould and said:

We accept, on 1 condition. We'll each be partners, you, my niece and I, and we'll each share the profits equally.

Gould replied:

Impossible. This is what we'll do: you'll share ½ and I'll take ½.

My aunt hesitated and then said:

Okay, then, Karen gets 25% and I get 26%.

Aha, Gould said. You 2 want to make sure you retain control.

And I, who was listening on the other line, said:

No, we want to have more than you.

Gould laughed and said:

I love a straight answer.

And that was how my aunt came to stake her future as well as mine and that of 800 fishery workers on the brilliant 10% of the brain of a woman who fell somewhere between imbecile and idiot and took on an all-or-nothing bet that would lead us to the little island of Nogocor in the African Mediterranean.

I'm going to have another glass of water.

13

The bronze bell.

The slender Japanese man standing on a wooden box in the depot of Tokyo's Tsukiji Market stopped it against his knee 1 Monday morning at 5 o'clock.

He swung the bronze bell in an arc above him and flicked his wrist, now above his shoulder, to make it ring. He flicked it again and again, peal after peal.

Me and Gould, along with Miss Yasuko, DBA, captain of Gould's fishing industry, stood behind a rope in blue parkas with lime green ear muffs with the rest of the spectators at the auction, and behind the bell ringer in 3 rows were the 50 orange-colored refrigerated coffins, each with a serial number on the side and our bluefin tuna submerged in crushed ice.

The ringing stopped and the slender bell ringer began shouting in Japanese, reading the bluefin tuna's numbers from a square ledger. 5 metres from him, on a wooden counter with a block of ice, were 5 slices of 1 of our bluefin tuna.

5 buyers dressed in blue uniforms and blue aprons and black plastic boots made their way along the coffins on the floor, and the spectators let out an ooooooooooooooh.

Those are the fiercest buyers, Yasuko whispered in my ear in her thin, little girl voice, enunciating each syllable separately.

The 5 fiercest buyers approached the counter. They contemplated the slices.

With their thumbs they pressed the red flesh. They took magnifying glasses and flashlights out of their aprons and shone them on the flesh to better see its striations. 1 pinched a fatty area between 2 fingers, cut the fat with his fingertips, brought it to his nose, and sniffed. Another—a tall man with a shock of black hair covering his eyes—pulled out a knife that hung sheathed at his waist and another ooooooooooooooh erupted among the spectators.

That's Atsuko Yamura, Yasuko whispered, and when he takes out his knife it means that he is very interested.

And who is Atsuko Yamura? I asked.

The greatest expert in bluefin tuna at Tsukiji Market; his family has had a stall here for 15 generations.

Yasuko's voice, faltering, left little puffs of steam, and I pushed her with my right hand so she would stop leaning over Me.

The tuna master cut off a centimetre of tuna, skewered it with the tip of his knife, and brought it to his mouth.

Bluefin tuna belly—*toro*—is very fatty. When it hits the warm roof of a person's mouth it melts, turning to oil. They say that Tsukiji tuna masters are the best in the world when it comes to sampling: just by tasting, they can discern how much flavor has been lost to the ice, how much time has passed since the tuna died, how much it suffered when it was killed.

Suffering, storage after death, refrigeration: each of these things leaves an aftertaste in the fish's flesh.

The other master buyers also cut off 1 cubic centimetre of red flesh and placed it in their mouths, the faces calm, expressionless.

The bell ringer swung the bronze bell over his shoulder once more.

And as the bell rang, he began to shout, Yasuko explained, the numbers under which each of our tuna were registered.

Atsuko Yamura raised both hands, turned backward, then

raised only his middle fingers, the others folded down, the way people in the United States do to say fuck you.

Oooooooooooooh, the crowd said in unison.

And then began the intense exchange. The crier on the wooden box announced Atsuko Yamura's offer and then repeated it and repeated it until other buyers raised their hands with other hand gestures that the crier cried, and Yasuko's translation slowed down and got garbled until she finally said:

I will explain when the auction is over.

In total, we sold 35 tuna for a high price and 15 for a good price.

Gould asked Yasuko:

So, how the hell did we do?

Good, she said. Not bad.

It was still dawn as we made our way through the enormous market: merchants pulled the tarps off of their stalls; industrial forklifts drove down the aisles loading and unloading boxes of fish and seafood, some still alive. The world's largest fish and seafood market.

We entered a shop on an adjoining side street, blanketed in mist, to get something hot to drink.

There were no employees. There were, however, 15 different kinds of vending machines lining the walls and for 100 yen they sold: coffee (hot and cold, with multiple possible combinations of milk and sugar), tea (also hot and cold and with multiple options), chocolate (hot and cold), pastries (30 varieties), personal hygiene items (brushes—tooth and hair— and combs, for women and men).

Karen! Gould called out to get my attention, rapping his knuckles on the Formica table where he and Yasuko had taken a seat, adding:

The action's over here, Karen. We didn't come to Tokyo so you could fall in love with the vending machines, so let's discuss our situation.

I went to sit down with 3 cans: 1 of hot black coffee, 1 of cold chocolate milk, and 1 with a hairbrush.

Thank you, said Yasuko, and I didn't know why.

Until Gould and Yasuko, without stopping talking, each took 1 of my cans, leaving Me, unfortunately, with the hairbrush—Me, the 1 with the crew cut.

Anyway, Yasuko explained the situation. Having sold our whole consignment was good, definitely not bad, but what mattered even more was that on the same day our buyers in turn be able to sell to the restaurant buyers from the most honorable sushi and sashimi restaurants in Tokyo, *sushi ya san*.

224

All of that in her high voice, carefully enunciating each syllable, her cheek beside mine. I took hold of her shoulder and pushed her to 1 side.

From the massive window in my hotel room on the 37th floor, Tokyo's business district looked like a light-brown marble anthill, with thousands of tiny humans dressed in black scurrying along the sidewalks.

The room was decorated in different shades of gray, from pearl to coal, and had a mesmerizing number of electrical and mechanical devices: a digital clock, a battery-operated clock with hands that rotated around the dial, a sound system that had a radio with AM and 4 FMs and a CD player, lights with 6 different brightness settings, a TV with 304 channels, a bed with 7 comfort settings.

I played music on the radio and was happily switching from channel to channel on the TV when I pushed the wrong button on the remote control and discovered that the screen could be split to let you watch 2 channels simultaneously, or 4, or 12.

But what I remember most is the toilet.

It was alive. When I approached, the lid lifted by itself, which startled Me. I pulled down my pants and when I sat, the seat became warm, causing Me to jump up, distressed. I sat back down and felt its warmth and discovered a console to the right with 9 buttons, each explained in Japanese.

Having spent my childhood in a basement with a hole in the wall looking out at the sea eating handfuls of sand, I was enthralled by all of the toilet's buttons.

1 caused a jet of water to spray directly into my anus, which made Me giggle; another caused a jet of water to spray directly onto my clitoris, which flustered Me; another seemed not to do anything at all for a while, until I saw a cloud of flower-scented perfume form between my legs; another intensified all of the jets.

I pushed several buttons at once in an attempt to stop all this activity but instead managed to intensify it even more, and then 2 things happened.

1. I felt tremendous pleasure in my anus and clitoris, a sensation that climbed up my spine vertebra by vertebra, causing Me to arch my back and close my eyes, overcome by the sensation, and then to groan and sweat inexplicably, until my body cried out.

2. When I opened my eyes, I found myself enveloped in an asphyxiating cloud of perfume and when I stood, dizzy and disoriented, the jets of water sprayed the ceiling and mirror and I couldn't find my way out and then the toilet roared,

causing Me to fall backward into a plastic curtain. I landed in a tub where I lost consciousness, whether from the fear or the impact I don't know.

When I came to, the bathroom insanity was still going strong. I extracted myself from the tub, dripping wet, decided to call reception, and feeling my way through the nauseating floral mist I finally groped my way to the door. But the moment I crossed through the threshold, the toilet serenely closed its lid and everything ceased immediately.

In my diary this adventure is entitled How I Got Lost in a Tokyo Bathroom and Had What I Believe Was My First Sexual Encounter.

The honorable sushi restaurant was located on the 60th floor. When the elevator doors slid open, Gould demanded that I turn around—I'd been standing with my face to the corner formed by 2 steel walls—and get out.

But when I did 10 men dressed in red shouted at us in unison:

UUUUUUUuuuuuooooooOOOOOO!

Yasuko whispered to Me in her itty-bitty voice:

War cry, to welcome you.

I'll say something about the Japanese. As a race, they

exhibit a high degree of autism. They don't shake hands. They greet each other from a distance, nodding their heads. They are either sweet and as friendly as little ducklings or as ferocious as sharks. And they are more attentive to things than they are to people.

Anyway, I was terrified by the damn welcome cry delivered by a gang who turned out to be, said Yasuko, the waiters.

Then Gould bowed before a Japanese man sitting in a chair sleeping—or at least his eyes were closed. I, on the other hand, went straight to find our table, because I hadn't eaten since our arrival in Tokyo at midnight the night before and I was starving. Unfortunately there wasn't a single table in sight.

Do as I do, Yasuko whispered.

She knelt on the floor at a block of wood 30 centimetres off the ground, which turned out to be the table.

So I knelt beside Yasuko right in front of the man who was sleeping, or had his eyes closed. It was hard to tell because the flesh under his eyebrows was swollen over his eyelids and he had puffy bags beneath his eyes, so between the pocket of flesh under his brows and the pocket of flesh under his eyes there were no eyes to be seen.

Gould rapped his knuckles on the table.

Karen, please, the action is not on the man's face.

I lowered my gaze to the table.

Yasuko translated the conversation back and forth, between Gould and the sleeping man.

Sleeping man:

Happiness that you choose me as the first in Asia to taste your *toro*.

Gould:

It's an honor, friend. An honor, too, for my partner Karen Nieto. Please, sir, order the *toro*; it would be our pleasure. Isn't that right, Karen?

I looked up but the sleeping man didn't so much as glance at Me. Instead he reached out his hand to take the menu from the centre of the table.

He studied it for an instant and said:

Maguro.

That is the least fatty part of *toro*, Yasuko whispered to Me, and therefore the least expensive.

No, no, order the best, Gould insisted.

Chutoro! The sleeping man exclaimed.

Otoro! Gould cried.

Otoro, Yasuko whispered to Me, is the fattiest and most expensive part.

Otoro for everyone, Gould said, turning to Me to ask, Don't you think, Karen?

No matter how Gould tried to include Me, the sleeping man never turned to face the women.

It was served on white plates, 2 bites of red meat from blue tuna caught 20 hours earlier on the other side of the world with no excessive violence, only a short period of agony, and kept cold, but not frozen.

120 dollars for 2 bites.

I thought about Ricardo, who years ago on a small boat on the huge sea had told Me about restaurants where a bite of tuna cost its weight in gold.

To 1 side of the *otoro* the waiters placed a white cup of white rice, a tiny little plate with a tiny little mound of spicy green wasabi, and another little dish of soy sauce. And in the center, a white ceramic glass of steaming green tea.

Since I don't eat fish or any other animal, I drank the tea, starving to death.

At the first sip, I became lost in the memory of my afternoons with Ricardo on the boat on the high seas, though the tea was not made of lemon leaves.

Suddenly we were surrounded by 5 photographers.

Cameras flashed at Gould and the sleeping man, each as they raised a bite of tuna to their mouths with chopsticks.

At the second round of flashes 2 creases on the sleeping man's face expanded and 2 little black eyes appeared and he exclaimed joyfully that he had really, really, really enjoyed the *otoro*, that it was in fact the best *otoro* he had ever tasted in his life. The photographers snapped more photos and then withdrew, silently walking backward, and finally left through a red door at the back of the restaurant, still backing up.

And the man closed his eyes once more.

From inside his jacket Gould withdrew a check folded in 2 and slipped it into the man's outside pocket and said:

Happy origami!

The sleeping man nodded, no expression on his face.

We drank green tea in silence, the man stood, bowed at Gould, ignoring Yasuko and me, walked straight to the elevator awaiting him with open doors, and the next morning in the hotel dining room I saw him again, on the front page of a newspaper, the bite of our *otoro* suspended between his chopsticks, 2 centimetres from his mouth.

It was a Japanese newspaper, and Yasuko translated the caption beneath the photo for Me.

The Minister of Agriculture, Livestock and Fisheries Met with Scottish Entrepreneur Ernest Gould to Discuss the

*Construction of a Multimillion-dollar Household Appliance
Factory in Kyoto.*

I don't understand, I said. Aren't we here to sell tuna?

Yasuko whispered:

The part about the factory is a lie. What is important is
that the article mentions that they met at an honorable
restaurant—where we had dinner last night—and that the
minister exclaimed it was the best *otoro* he had ever tasted in
his very long life.

Oh good, I said, not fully understanding.

Very good, Yasuko smiled.

Every morning Yasuko met Me in the hotel breakfast room
with another piece of news from another newspaper in which
our *otoro* appeared both in a photograph between 2 Japanese
people and in the written text.

We're entering the collective consciousness, she announced.

And then it took her ½ an hour to explain to Me what collective consciousness meant.

A month later, 2 people with long black hair appeared on
the cover of an incomprehensible magazine, crying over 2
plates of bluefin tuna sashimi.

Yasuko said:

Those are 2 movie stars beloved by the Japanese public.

Their emotional breakup in an honorable restaurant where they ate our otoro is on every TV channel and in every magazine.

Lucky for us, I said.

Yes, very lucky, Yasuko replied. And ½ of Japan is about to jump into the ocean.

Strange woman, Yasuko, at least to Me. Very thin, very pale, in sharp contrast to her tailored black pants suit and her black leather boots with stiletto heels. Capable of delivering brutal news like this in her little-girl voice:

½ of Japan is about to jump into the ocean.

They are? I asked.

She sighed.

Don't be upset, Karen, it's not true, she said. I just wish it were.

I don't know why Yasuko hated the Japanese so much given that she was Japanese. I think she might have explained it to Me once, but right at a time when I turned off my Relating Mode, so all I saw was her crying many tears over things that didn't exist.

I, on the other hand—as I've already noted—think the Japanese are the greatest people on Earth, for reasons already stated and for a few others that I discovered over the course of the year I spent in Tokyo.

They don't shake hands. They always keep at least 50 centimetres of distance between themselves and you. They don't stare into your eyes. They never invite you to their houses for dinner and never ask about your personal life. 99% of them are shorter than Me. And, okay, they talk a lot, like all humans, and often in fluty voices that can hurt your ears—that is, if you pause to listen to them carefully. But luckily for Me, they speak in Japanese, which I don't understand, so I was able to be among them on the street and in stores and on the metro and it was as if I were just walking in a forest of short ambulatory bushes full of little tweeting birds.

Here's something else I like about the Japanese. They celebrate Shinto holidays, because most of them belong to the Shinto religion, and they celebrate Buddhist holidays, because being Shinto doesn't mean they can't also be Buddhist, and they celebrate Christmas, just because they like to celebrate.

As a matter of fact, I have never heard Jingle Bells so many times as I did in the winter of 2002, in Tokyo.

On December 24, while the Japanese were at home pretending to be Christians and celebrating the birth of the son of a god they don't venerate the rest of the year, Gould called us to his suite on the 70th floor, the hotel's penthouse.

In a room of pale gray armchairs, he began by saying that it was time for him to leave Tokyo.

This is how he explained it, first to Yasuko and then to Me. To Yasuko:

The demand for our tuna exceeds our weekly consignment, and the price can only go up. So my work here is done. To Me:

We don't want to catch more tuna and lower the price, do we?

No, I agreed. The beauty of humane slaughter is that it's also sustainable, it has to enable the species to survive.

That's right, Gould agreed as well. Now then, I'm going to raise you up, Karen. You're going to take over the 70th-floor penthouse suite, and Yasuko will be here with you. All right?

Yasuko pressed her fingers to her lips, overcome.

And finally, Gould said, I have a present for you, Karen.

We all stood and followed Gould to a wall.

This is it, he said.

A black painting, 4 by 4 meters with a round gold drop in the middle.

It's a Yoshida, Gould announced. Japan's most transcendental 20th-century painter.

Gould, Yasuko, and I stood in silence before the painting.

It's called *Life Force*, he added. And, this is very interesting, every painting he did over the course of his life has the same title: *Life Force*.

Why didn't he paint this 1? I asked, because no matter how hard I looked all I saw was a drop of gold on a black background.

Gould replied:

I don't know, but it's worth 500,000 dollars and this is my way of telling you how much confidence I have in you as a partner.

Gould poured 2 whiskeys, 1 for him and 1 for Yasuko, and a glass of milk for Me.

The 3 of us stood, and Gould held out his whiskey and said:

Karen, sweetheart, I love you like the daughter I never had.

1 of those impossible sentences that only human fantasy could come out with. Gould loved Me as much as a non-existent girl. At any rate, after taking a sip, and after the 3 of us took our seats back on the comfortable pearly gray arm-chairs, he added:

Given that you're not moved by the Yoshida, I'll have it taken back and you can ask me for whatever you want. The sky's the limit.

A Nobel, I said.

Gould hooted and Yasuko laughed quietly, lowering her eyes.

That's the first joke I've heard you make, he said, his blue eyes sparkling. If you keep it up, pretty soon you won't even be autistic.

That's not true, I countered, distressed.

All right, he laughed again, you'll never be like us, luckily, Miss Different Abilities.

He and Yasuko then moved on to other matters and I went into Non-Relating Mode and just existed, sitting there on the comfortable sofa, taking sips of milk, and watching the snow fall out the window.

Rather: the windows.

There were 15 windows in the penthouse suite and by turning your head slowly you could see white-white flakes of snow, falling and falling among the motionless stars in all 15 of them.

It was strange. As soon as Gould walked out the door at 5 am, dressed in blue jeans and an enormous black overcoat, my uneasiness set in.

It was raining.

I called my aunt on the phone but her Zapotec boyfriend answered groggily and told Me that night was just beginning in Oaxaca, on the other side of the world.

Isabelle is asleep, he said as if it pained him, and I can't sleep because I can't stop watching her. She's the most beautiful woman life has ever given me.

Okay, I said and hung up.

I decided to make the most of my time by shaving in the bathroom.

In the bathroom mirror, using my electric clippers, I evened out the 4 centimetres of brown hair on my scalp. I inserted a blade into my razor and shaved the back of my neck. Sitting on the edge of the bathtub, I shaved my armpits and legs. Standing, I removed my triangle of pubic hair.

Outside, in the penthouse's main room, Yasuko had already turned on 6 laptops. The screen of each displayed different color bar graphs.

Shall I explain to you what they mean? she asked.

That's not necessary, I replied.

I went into the master bedroom and lay down naked on the bed and tried to sleep.

I couldn't.

I got out my suitcase and took out my portable harness, which I hadn't needed once during my stay in Japan. Standing on the bed, I hung it from the ceiling and then, dressed in my wetsuit, I hung from the harness.

Yasuko looked at Me from the doorway, and—hanging in my harness, floating in the air in the wetsuit's warm, even embrace—I watched Tokyo, 70 floors down, coming to life in the still-dark night sky and the rain, beginning its workday.

Beneath a sliver of moon: Tokyo, its dark glass-and-marble skyscrapers, its double- and triple-decker beltways criss-crossing, full of tiny cars with 2 headlights in front, green specks that were public parks, holes down to the metro and from which streamed hundreds of millimetric humans, joining the thousands already walking down the sidewalks and entering buildings that, window by window, began to light up.

14

I don't know exactly how it happened. 1 moment we'd be sitting in an honourable Japanese restaurant in Moscow, talking to the fat Russian owner, arranging shipments of True Blue Tuna. The next moment we'd be in another luxurious Japanese restaurant in Montreal or Toronto or Las Vegas or Paris or Dubai. Always talking to someone who wanted more True Blue Tuna.

But why do I have to actually go to all of the restaurants? I complained to Gould via cell phone.

To experience the whole process from start to finish, he replied from another continent. What the eye sees, the brain won't dispute.

So we kept traveling to different restaurants and in

between we flew in planes and walked down long, noisy air-port corridors.

I'd watch diners at their tables open the menu. Their eyes would flit back and forth to the diminutive silver-plated True Blue Tuna logo: the idea of placing a silver-plated label in each menu had been mine; managing to get a patent for the exclu-sive use of the word *true* associated with the words *blue tuna* had been Gould's doing. That was what distinguished our cruelty-free, never-frozen tuna. And if diners finally decided to order it, and if they then chose the most expensive of the 4 types of tuna available—the famous True Blue Tuna *otoro*—then when the white plate with 2 unadorned bites of red flesh was placed on the table, an expectant silence would descend.

In silence they would lift the tiny morsel of flesh with their chopsticks, place it between their lips, close their eyes, and make astonished noises.

Ooooooh. Aaaaaah. Mmmmmm.

All this as the bite of tuna dissolved into oil between their tongue and palate.

60 dollars per bite. It was a good thing they didn't eat fast.

It's the host wafer at a rich man's mass, Yasuko told Me.

And then it took her ½ an hour to explain the metaphor to Me. I'll try to explain it faster here.

It turns out that in the early 21st century, the number of millionaires increased drastically and therefore the number of humans who could afford to pay 120 dollars for 2 bites of bluefin tuna belly did as well. Or rather, not just the number who *could* but the number who actually *did*. Or rather, the number who thought that doing so proved to the world that they were winners.

Going to a luxurious Japanese restaurant and ordering real True Blue Tuna *otoro*—the so-called foie gras of the sea—and not the cheaper versions was like proclaiming to those at the table, and to themselves (and here I'm quoting Yasuko): I could spend enough to feed an entire family in Africa for a month on just 1 bite.

That's the cruelty of Yasuko. Or of the rich. Or of money. I don't know.

At any rate, by selling it for that ridiculous price our profits were ridiculously high and we were able to buy several neglected fisheries on the bluefin route and transform them into natural fishing preserves, which was the euphemism Gould preferred over humane tuna slaughterhouses.

I drew the plans on the 70th floor of the Tokyo hotel, in a room where the blinds were always closed and the ceiling light was always on so that night and day didn't interfere with my drafting rhythm.

7-by-10-metre technical drawings took up the entire bedroom floor, and on 1 wall, which was also entirely covered, I projected an aerial view of the sea and coastline where the catch would take place.

I'd lay on top of that paper rug with my black Variety pilot pen, my face pressed to the paper, and sketch each step of the process with equal precision, whether big or small. I spent the same amount of time on a circular helicopter-landing pad as I did on a polyethylene ball, and each item was accompanied by almost microscopic notes.

> *Polyethylene buoy to be the exact shade of blue as the sea here.*
> *Black plastic pulley with minimum noise.*
> *Rubber conveyor belt the exact color of bluefin tuna.*
> *Flashing neon light, <u>must</u> be neon and no other light.*

Then I'd travel to each site to ensure that everything was as it should be. Or, more often, to correct the things that were not as they should be. I drove the sailors crazy and vice versa.

Why the hell are the underwater crates so big? demanded a Portuguese midget disguised as a frigate captain who stood waving his arms around at the fishery in Porto de Caeiro, Portugal.

Fuck! he continued in his halting Spanish, cages are 10 by 7 metres each, and you want 30 of them!

I had to stare at him very carefully, because for a minute I thought it might be Peña the cheapskate autistic who'd somehow surfaced in my life once more.

What is your objection, sir? I raised my voice. Please express your objection in words; I don't understand the language of arm-waving!

It's a lot of fucking iron, that's my objection!

Listen, I said, lowering my voice so as to lower the tension between Me and the fucking imbecile midget, I'll explain it to you, okay? So listen to Me, are you listening?

I'm listening, he said.

And using my best Friendly Voice, I said:

I'll give you 2 reasons. First, the cages are that big because they're not for you. And second, why the hell do you care, if you're not paying for them?

But he did care. And he had 2 reasons, too. First, he didn't think it was right that the tuna had more square metres to relax in than he and his family did in the proletariat apartment building where they lived.

And second, lady, it's a lot of fucking iron! He barked in my face.

So I took the peak of his sailor's cap and: splash! straight into the water—the Portuguese midget, I mean, not the pretty white cap, which was the property of True Blue Tuna.

With 1 hand I held the cap in the air, and with the other, I grabbed the little man, hauled him over the edge of the dock, and dropped him.

I'm explaining this because of something that happened later in Porto de Caeiro, something that unfortunately turned out to mean that the damn Portuguese imbecile was right and fortunately was to change my life.

I'll admit now that, unquestionably, it was a lot of iron— too much.

1 afternoon a few weeks after the incident with the Portuguese midget, in the calm waters of the bay 1 kilometre from the dock, which were bathed in amber light, I was in my wetsuit, wicker basket on my back, distributing bonitos to the 7 tuna in a cage, when something took Me by surprise.

The cage door began to swing outward, opening very slowly.

Had I forgotten to close it all the way and bolt it shut or had it opened by itself?

I dangled an orange bonito by the tail and a tuna swam

over to Me and downed it in 1 bite. Then I held out another bonito and another silvery tuna swiftly plucked it from my hand and swished a quick U-turn to go off and gobble it up.

And the door to the whole sea was wide-open and the tuna didn't notice.

I don't know why I did it. Often, the most intelligent things I've done, my body has done without consulting my brain. I swam out of the crate and all 7 of the tuna followed Me, 1 after the other.

They surrounded Me.

I kept offering bonito after bonito and they kept gobbling up bonito after bonito.

All perfectly calm, with no attempt to escape.

I swished my fins and swam back into the cage. I swam down onto the sand bank and deposited the basket of boni-tos on the sea floor. I uncovered it. A cloud of bonitos emerged and began to scatter and the tuna began to scatter after them, to gobble them up.

And inside my mask, I murmured to myself:

What if I left the cage open all the time?

I thought about the Killer in his classroom, making fun of my bird trap, the 1 that had no trap, or at least no death chamber. The other students had laughed on noting the folly:

my trap was a net, that is, a cage made of string, stretched around the foliage of an ash tree where the birds could fly in, flit around, sing, hop from branch to branch, and finally fly away, up into the sky. Yes: a no-trap trap, a trap with no prey, and therefore imbecilic, according to the Killer.

But there among the tuna there was nothing funny about it, nothing imbecilic. The tuna swam in the cage because the tasty bonitos were there, and because they were comfortable in the warm, amber, afternoon water; they had no reason to escape.

It was so simple to understand them; they simply didn't know the whole plan, didn't know the part they played in the process. They couldn't guess what was going to happen 3 months down the line, at the end of spring.

Well fed, grown, their muscles saturated with fat, they'd be hauled onto a conveyor belt, a neon flash would dazzle them for 20 seconds, on regaining their sight they'd be asphyxiating, the compressed air pistol would be fired into their brains, the following day before dawn each 1 of them would be lying in an orange plastic coffin filled with ice in a market somewhere, and that same night their ventral muscles—or small pieces of them—would melt in the warm mouth of some rich man and slide down his oesophagus and into the red cave of his stomach.

The tuna were still following the last remaining orangeish fish into the cage and again I thought:

I am about to have a very, very, very great idea.

I kept waiting for the great idea to come.

It didn't come.

I spent the rest of the afternoon going from cage to cage, feeding groups of tuna.

In the 10th cage, just after a tuna took a bonito from my hand, I thought:

Why do we keep them separate? Are we afraid there's going to be a tuna revolt?

I laughed out loud and a cloud of silver bubbles escaped from my mask.

Back on the dock, taking great floppy steps with my frog flippers, I pulled off my mask and said aloud:

We'll build the Portuguese fishery with very little iron. A lot fewer bars. We'll only build 1 big cage so all the tuna can live comfortably inside it and use only enough bars to protect them from sharks.

What we'll do, I thought in the hotel elevator, dressed back in my white jeans and T-shirt, is make an aquatic paradise full of sun during the day, cool at night. With regular feedings. We'll plant an underwater forest of black algae and another forest of anemones—red ones. So the tuna can have fun. And so their flesh will taste better and be redder. A paradise for tuna, where there's no hunger, no fear, no danger.

No ferocity.

A paradise with no ferocity: I had learned those words from Rabbi Chelminsky late that night in Mazatlán when he spoke to Me about paradise.

In the hotel, in the bathroom, in a tub of hot water, I sank down and heard myself think:

Would they reproduce in a paradise with no ferocity?

In Japan they tried to get female tuna to ovulate in tanks of water, and it worked. In Bali they built ocean pools for them to ovulate, and it worked there, too. In Panama, they got the females to ovulate in tanks and some males to ejaculate to fertilize the eggs. But they've never gone any farther than that. Further: they've never gotten the eggs to develop into tuna larvae. Despite strict controls of water temperature and salinity.

Going against all human experience, I thought:

But what if they *did* reproduce, here? What if the trick is to do less than the farmers in Japan and Bali and the lab scientists in Panama? What if we just leave them in peace and let them go about their lives without controlling the water or them? And we plant a great island of red coral in the center of the great big cage?

I laughed.

What the hell would the island of red coral be for? I asked out loud.

And I responded to myself out loud, too:

No clue.

Maybe, I thought, to tempt them to procreate at the right time, the time when they would have reached the end of their journey if they were free, when the females would be laying eggs in a warm coral reef, maybe a red 1.

What I was thinking made no scientific sense but my entire body was telling Me I was right.

If I were a tuna, I thought in the warm tub, I'd love to be able to stick my nose in the red coral and I'd love to slip through a forest of black algae and decide suddenly to stop and nibble at the blue branching seaweed, that sky-blue-colored sea lettuce that you sometimes find at the bottom of the deep blue sea. Yes, we were going to plant blue sea lettuce on the sea floor of our aquatic paradise, too.

I got out of the water feeling light, as if the air were water and I were a tuna, floating upright.

Then I went out into the main room, where Yasuko was working, surrounded by 4 open laptops full of colored bar graphs and, dripping water, I said to her:

Yasuko, I just had the greatest idea of my entire life.

THE WOMAN WHO DIVED INTO THE HEART OF THE WORLD

Well, I was wrong. The idea of creating a tuna paradise was just part 1 of an even bigger idea. A truly great idea that would take 3 more years even to be fully formulated in my head.

Now that I'm writing this, it occurs to Me that 3 years seems like too long to have a single idea, but I've never claimed to be quick-witted.

Meanwhile, other things—big and small—continued to occur. The first: a suicide. Someone with religion would have seen it another way. Someone with philosophy would have seen it still another way. I, who don't use either religion or philosophy, because I know that things are what they are and that they actually exist outside of my head and even outside of human language, simply saw it with fear.

The BBC online news reported that Japan's minister of agriculture, livestock and fisheries—the same sleeping man who'd claimed in Tokyo that our *otoro* was the best he'd ever tasted in his long and honourable life—was found hanging, in white pajamas with blue stripes.

He hung himself in his pyjamas with a dog leash, from the living-room door in his apartment in the center of Tokyo. He was scheduled to appear before parliament that day to respond to charges of corruption: it was alleged that he'd accepted bribes from large corporations. But before he could defend himself, well, as I said, he killed himself in his pajamas.

For the BBC and the other news agencies and of course the Japanese police, it was all very clear: the minister couldn't face being dishonoured in parliament and committed suicide, end of story. For Me, however, it became an obsession.

How does a man hang himself from a door with a leash? There were no photos of him hanging on the Internet, just pictures of his body being taken from the building on a stretcher, with a sheet over him. So I decided to investigate myself. I took 1 of my leather belts, knotted it around my neck, slid the strap through the buckle, tied the end of the strap to the door handle, and tried to hang myself. And this is what I discovered.

From the handle to the floor there's not enough space to hang.

And, if you hang the leash from the upper part of the doorframe it just falls off, because there's nothing to attach it to.

Therefore, it's not possible to kill yourself quickly and on your own if you do it from a door and with a leash. You would need a ladder to get up there in order to be able, with hammer and nails, to make the end of the leather leash stay up, which requires both time and serenity.

Additionally, would a person who truly wanted to save his honour commit suicide in pyjamas? Hanging himself from a door?

I called Yasuko on my cell phone and she told Me something very interesting.

Committing suicide is considered very honourable in Japan, but being seen in one's pajamas is not considered honourable in Japan. Therefore, hanging yourself in your pajamas is idiotic, mixing something honourable with something dishonourable. And what is plainly an obvious dishonour is being strangled to death with a dog leash.

In Japan, Yasuko explained, the most honourable thing to do is to kneel and disembowel yourself with a knife and then have a friend slice off your head in 1 go, using a samurai sword.

I kept searching online for more details. Which multinational companies were to have bribed the minister?

Very quickly I came up with the name Miau Co., a canned cat food company. I checked out the Miau Co. Web site. Miau had been granted permission by the minister to use the Sea of Japan and to hunt all the whales it wanted, despite the fact that they were an endangered species; then Miau could chop them up and can them and sell the cans as cat food that was labeled—quite resourcefully, in my opinion—"Miau, natural food for cats."

Next, my Internet search led Me to a strange Web site for ALF, the Animal Liberation Front. A joke page, I thought, because it showed photos of cats, dogs, monkeys and rats in black berets with pistols and machine guns at the ready. It also had a photo that left Me with my mouth hanging open: the minister, in pyjamas, hanging from a dog leash attached to the upper corner of a doorframe.

No, this was certainly not an honourable suicide. The man's tongue was hanging 10 centimetres out of his mouth, and his flaccid penis hung another 10 centimetres from his pyjamas.

Which is only natural in the strangulation of any mammal possessing both tongue and penis. Technically, compressing the trachea forces the tongue out of the mouth and compressing the carotid artery in the neck interrupts the flow of blood to the body, which induces an erection. So the minister's erect penis must have slipped out through the fly of his pajamas and after 20 minutes hanging there, it just hung there.

I zoomed in on the image to try to see what really intrigued Me: how the leash had been attached to the door. All I could tell was that it was definitely hanging from the upper corner, attached with nails or something similar, as I'd imagined. Zoomed in, I looked around for a ladder or little stool and then I saw, on the floor, 40 centimetres from the hanged man's bare foot, a small white object with black markings.

I zoomed in further: it was a toy whale with something written on its side.

I zoomed in even further but the image became blurry.

Still, what was clear to Me was that the minister had not committed suicide but rather had had suicide committed upon him. By whom? ALF's black-bereted cats.

I laughed. That last part was highly unlikely, but ALF was involved.

That determined, I went back to my technical drawing, lying on top of the paper covering my bedroom floor like a rug—the sketch of the Nogocor tuna paradise—and didn't think any more about the whole thing. As it happened, I wouldn't think about it again for the rest of that year or the next 1, while we were building tuna paradises at our 7 fisheries.

In Paris, I won an award. The prestigious Coup de Coeur, an award the French give every year to the best gastronomical product, sort of like the Nobel Prize of Food.

Elated and tense, I get up from my chair in the theatre and make my way to the stage. Yasuko and my aunt decided that I should wear white. A thick, collarless, white silk blouse and white jeans and the same yellow-leather work boots I always wear, but new ones. I walk past the most prestigious chefs in the world the only way I know how: like a sailor, planting each foot squarely on the ground with every step.

When I reach the stage I hear braying in the audience. Whistling. Impassioned words in French. Since I don't speak French I assume that it's praise. They—the French—are, after all, giving Me the Nobel Prize of Food, as far as I understand. I hold up an arm and put on my Proud Face (big smile and eyes opened extremely wide).

The MC, a very slender man in a red bow tie, holds the gold trophy out to Me with both hands.

I assume I'm supposed to take it from him, so I take it from him, and the braying increases, as do the whistles.

Merci, I say into the microphone, that being the only word I know in French.

Then amid the braying from the little black-haired heads in the audience comes a voice speaking the kind of Spanish they speak in Spain:

They're whistling because you *bought* the prize. Because

they say your government, the Mexican government, bought it for you.

I lean into the mike and say in Spanish, and in my autistic monotone that comes out shrill because I'm nervous:

No idea! I haven't been in Mexico for 5 years and even though I did meet a man who ran for president he lost the elections and now a different man who I've never met is president.

Laughter here and there.

Someone with a French accent shouts:

Viva Mazatlán!

The braying and whinnying intensifies and the Spaniard explains loudly:

Now they're saying that you stole the prize from a French farmer who cultivates truffles in pig shit. And, that your tuna foie gras isn't foie gras, because how the fuck can you make foie gras with no geese, so you're a thief and a liar.

I'm so scared I have to pee, urgently. Then the MC starts exchanging mysterious remarks and gestures with people in the audience and I bend down to deposit the trophy on the hardwood floor, because the French sound really angry and there are a lot of them and I really have to pee and besides, as far as I know I never even put my name in for the damn

Coup de Coeur prize, which after all is *like* the Nobel Prize of Food but it *isn't* the Nobel Prize of Food, so I climb down off the stage and head straight for the exit and while advancing across the red carpet I get a red tomato right in 1 eye and with the other eye I can see the attractive Clean Seas banner with its blue circle representing the planet Earth.

Killer! they shout—and these people shout in English, which I do understand.

¡Asesina! In Spanish.

Assassin! In French.

Fists raised, they stand behind 12 police officers whose hands are joined to form a human chain that prevents them from attacking Me.

Then someone from Clean Seas spits on the sidewalk and apparently the rest of them all think: great idea! Because then they all spit on the sidewalk, and to my right Yasuko calls Me from inside a white limousine where she's sitting, holding the door open.

The next morning I hang my pretty white silk shirt—now stained red—on a hanger and open the door to hang the hanger on a hook outside the door for the hotel dry cleaner to pick up, and standing right in front of Me, leaning against a wall, wearing dark glasses and a khaki raincoat, is a very strange man, smoking, his boots crossed at the ankles.

He speaks in English with a heavy French accent, exhaling smoke as he talks.

I am waiting for you; let's go.

I step back into the penthouse and quickly try to close the door but the man jams his cowboy boot between the door and frame and then shoves in a hand with a gold badge that says, in raised letters, "Département de Justice."

So I open the door back up and turn myself over to the French Department of Justice.

Follow my steps, he orders.

And I obey, walking in stride beside him and imitating each step he takes down to the centimetre.

We step into the elevator, step out in the hotel lobby where a lady is playing the harp and 2 other Frenchmen in dark glasses are waiting for us, also smoking, sitting at a white marble-top table. They get up and I walk in between them to the street where a dilapidated jeep with no roof is parked, awaiting us.

It strikes Me as odd that the Department of Justice of France employs such run-down vehicles, and I step back.

Undercover vehicle, 1 of the men says, and he grabs my

elbow and that shocks Me and I elbow him and he says, Fine,
then. Get in on your own.

I get in on my own and the rest of them get in on their
own, too.

The jeep starts up and the same guy, now seated beside
Me, leans toward Me and I lean away from him and he
orders:

Relax.

So I swallow and I relax and he puts a band-aid over 1 eye
and another band-aid over my other eye and then orders:

Open your eyes.

People are morons. Obviously I can't, because the band-
aids are holding my eyelids together.

Then he puts black plastic glasses over my eyes that have
band-aids on them and my thoughts go dark.

Honestly, the French are more trouble than they're worth.
Their culinary awards are complete crap and their Department
of Justice transportation is even worse. They don't have tinted
windows and they don't even have a roof. But then again, I
think, therein lies the beauty.

Who would suspect that an open-topped jeep driving
around in Paris traffic is in fact an undercover vehicle?

After 30 minutes we've left the noise of the city behind
and, unable to see from behind the dark glasses and the

band-aids, I use my nose and recognize the wide-open country.

The smell of chlorophyll up above. The smell of straw in the middle. The sweet and spicy smell of quadruped mammal shit below.

15

They take the dark glasses off Me.

They order Me to take the band-aids off my eyes.

We're in a wood cabin, Me at a table with the 2 strange men from the jeep and another who's even stranger; all of them still have their dark glasses on.

Man 1 whispers:

15 years ago the bluefin tuna were twice as big.

That's true. But at Blue Tuna we raise our own in cages on our farms, I inform him.

Man 1 adds:

You raise them to be ½ as long but twice as fat. And you flavor and color their flesh by using spicy red algae to make them look appetizing and attractive and marketable.

I put on my Proud Face and confirm:

Correct. That's my contribution to the tuna industry.

Guy 2 intervenes:

Go to hell, bitch.

Man 1 gets back on topic:

And, 15 years ago there were 3 times more bluefin in the seas than there are now.

2:

Fucking son of a bitch.

I decide to ignore his apparent confusion about my gender and announce:

I suspect that you are not in fact from the Department of Justice of France.

To which he replies:

You're not the sharpest fucking knife in the drawer.

Now I am very confused.

Again 2:

We're the Department of Justice of ARM. Ever heard of ARM?

ARM or ALF? I ask.

3, really pissed off:

ARM! The Animal Rights Militia.

A vague memory surfaces from somewhere deep within. Yes. At some meat industry trade fair someone mentioned them and called them Those Crazy Terrorists and told us that 1 night they'd opened thousands of cages 1 by 1 at an industrial poultry plant and taken 900 chickens; another night some other ARM fanatics stole the minks from a mink farm.

Yes, I've heard of you, I reply. You steal chickens and minks.

2 leans toward Me in his black glasses.

Wrong, bitch. We free them. We lead them to a better life. The chickens we give to poor farmers so they can range free and lay eggs in big barns, and the minks we release in the forest.

I try to make sense of what he said.

I see, I say. So you're like the Clean Seas of chickens and minks.

3 is immediately furious.

Clean Seas are fucking mama's boys! They believe in meetings and talking to senators! They think they can change public opinion by publishing magazine articles! They believe in gradual legal reform in the hopes that somehow something might change 100 years from now! Stupid idiots, they stand around in front of fur shops and chant, Don't wear cadavers! Don't wear cadavers! They were the ones who called you a killer yesterday, shaking their little fists in the air.

He takes a breath and then quietly concludes:

No, that's not us.

Me:

I see.

3:

We, on the other hand, have lost patience. We're the ones who have crossed over to the other side of nonviolence; we're on the other side of the law. We're the armed wing of active compassion, representing nonhuman animals. We're the human extension of tortured and sacrificed animals. So when we act on their behalf, we act in legitimate defence.

2:

Got it, bitch?

1 informs Me:

We're the clandestine army of compassion. Our motto is, Fight terror with terror, murder with murder. And you, 1 of the biggest killers on the planet, are 1 of our biggest targets.

I inform 1:

I need, need a glass of water.

2:

You're out of luck, you fucking bitch.

I swallow hard, my knees trembling.

1:

You should know, Karen Nieto, that we're deadly serious. We injected rat poison into 700 dead turkeys in Vancouver this year and sent a warning out on the Internet. As a result, this December not a lot of turkey cadavers were bought in Vancouver, but 700 hardheaded assholes who just had to have turkey with their cranberry sauce spent Christmas having convulsions and vomiting. What do you think of that?

I, I, I don't know, I say.

Damn it. My stammer is back.

1:

We also poisoned a shipment of Mars bars in London.

Me:

Mars bars? The candy, candy, candy bars?

2:

Pretty tasty, aren't they?

Me:

But why? Do you defend chocolate, too?

2:

Lose the irony or I'll blow your brains out!

2 pulls out a pistol and holds the cold barrel to my ear. I begin to rock softly in my chair.

2:

Mars was conducting tooth decay experiments on monkeys. They gave them candy bars all day long but wouldn't give them any water to rinse out their mouths. Imagine a monkey with a toothache, locked up in a cage with nobody treating it. Can you imagine? It's nighttime and the monkey's rattling the bars of his cage, screaming in pain with a hella-cious toothache. Can you imagine that, Karen Nieto? I'm asking you a question. Can you imagine?

I, I, I can imagine it, I say, terrified, rocking the whole time.

3 perks up:

Well, Mars doesn't experiment using monkey teeth any-more! What do you think?

My voice almost silent, I say:

I, I, I think that's great.

1:

But let's talk about True Blue Tuna. That's why you're here, after all.

Me:

Okay but could you put your, your, your, um, sir, could you put your.

2:

Put my gun down?

3:

Put your gun down, asshole.

2 puts his gun down and 1 starts up again:

In the past 10 years you've wiped out ⅔ of the tuna species.

Not, not, not True Blue Tuna, I counter. There are 523 tuna fisheries, fisheries in the world.

1:

But True Blue Tuna is the worst. It's the biggest by far and catches 40% of the tuna, and what's worse, True Blue single-handedly made the price of tuna skyrocket. Turned it into the sea's biggest treasure. Hand me that magazine.

2 goes to a shelf and pulls out a magazine: The Economist. With a photo of Gould on the cover, showing all of his teeth as he smiles.

1 opens the magazine.

I'm quoting an interview with your partner, Ernest Gould. "The success of True Blue Tuna is above all conceptual. What we've done is put a price on tuna, and it's the price of silver."

Now then, 1 says, lowering the magazine, let me ask you something in all honesty.

And 2 interjects:

Fucking bitch.

1:

How do you convince a bunch of poor fishermen in Libya not to go out in their little sardine boats and catch all the tuna they can find? How, when a 2.3-metre adult tuna sells for 173,000 dollars?

With, with, with international fishing, fishing quotas, I reply, that's how you keep people from overfishing.

3:

Oh, sure. The quotas set by ICCAT, the International Conspiracy to Catch All Tuna.

No, no, no, it stands for the International Commission for the Conservation of Atlantic Tunas, Tunas, I stammer.

1:

At this rate, by 2015 there will be not 1 bluefin tuna left in the sea. Another species extinct. But who cares, right? You'll just find another 1 to value at the price of silver, right? The industrial massacre of marine species began in 1950 and by 2050 the ocean will be 1 huge death pool, just salt water and plankton lapping at the continental coastlines.

I, I, I have to pee, I say.

2, whispering in my ear:

Go ahead. Pee on the floor, like the orangutans in their cages in the zoo.

3:

By 2070 the planet Earth will be inhabited solely by humans. Maybe some dogs and cats, ants and rats. In the sea there will be nothing but slimy jellyfish. Though not even that is certain.

2:

If we let it come to that.

1 weaves his fingers together in front of his face and says:

Here's the offer, Karen Nieto. You have 6 months to close your fisheries if you don't want the plane you're flying in 6 months from now to blow up into 1,000 pieces in the sky.

2:

Boom!

My urine runs down the leg of my black jeans and forms a puddle in my boot.

The guy with greasy hair takes the dark glasses off my face, then takes off 1 band-aid and then the other 1. We're in front of the hotel again, both on the sidewalk, and he hands Me a card.

ARM

Animalrightsmilitia.net

I hand him mine.

Karen Nieto

Engineer in Humane Slaughter

0044 5678 9055

Address? he asks.

I don't have a house.

You go from hotel to hotel?

Yes.

But we can reach you on your cell?

Yes.

Here, he says. Going-away present. Hold out your hand.

I hold it out.

And the man places a 10-centimetre toy plane in my palm.

It's made of steel and has transparent windows and 2 rubber wheels on the bottom. I'm still inspecting the model when he says:

And another thing. Don't talk to the police or there will be grave consequences.

He climbs into the run-down jeep and takes off.

With tweezers, the man removes the plane from the palm of my hand by 1 wing and slides it into a plastic bag, which he seals and slips into his jacket. The Interpol detective.

I suppose you've already touched it all over, he says.

I tell him that I have.

Shame, he says. Still, there might be a fingerprint some-where. Don't worry. They're sloppy.

And he runs his hand through a shock of black hair. Grey

suit, black tie, cleft chin, impeccable British English even though he's Portuguese.

We're sitting in wicker chairs on the balcony of the middle of my 3 rooms on the sixth floor of Hotel Caeiro in Porto de Caeiro. My bedroom. My workroom. My assistant Yasuko's room.

Not a cloud in the sky. Red roof tiles on buildings gleaming in the sun.

What makes you say they're sloppy? I ask.

Imagine. An organization with no leader. No hierarchy. No money. No central control. A Web site, that's all they've got. In short, an organization with no organization.

Let me tell you about 1 of their early triumphs, he continues. A guy planted a bomb in the pocket of a sealskin coat and hung it with the rest of the coats in a fur shop, and when it exploded he claimed victory on the ARM Web site. So another guy in another country read it, found a bomb-making manual online, printed it, made a bomb in his bathroom at home, stuck it in another animal skin—this 1 a lambswool vest—and hung it in another fur shop with the other garments, but the idiot didn't assemble it right so it never went off and nobody found out about his failure except us, when the owner phoned us a year later, hysterical because he'd discovered a bomb in his shop.

So they're like an ant colony, I say.

An ant colony? What do you mean?

That's how an ant colony works. No centralized authority. No set goals. It just functions by imitation. 1 ant starts to line a hollow with a piece of leaf and other ants stop to watch. If it seems like a good idea to them, they cooperate; if not, they keep marching down the tunnel.

Ah, the detective says. But what about the queen?

What about the queen? I ask.

Well, doesn't the queen control the colony?

No. The queen lays thousands of eggs; technically, she's the mother of every ant in the colony, which is why she's so important. But she has no control over the other ants.

So why is she queen, then?

Because when human beings started studying ant colonies 24 centuries ago, they asked themselves, who's the boss in this society? Someone had to be the boss, in their view, because human beings had only ever invented societies where someone was the boss and the rest of them obeyed. And then they noticed that the ants took very good care of the mother ant and that she did nothing but lie there reproducing and they said: Of course, that 1 there who doesn't do anything and everyone attends to must be the boss, and they called her the queen.

Aha, says the detective. That was 24 centuries ago. So why do we keep calling her the queen ant today?

Stupidity.

Aha, he repeats. Of course, of course, and he scratches the top of his head. Now, forgive me for asking something so silly.

And then he asks a very odd question:

Are there ant police?

What do you mean, ant police? I ask.

I mean, ants that make sure that the rest of them are all doing their work and not getting out of line, out of their ant lines? There must at least be someone to maintain order, make sure those ant lines don't get messed up. I mean, if not, the colonies wouldn't be so orderly.

No, I say. No ant police.

The international human police officer seems very troubled by the lack of ant police officers.

Furrowing his brow, though, he continues:

Well, so yes, that's how it is with these anarchists. They have no centralized power structure, no hierarchy, and yes, they just imitate each other. In 2004, for example, there was a series of attacks on poultry farms. First 1 cell freed all the hens on an industrial farm in Canada and the news spread on the Internet. Then other cells got inspired and did the same in Denmark, Belgium, Sweden, Finland and North America. These sons of bitches let loose millions of hens from dozens of poultry farms—millions of dollars were lost and the egg industry panicked. Finally, near St. Petersburg, another cell was opening cages at a farm when the Russian police intervened, captured them, and sent them to Siberia, where all the chicken liberators disappeared. Just like that, vanished into the snow. And that was the end of it. Until today, that is.

A waiter deposited 2 glasses of orange juice on the little table between us.

Of course, that's also what makes it impossible to destroy them, the detective continues, worried again. The fact that they're like a colony of ants, with no central control. In other organizations you get rid of the head and the organization falls apart. You steal their files, get their membership lists, their organization chart. But with these guys there's no head, no files. No sense infiltrating their ranks because nobody knows anyone outside their own cell.

He raises his glass and takes a sip of juice and I think that ARM is not sloppy at all; I think they're a very effective organization. And I go into Non-Relating Mode while the detective continues with his bla bla bla on my left.

Until I distinguish from his bla bla bla a few words that catch my attention.

So, about your death threat.

Excuse Me? I ask, anxious again.

Look, try to just forget about it. Ecological terrorists have very few rules, but 1 thing they won't do is harm living creatures. They might damage property, make threats, sure. Scaring people is what they do best. But they've never killed anyone. Murder would be illogical for a group that carries out active compassion, as they themselves proclaim.

Even though they said they're going to kill Me? I ask.

The detective takes a sip of juice and places the glass down on the little table between us.

That's right, he says, even though that's what they said. Our statistics indicate that they usually make only 1 threat. They find someone they hate, make a threat—even a death threat—publicly celebrate it on their Web site, and that's the end of it. Let me put it to you this way: if you haven't heard from them again in 6 months, you can take it as a sign that you've become a party piece, a story circulating at radical green get-togethers.

What about the murder of the Japanese minister of fisheries and agriculture? I ask.

What are you talking about?

I summarize what I'm talking about.

Since he still doesn't fully understand, I take out my notebook and sketch a door and a man in pyjamas hanging from the door on a dog leash nailed to the upper corner of the frame, his tongue and penis hanging out, and explain the unlikelihood of his having decided to hang himself in this fashion.

The detective looks at my drawing for a long time.

This looks like a photograph, he says, still staring at it.

Almost like a photograph, I amend.

You even put stripes on the minister's pyjamas, he says.

That's because the minister's pyjamas had stripes. White pyjamas with vertical blue stripes.

Can I keep this? he asks.

I say yes and the detective pulls his briefcase onto his lap, opens it, takes out a brown, letter-sized envelope, and slips my drawing into the envelope that he slips back into his briefcase.

I keep insisting:

A month after the suicide, news of it appeared on the ARM Web site but they called it a murder and attributed it to 1 of their Japan cells.

They do that. Claim responsibility for a whole host of things. Did you know they claimed responsibility for the tsunami in Sumatra?

I find this very upsetting.

Really? I ask.

Really. Giant waves razing villages all over the island,
killing tens of thousands of people, leaving more homeless,
and these bastards try to claim that Mother Nature was taking
revenge because they'd murdered whales—they see themselves as Mother Nature's next of kin.

I consider the possibility: those chains of cause and effect
and that configuration of kinship. I wouldn't be so quick to
reject the idea, but the detective starts up again.

Anyway, I'll make note of your, uh, hypothesis we'll call it,
about the Japanese minister, but I will also reiterate that
according to our reports neither ALF nor ARM has ever killed
anyone. Their rhetorical rage aside, ecological activists
emphatically declare love for all life.

He directs his eyes to mine and I look the other way.

Don't be offended, he says. I apologize if I offended you.
I'll circulate your hypothesis at the agency, I promise.

He continues:

Now, about your property. That, they may try to damage,
and I have orders from your partner, Mr. Gould, to spare no
expense to protect it. We'll bolster fire safety at all of the fisheries, install alarms and controls, get you some guards, metal
detectors at the entrances, and we'll install cameras to record
activity in every area. Which, by the way, is not only good
protection, it'll also help you keep tabs on your employees.

He does something very strange. He closes 1 eye at Me and I stare at the black tip of 1 of my boots.

And as far as your own safety is concerned, I hear him continue, I personally will speak to management at the hotels where you stay about precautionary measures.

What kind of precautionary measures? I ask.

The most important 1: I'll give them letter scanners if they don't already have them. In the past, in the 90s, ARM sent letter bombs to several scientists and the British prime minister. None of them added up to more than a few burned hands and faces for the recipients but they got a lot of press write-up, which is of course what they're after—publicity.

He takes a white silk handkerchief from his breast pocket and wipes the sweat from his forehead.

Uf, the heat in Porto de Caeiro, he says. Great for vacation, terrible for work. So. You had a college professor, Doctor Charles Huntington, yes?

I straighten up in my wicker chair.

Yes. Does he have something to do with ARM?

Too much for his own good. In 2003 in the state of New York, ARM blew up his car and said they'd leave him in peace if he stopped building slaughterhouses. He ignored them and they burned down his house, though he was out teaching class at a nearby university so he wasn't even burned. He ignored them again and drew up plans to build a more modern house with the insurance money he'd received; after all, he knew they weren't going to hurt him directly, because of what I already explained.

And they hurt him, I said.

Not directly, no. What they did next has its beauty. The professor had moved into a motel while his house was being built. And what they did was dig up his mother's grave and put her body in his bed at the motel. It seems that, like any good bachelor, Huntington wasn't too meticulous when it came to bedtime rituals. That night he was very tired when he got back to the room, so he took off his shoes and his jacket and went to bed fully clothed.

In his tie?

Well, maybe, or most probably yes, in his tie. I see that surprises you.

When I was his student that's how I imagined him. Wearing a tie in bed.

Odd.

Yes.

So, as I was saying, he stretched out in bed, perhaps in his tie. And when he woke up in the morning, he saw that he'd spent the night beside his mother, or rather, the corpse of his mother. Well, that was when Huntington snapped. He started suffering panic attacks. Insomnia. Began roaming the streets at night, barefoot. He retired—he was 82 years old, after all— and started living in a psychiatric asylum. What's interesting is who was in the cell that was behind all this psychological torture that drove him crazy.

Who?

Guess. Someone you know.

An old student of his?

No. Try again.

No idea.

The cell contained exactly 1 person: the man who'd been his assistant for 30 years, Gabriel Short.

I say:

I don't know what to say.

I know. Shocking, isn't it?

And could Short be behind my kidnapping?

Impossible. Poor devil's in jail, and that's where he'll stay for the next 19 years.

He crosses his legs; his black shoes look like ballet slippers: thin, flexible leather.

And that's how I spend the whole morning, listening to Detective Iñaki Belloso's monologue and learning the triumphs and failures of ARM.

*

When he's finished, he gives Me a few orders.

Notify us immediately of any contact they make with you, if indeed they even try. You say you have only a cell phone, no landline, so make sure to take note of the number they use if they call. And, if you receive a letter with no return address, or a return address that you don't recognize, don't open it. And call me immediately. Finally, about your luggage, when you travel.

I don't take luggage when I travel, I say. Just a briefcase with jeans, a spare shirt, and my laptop.

Ah, he says.

And then he asks happily:

Will you sign that drawing?

He pulls out the drawing of the minister hanging in his pyjamas and places it on the little table and I sign it in the corner.

There will always be troublemakers, the elegant detective assures Me, standing. The mentally disabled, good-for-nothings, misfits.

He smiles at Me and I stare at my boots and prepare to explain to him that even though I am disabled in some things I am exceptionally able in others, but then he asks Me the 2 most surprising questions of the morning:

Do you know Bar Alberto, over on Punta Azul in Porto de Caeiro? That little bar with a balcony overlooking the sea where you can have a glass of champagne and talk in the moonlight?

No, I reply. I don't drink.

Ah, he says. I see. And do you like movies?

Not in the slightest.

In the silence that follows, a black tern flies in the sky above us.

Iñaki Belloso says:

Pleasure to have met a gentlewoman like you.

He bows and then walks away on his supple black slippers.

16

1 afternoon my cell phone rings in my Porto de Caeiro hotel room.

Good afternoon, doña Karen. They're spawning.

10 minutes later I'm on the pier in my blue wetsuit, mask on my head, surrounded by fishermen and captains who are as thrilled as Me.

Doña Karen, the females are laying eggs! they shout.

Doña Karen, this has never happened before! Females in captivity have never laid eggs!

That's not exactly true! I shout back excitedly. In 3 places they have! We'll have to see if tuna actually hatch here!

Nobody pays any attention to my autistic rectifications, not even Me, and I order:

Get the video camera! A boat! You, you and you: meet Me underwater!

I drop off the side of the boat, the heavy camera on my back, and descend 5 metres, 10 metres, and swim over to the bars of paradise.

I hold the camera up and zoom in: beyond the cage bars the tuna are circling the red coral island in clearly ritualized behavior.

Ritualized behavior: the ordered, reiterative conduct of a living group.

Suddenly 5 tuna separate from the school circling the island, quickly accelerate, and swim away. Then in the distance, they decelerate. And accelerate again, chasing each other, their chase forming what looks like a sideways 8.

Like this:

$$\infty$$

1 tuna expels a reddish cloud. Those must be microscopic eggs. A reddish cloud that keeps floating as the 5 tuna reenter acceleration phase.

They quickly shoot through the reddish cloud and the other 4 tuna expel something white.

The 3 captains in their wetsuits kick over to Me and aim their binoculars toward where my camera is pointing.

Then another group, this 1 of 4 tuna, breaks away from the tribe circling the red island. And this group, too, chases each other in fits of acceleration.

The female expels a red cloud of eggs nearly invisible to the eye. The males swim through the red cloud and penetrate it with their clouds of semen.

1 after the other, just like that, 7 groups of tuna fertilize eggs that afternoon in Porto de Caeiro. And the afternoon turns to night.

The water has got cold, it's dark, we return to the boats, and under the star-filled night sky we return to the fishery talking about the thousands of years it took for life to perfect the spawning of tuna: fertilization occurs on a warm, orange, sunlit afternoon so that at night the cold, dark sea acts as an incubator.

We change into dry clothes and, leaning against a white wall with the other captains, study the video footage.

With each red or white cloud expelled by 1 of our tuna, those of us gathered in the screening room applaud and shout: Bravo!

When the lights go on, 1 captain opens a bottle of *sidra*. Pop! Fizz spills from the bottle into glass after glass after glass, as another captain passes out cigars.

Have a cigar, boss, he says in a Uruguayan accent. After all, these fertilized eggs are your kids!

No, I correct. Only if we get larvae and the larvae survive and turn into tuna. And that has never happened in captivity.

But the captains' optimism is untroubled by reason. They laugh and I don't. I take the cigar, sombre, place it between my lips, someone holds out a lighter, and I inhale and choke on the smoke.

Boss is the Wizard of Oz of tuna! another captain laughs.

They nod, blowing out smoke.

Boss is the Pied Piper of Tuna of the Atlantic, says another.

I have no idea what they're talking about and leave them drinking and smoking and go to bed.

Gould's call wakes Me up in the middle of the night.

Karen, I got the video. This is the first footage of tuna laying eggs in history. Do you realize that?

I realize that, I say, my head under the sheets.

Karen, sweetheart, listen carefully. This is as big as the first moonwalk.

Not true, I respond into the cell phone. It will be, I amend, if tuna are actually born of the fertilized eggs.

If tuna are born in captivity, I explain on the phone to my aunt Isabelle that day, strolling on the dock that leads to the sea sparkling with sun, this will be the start of a new relationship between tuna and humans.

You have to write about it, she says, from the night of Oaxaca. Let me call a friend at *Nature* magazine.

That afternoon it happens again. The school of tuna ritually circle the red coral island. Groups of 3 or 5 males and 1 female break away to form their horizontal 8 and lay eggs and ejaculate.

And the school of human lookouts, and Me—the hybrid— capture it on video from outside paradise.

This goes on for 14 days in the sea at Porto de Caeiro.

Until 1 afternoon the camera captures the first tuna larva floating on its own in the water. I have the camera zoomed all the way, so the larva must be tiny: a blue, translucent larva, a miniature tuna with all of its parts in place but 1 eye looking too big.

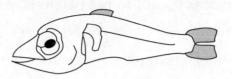

When the captains and I watch the video of the 54 tuna larvae, the silence is so utter that you can hear the projector buzzing.

And when the lights are turned on, once again bottles of *sidra* are uncorked and once again someone passes out cigars. Then the Uruguayan captain tells Me that we all have to go to the dining room next door because they have a surprise for Me.

The image of a tuna larva fills 1 entire wall.

I think about it for 30 seconds and finally pronounce:

You enlarged an image from the video.

The Uruguayan takes off his captain's hat, tucks it under his arm, and raises his glass of *sidra*.

To the boss's first child! he exclaims.

This makes Me furious.

LOWER YOUR GLASSES! I shout.

As is so often the case, I find the human penchant for metaphors dangerous and try to make them understand. I ask:

What happens if the press hears I had a tuna-child? That would sure contradict Darwin and everything in the history of human experience. So I forbid you to ever say that I am the mother of that larva. Or its Wizard of Oz or its Pied Piper or any of that metaphor shit.

A month later, 103 tuna larvae are growing tails at a sustained pace. They double in size every 3 days. And the adult tuna have stopped their ritualized behavior and now become angry with each other: head butting, tail swishing.

Things on land have changed, too.

The press pays us a visit every day, interviewing captains and leaving with larvae photos that the captains give them. The news spreads on the Internet, on aquaculture and animal husbandry sites. The *National Geographic* channel broadcasts images of larvae turning into fish. Japan is the only country in the world to report the news on broadcast television, in a report in which the disaster I'd been fearing finally occurs.

According to what Yasuko tells Me on the phone, as the 2 of us watch a video of the report on laptop, they say that Karen Nieto is the mother of hundreds of tuna and that every afternoon from a boat she feeds them 1 by 1, using a baby bottle.

Well, I say. That explains the fucking picture.

The picture of a boat in the distance on which a woman with close-cropped hair in a white T-shirt leans over the prow holding a baby bottle from which a young tuna—its head barely peeking out above the sea's surface—suckles.

Yasuko says:

You look good. Muscular. Trim.

Don't you get it?! It's a photomontage, damn it! A fucking metaphor that became just another lie. Which is precisely why I don't allow metaphors in my language system. Metaphors undermine the truth of your information. Why the hell can't you people live without metaphors?

Yasuko's voice comes softly through the cell:

That's just the way it is. Simple reality is insufficient.

What are you talking about? Insufficient for what?

I don't know, Karen. Simple reality is frightening, I suppose. Maybe we use metaphors as a way to isolate reality. To separate it from us. To disguise it.

Of course reality is frightening, I say. It's worse than that. Reality makes people go hungry. Reality makes people sick. And reality will definitely kill you. But reality is the only thing that's real; everything else is ... a metaphor in your fucking head!

If-you-e-ver-shout-at-me-a-gain, Yasuko says in her soft little-girl voice, I-will-re-sign.

I hurl the phone against the wall, where it crashes to the floor in pieces.

Then 1 afternoon we find something that truly unleashes my fury: a scuba diver armed with an underwater camera swimming near paradise.

They bring him to Me at the hotel, his mask still on and everything, green fins over 1 shoulder, heavy camera over the other, and on the balcony the guy refuses to pull off his mask or give Me his camera.

Take it off and hand Me that, I insist.

Flanked by 2 captains, he shakes his head. A brawny guy of about my height, that is, approximately 1.85 metres.

I approach him, wrap 1 hand around his neck and use my thumb to apply pressure to his carotid artery while with the other I yank first the mask off his head and then the camera from its strap.

When I let go of him he begins screaming in English that sounds like a cat meowing, saying that he's going to sue Me and other nonsense. He has almond-shaped eyes and turns out to be Chinese.

I examine his camera. It's good: an Olympus 8080, but mine is better—a Sony 9556—so I ask reception for an ax in order to destroy it.

They tell Me they don't have an ax. They bring Me an

approximation: a baseball bat. I place the Olympus on the floor and smash it to bits with the bat. The Chinese diver shouts himself hoarse the entire time and my 2 captains stand by, arms crossed, waiting.

That afternoon I call a meeting on the dock with the captains of the fleet. They're all smiling in their suits and impeccably white sailor hats.

I, on the other hand, am tense and nervous.

So, I say, it's time to move.

Doña Karen, the Uruguayan captain demands, at least greet us before you start firing off orders. After all, we made nearly 110 tuna babies with you.

Fine, I snort, trying not to get pissed off. Good afternoon, Captains.

Good afternoon, Mama Karen, they reply in chorus.

And they all erupt in laughter.

I wait until they quiet down and I can hear the afternoon sea crashing intermittently against the cement dock once more.

So, I begin again, now that they've reproduced, the tuna are ready to go; they're restless.

Everyone nods.

And you're restless, too. And Me. Technically, it's referred to as a behavior of uncertainty.

They nod again.

So, I continue, what we need to do is move to our behavior of certainty. Prepare the conveyor belt, the air guns, fill the coffins with ice, schedule the plane pickups, notify the markets.

The captains stand motionless, staring at Me with blank faces, except for the Uruguayan, who twirls his hat in his hands and finally ventures:

We're going to kill them?

I respond:

To my knowledge, killing them is how we make our living.

He stands, twirling his hat in his hand for another moment. And then all at once we begin to move, going about our business.

17

The next few months are a series of big things and little things with no major turmoil.

They award Me the Committee for More Humane Animal Slaughter medal, the same 1 that's hanging from a nail on the wall in my room in Mazatlán—although that 1 belongs to Charles Huntington—and Yasuko goes to accept it on my behalf.

I finish revamping the 7 fisheries on the Mediterranean coast and install a tuna paradise in each 1: a provisional paradise that will last until the day of their slaughter.

I write an article for *Nature* magazine and give it a title that I know in advance will be controversial: "The Dynamics of Spawning, Courting, Fertilizing and Larvae Growing for Bluefin Tuna in Captivity."

Outcry from the meat and fishing industry! Chaos throughout the biology departments of the world!

As the hundreds of e-mails to *Nature* have proven, 2 things in particular are the cause of such outrage. First, my article contains no citations and second, my synoptic charts and diagrams comprise the majority of the article.

So *Nature* invites Me to publish whatever I want, whenever I want, in their journal.

For my next article, I choose an even more scandalous title: "The Dynamics of Training *Homo sapiens* Using Descartes' Instructions (or Why Darwin Has Not Been Accepted into the Repertoire of Human Conduct)."

They don't publish it; they want Me to write only about what they call "the evolution of 21st-century fishing and aquaculture." So I do, but in my next article I surreptitiously slip this paragraph into a footnote by way of a reference.

It is a shame that after the publication of On the Origin of Species *by Charles Darwin at the end of the 19th century, all of Descartes's books were not piled up and burned. If such an act had occurred, new ways of relating to animals would have been invented in the 19th century and not the 21st, when the*

planet's fauna are already endangered. It's time to make that
bonfire with Descartes's books once and for all. Burn them!

This time the article is published but the footnote is not, and I receive a brief e-mail.

Nature *does not publish hate speech, and certainly not discourse that incites the public to burn books.*

Frankly I cannot understand why we should not burn incorrect books. They serve only to distract attention from books that make fewer mistakes in their way of thinking, and thought ought to be a progressive science. That is to say, the human species over time should learn to think better, more easily and more happily.

That is to say, if I were world secretary of education, I would burn all of Descartes's books, and not only his but also all books by all writers who think like him—approximately 99% of those published in the past 3 centuries—and students, trees and fauna would thank Me for it.

Gould, for his part, publishes his book *Profit (A Love Story)*. The book tops the bestseller list in the United States for 11 consecutive months and is translated into 17 languages. No idea if anyone gets rich by reading it, but what is clear is that

Gould earns a fortune; with his royalties he buys a new jet and gives Me his old jet, with a pilot who wears a black uniform with gold insignia and everything.

Yasuko and I walk across the runway toward a white plane with a G on the tail and an elegant pilot dressed in a black uniform with gold insignia. Yasuko whispers:

Gould is lying to you.

Gould never lies, I reply angrily.

Ha! Yasuko says dryly. He's not being so generous to you because of his book profits. It's the profits from your fly killer, the best business venture Gould has ever made in his life.

We go up the plane's steps and it occurs to Me that it might be true. My electric fly killer, which I rarely even think about, is now used all over the world, and better designed so that the bulb and tray water form a single piece.

Restaurants small and large, food-packing plants, hotels in places with hot climates. Even the Saatchi Gallery in London has 1: an artist hung my electric fly catcher in a display cabinet with a rotten cow's rib to ensure a perpetual supply of flies to the light where they burn with a bzzzzzzt.

The same artist, by the way, who years earlier stuck a sheep in a tank of formaldehyde, the 1 considered to be the founder of postmodern art (!) about whom Gould told Me 5 years ago on the 132nd floor of his Shanghai office:

He's a marketing genius.

Yasuko says, as we enter the plane:

You're Gould's ideal partner. You work and you sleep, that's all you do. You pay no attention to your percentage of profits and your expenses are negligible. All you want is frozen yogurt brought to your hotel room.

The elegant pilot invites us to take a seat in the honey-colored armchairs and we sit and I order a martini—with lots of alcohol, I add—and while Yasuko carries on crossly about how Gould is cheating Me, I disconnect from Human Language so that all I can hear is a buzzing sound and I press all the little buttons on the armrest, making the seatback recline, raising the footrest, making the entire chair go horizontal and turn into a bed, turning it back into a chair once more.

When the captain returns with the martini on a little silver tray, I tell him:

It's for Yasuko.

And finally, Yasuko stops complaining about Gould and drinks it.

Now, I know that Yasuko is the one with an advanced

degree in business but a white jet for a fly killer seems like a pretty good deal to Me.

Something else begins happening during that time. Every 15th of the month, no matter what port I'm in, I receive a white envelope at the hotel with no return address and 2 razor blades inside.

Yes, yes, I know, in retrospect, I know I should have informed the Interpol detective immediately, but the first time I got 1 of those envelopes I could tell that there were 2 flat objects inside, which made Me think about Ricardo and the lemon leaves he sent Me at college for years in a white envelope, and I opened it.

So why do I keep opening the other ones without informing the detective about it? For 3 reasons, all of which are very personal.

1. As I said, they make Me think of Ricardo and the 2 lemon leaves he used to send Me.

2. I am 1 of the few people left on the planet Earth who still uses actual razor blades to cut my hair and I know how hard it is to find anyone who stocks them.

3. They're just 2 razor blades with no threats written on them that I can see.

At any rate, not calling Interpol turns out to have irreparable consequences, for Me and for a lot of people, but what I do every month when I receive the blades is hold on to them, and 1 night I see in the mirror that my hair is 7 centimetres long and I open my briefcase, take out 1 of the 5 envelopes that I keep paper-clipped together with the razor blades inside, remove 1 blade, and finally put it to use.

I insert it into my steel safety razor and shave, from my ankles to my neck. Legs, pubic hair, armpits, the back of my neck. Then with my electric clippers I cut 6 centimetres of hair off of my head.

And then my cell phone rings.

It's Gorda, which makes Me happy.

Hello, Gorda, I say. You've never called Me before. Is it daytime in Mazatlán?

Your aunt is very sick, she responds.

I fly backward through time zones and arrive the day before I left and the house in Mazatlán is filled with the scent of white spikenards. All over the house are vases filled with white spikenards.

*

Spikenards on the shelf in the entryway. Spikenards on the table in the living room with the checkerboard marble floor. Spikenards in a cardboard cube by an open window through which I can see the Zapotec painter out on the beach standing before an easel, painting, his white shirt luminous in the noonday sun.

Spikenards on the table in the library where Baldy holds a book before his bloodshot eyes.

I feel terribly afraid when I open the door to my aunt's bedroom. There, a third man, older, with gray hair, wearing a cream-colored 3-piece suit, nods when he sees Me.

You're the doctor, I say.

Yes. I'm also your aunt's first husband.

He says it in English.

Over his shoulder I see an open red parasol on the balcony. I go outside. My aunt Isabelle is lying with her back to Me, on a rickety old wooden bed with a white mattress, her linen shirt billowing in the breeze, the noonday sun the color of steel.

I sit on 1 edge of the mattress and touch her shoulder. I hear her say:

You can't see me all at once. Wait 10 minutes and I'll turn around slowly. Okay?

Okay, I agree.

We'll see if you even recognize me.

Beneath 1 centimetre of even white hair, her scalp is pink. There's a 9-centimetre scar on the crown of her head. When Aunt Isabelle turns a bit more to let Me see her, I note that her green eyes are as big as ever, but now on such a skinny face, her skin spread thin over her cheekbones and jawbone, they look bigger than ever.

I'm almost, she says and then pauses to swallow.

She completes:

Almost a skeleton, aren't I?

I say:

That's right.

She smiles:

We look like twins, Karen. The same hair ...

Haircut, I finish for her. What happened? I ask.

She speaks so slowly that between sentences the sea has time to crash.

Fucking brain haemorrhage.

The Nieto women.

Always bleed between our legs when we turn 15.

And have a fucking.

Brain haemorrhage.

At 67. Genetic.

Your mother died at 67. Remember?

No, I say, I don't remember.

I take 1 of her very white, bony hands in mine, her knuckles the widest thing on each finger. Her hand in mine is like a little girl's and weighs approximately 100 grams.

I say:

I don't remember anything before you.

Yes, well. Your mother had a goddamned brain haemorrhage just like this, and then she took off in her jeep.

She inhales deeply so that she can finish:

And kept driving straight when the road turned and flew off into the void.

I lie down behind her, press my body up against her back. Like I used to when I was a kid. I raise her head and put mine beneath it so that her head is resting on top of mine.

I hear her say:

I'm going to miss this.

The sun.

The sea.

My 3 husbands.

And especially you.

I only made 1 mistake with you. The fishery.

You liked animals more than people and I sent you to off to a tuna slaughterhouse. What a terrible mistake. But.

But we're born into this ancient world. Full of things created by our parents. And our parents' parents' parents.

We're born into a tomb full of relics. Ancient words. Fixed sentences. Fixed customs. Ways of living are passed down from those who've already lived.

My grandfather's tuna fishery was there before I was born. The idea that you, my niece, the only other living Nieto, would inherit it from me was there, too, centuries ago.

God forgive me, my aunt sobs.

You're talking about God, Aunt Isabelle?

I haven't changed my opinion, she says. God is everything we can't know. If a question has no answer ...

The answer is God, I reply, completing the sentence she taught Me.

Exactly. That's why I want God, who is immense, to forgive me, who's so tiny.

We lie there watching the sun, the sea, speaking intermittently, my body pressed against hers, her head on my head, until she stops speaking.

She falls asleep and her head purrs on my head.

Dusk falls, the sky and sea turn shades of orange, a sliver of moon appears in the East, and the tiny diamond of light of Venus.

18

In the days that follow, my aunt Isabelle begins losing words. She glides around in her wheelchair, dressed in a white linen dress, her white hair cropped close to her head, and in the middle of the marble checkerboard floor she stops the chair and looks around, befuddled.

She searches out my eyes.

She licks her dry lips. She wants to tell Me something. She can't find the words.

She proclaims:

Airport.

No, that wasn't the word she wanted and she shakes her head and laughs. I laugh with her. Her men never laugh; each time my aunt falters and finds the wrong word they look horrified.

The Zapotec painter spends all day walking the beach, his hands thrust into the pockets of his jeans, his shoulders high, barefoot, crying.

Baldy has taken a sudden interest in alphabetizing Great-grandfather's library: 10,000 books that have lived in disorder for 120 years.

The doctor takes my aunt's blood pressure 16 times a day. He undresses her and puts her to bed in a bed with clean sheets and gives her 4 injections. He listens to her heart with his stethoscope another 16 times. He performs a urine analysis on a tiny drop of urine under his microscope every 8 hours. Then at night he stares into a telescope he's set up on the balcony in order to monitor, he says, the birth of a star, which is supposed to be born this month—September—and take 1 year to reach its stable size.

From staring into the microscope at a drop of his wife's urine to staring into the telescope where he watches the birth of a star that isn't actually born, the doctor spends his days. And in between the 2, he reads to her. I find the 2 of them on the balcony or in the bedroom or by the pool, the doctor and my aunt sitting side by side, he reading aloud from an old green, or blue or yellow book. Until he realizes that she's snoring.

I should say that she's purring, because my aunt is so elegant that when she snores, she really purrs.

At dinner Baldy and the doctor tell stories in which only 1 of them and Aunt Isabelle were present. My aunt, at the head of the table, nods in agreement.

Sometimes she concurs with a word intended to approximate yes:

Complete, for instance.

Or:

Pigeon.

And whichever lover is speaking continues with the tale of how he and she ate the most extraordinary oysters at the restaurant in the Eiffel Tower and then strolled along such-and-such a river and then this or that or the other thing, and the lover who wasn't there becomes incensed and begins preparing his next anecdote in which he and my aunt traveled the length of India and memorized murals depicting 57 ways to breed and then engaged in way number 15 and after that in way number 32.

And the Zapotec painter says nothing, drawing things that are invisible on the tablecloth with his finger.

1 night my aunt murmurs:

Karen, give him a. A.

She searches the air trying to locate the missing word; her glance catches on a fly that lands on my electric fly killer, sizzles, and drops into the tray.

My aunt tries again:

Give him a knife. No, tweezers.

I go get 1 of my black Variety pilot pens and when she sees Me hand it to the painter her green eyes light up.

That! she says. That. A ...

Pen, I finish for her.

Pen! she cries jubilantly. Pen! Pen!

From that night on, over dinner while my aunt's 2 vocal lovers tell competing stories, the mute painter draws on the tablecloth: rabbits, deer, bulls mounting deer from behind, lizards entwined around naked women, naked women with high heels bolted together, stars with seahorses sprinkled in among them and the sky, and land horses.

We get up after dinner and he stays there drawing.

In the mornings Gorda spreads the tablecloth at the foot of Aunt Isabelle's wheelchair and she is delighted by the draw-ings and saddened by the smears where he's cried, the painter standing barefoot beside her, silent and wearing an expression of fear, hands in his jeans pockets, shoulders high.

In the end it is the silent lover who merits more of her time.

Gorda stores the cloth, carefully folded, in a closet, and every afternoon she covers the table with a clean, new white 1.

1 afternoon we're in her bedroom together, my aunt at a little table eating oatmeal, and a spoonful of oatmeal falls from her mouth onto her white linen trousers.

She sits gazing at the stain: oatmeal on a white linen trouser leg.

I go for a towel. I kneel to wipe away the little disaster. I sit in a chair beside her and feed her, 1 spoonful, then another. A tear wells up and brims over the corner of her green eye, slides down her cheek.

Karen, she says, I want to show you something.

She searches for the words. She says them:

Show you my co-op.

She shakes her head.

The cooperatives, she insists, desperate. The, the plots, the, those things. The agrarian reform. Fuck it! The, the plan to.

Your will, I guess.

She nods.

I go to the safe for the will.

I sit in the chair across from her and read it to her.

She nods after each clause. And suddenly she stops nod-ding. She's gone, with her eyes open. She's breathing but she's gone.

She wakes up, recognizes Me, recognizes the will in my hand, says:

Now tell them to. To.

She thinks. Shakes her head. Another tear brims in her green eye. Weary of her own mental torpor. She brings 3 fin-gertips to her lips and then with her 3 fingers waves good-bye.

I gather them—my aunt's lovers—in the library and tell them:

She wants you to leave.

The doctor, Baldy the librarian, and the painter: 1 by 1 each of them goes through to her bedroom to be alone with her for a moment and then all 3 walk single file out the front door, carrying their suitcases.

Through a window my aunt Isabelle watches them climb into 3 different taxis that will—I think as I watch from the kitchen window—all arrive at the airport at the same time.

And that's when Gorda hands Me the sixth white

envelope—stamped but with no return address—containing 2 razor blades.

Use them for something, I tell her, handing the envelope back. I have 9 more of them.

Strange: as soon as her lovers leave, Aunt Isabelle becomes very chatty.

The sea, the sea, she says on the balcony staring out at the sea. I see the sea sow the seeds of marvel, marvellous maritime marvel of velvet waves and salt and sun. And age and sun. And ancient son.

She explains:

Some poems I learned in my.

In my.

When you were a little girl, I say.

A little girl! she exclaims. You're a little girl and then you turn around and suddenly you're a. A. Fucking aneurism.

An old mammal, I complete.

She giggles.

An old mammal, she says.

Even stranger: that week she can recite poetry she learned in school when she was a little girl, or at least recall its rhythms, but she can't create any new sentences.

Spreading its wings, the dream; spreading, it swings the dream, its springs, it brings its wings, it sings its strings, spreading its dreams.

The following week all she can do is play with syllables:

Bla ble blu blo, plo pla, ple.

At any rate, the following week her desire to inhabit the sonorous world evaporates. We sit in silence on the balcony, she in her wheelchair, Me in a chair, watching the sea and the sun. Suddenly, a V of seagulls.

A little sailboat on the horizon.

Every now and then she becomes agitated and waves 2 fingers—the middle and index—and I know she wants a cigarette, I light it for her, pass it to her, she smokes slowly, and then suddenly looks down at it, confused, and says:

Damn thing, and drops it onto the red paving stones.

Those days, the longest of my life, the calmest, we spend our time—my aunt and I—on a careful mission just to exist.

To exist, which for Me is to unlearn to rush. To relax the muscles of my heart and let it beat in its own time. To be in the heat of the sun without thinking heat. To eat when hunger is hungry and give in to the tiredness that arrives with nightfall and darkness covers things and things in the darkness can rest.

Just to be. To be and to see. And to see all that is as it is, while it is, today, because we don't know if it will be, tomorrow.

I read in my diary:

Doctor Brady, her first husband, explained to Me that an artery in my aunt's brain had burst and the blood had soaked the part of her cerebral cortex that regulates language.

At first he thought it would be possible to suck the blood out with an extractor and he cut open the crown of her head to introduce a miniscule extractor.

It was impossible to extract the blood, so he introduced a miniscule camera and videoed the damage.

Then, together, they watched the video on the television in her hospital room and he told her to decide if she wanted to have that portion of her brain—the blood-soaked part—excised with miniscule scissors, which would cause a partial or total loss of consciousness.

Impossible to know. The brain, the doctor confessed, is 1 place on Earth we know very little about.

Aunt Isabelle said she didn't want to lose consciousness, partial or complete. She said what point would there be living without full consciousness. She said she was her consciousness.

Then the doctor brought her back to the Mazatlán mansion in the hopes that her brain would reabsorb the blood by itself.

Instead something else happened. The blood spread through the soft tissue of her cerebral cortex. 1 week her nouns were blurry. Another week it was her syntax. 1 day she'd be off balance.

By the time the doctor left, my aunt could no longer walk or eat by herself, nor could she read or write or speak clearly. Worse, she couldn't think clearly. But the very day the doctor left she began to recite poetry she'd learned as a child.

Every morning I wake up wondering where the blood in my aunt's cerebral cortex will have moved to that day. Will she be lucid? Will she be able to speak and understand or will she be outside the realm of language again?

Last night, still asleep, she suddenly turned to Me, opened her big eyes, and said:

My God, what next?

And yet today she woke up fine. She can't walk or coordinate her movements but she is speaking clearly and fluently. She's happy. I'm happy. When the doctor called I told him and he answered that it was perfectly feasible that she'd remain like that for some time.

A year? I asked.

Perhaps, he replied. Why not? But it could be just a few hours.

I carry her to the bathroom, sit her on the toilet. She looks at Me with laughter in her eyes. I tell her about the toilet in Japan; she laughs at the fact that I had an orgasm courtesy of water streaming from a toilet.

She asks Me if I ever saw Ricardo again. I say no. She tells Me to look for him. She confides that she has a phone number for a house in Sicily where he might live or they might know something about him.

Call him, she insists.

What do I need Ricardo for? I ask her.

You really don't know what for? my aunt asks.

No idea, I say.

And she laughs at Me.

Then together, completing each other's sentences, we reminisce about how Miss Alegría complained that I didn't understand that pooping is considered shameful and wanted to poop in the bathrooms of Mazatlán's museums with the stall doors open so I wouldn't feel trapped.

My aunt says very seriously, and speaking in complete sentences that stun Me:

That was the other mistake I made with you.

Another 1? What?

Letting Miss Alegría try to make you embarrassed of your anus. It's wrongheaded thinking but it's a mistake of our whole species, an ancient 1. To the civilized human eye, shit is taboo. Because we kill in order to eat and what we eat we then shit, humans refuse to allow it into their consciousness. We're blind to abattoirs and sewers and that blindness—that disgust and that blindness—is what distinguishes us from nonhumans.

I'll tell you a secret, she says, leaning toward Me. In their relationship to nonhumans, civilized humans are all autistic.

And I laugh with her, because it's so true.

I'll tell you another secret, she whispers, stroking my close-cropped head with both hands: I've never heard the sea, despite having lived in this house on the sea for so many years.

That's not true, I say.

Oh, it is, it is, she assures Me.

Listen, she says. I've never heard the sea for more than 30 seconds in a row. Drunk, maybe up to 1 minute and 30 seconds. I've listened to it drunk for a minute 30 or sober for 30 seconds before my thoughts carry me off somewhere else.

That's crazy! I exclaim.

Crazy! my aunt exclaims. The sound of my thoughts in my little round head block out the whole entire sea.

No, she says with a sad face, I've never truly heard the sea.

That's why you—she continues seated on the toilet, speaking with the fluency of a college professor and waiting for her lower intestine to expel her shit—that's why you, who are not alienated from slaughterhouses or from shit, who didn't let anyone separate you from Nature, who uses language but can leave language behind for hours, for days, you're my hope for the human race.

And I laugh at my aunt Isabelle's grandiose words.

You, she continues, stroking my head again, you're the mediator between animals who speak and animals who don't speak. You're a mutation of the human species and you can pull off another agreement with reality.

Do you understand? she asks.

I don't know, I tell her.

You will, she says, and you'll realize that it's true. Or—who knows?—maybe you'll never understand and maybe it will never be true. That's what's so distressing about reality: nothing is certain, nothing is definite, anything might happen—or not.

I carry her back into the bedroom and out to the balcony, where I sit her in her wheelchair, overlooking the sea.

I feed her spoonful after spoonful of oatmeal. But by the tenth spoonful she's gone. She's vanished. The oatmeal dribbles out the corners of her mouth.

I put my aunt into the bathtub. I take her out and wrap her in a big white towel and dry her, and then I sit her on the edge of the bed, naked. She's thin and fragile, like a girl, but her face is worn, like an old lady.

I tousle her white hair. I cut the nails of each finger of each hand. I kneel on the floor and cut the nails of each toe of each foot.

I put rose perfume behind her ears and elbows.

Give me a, she says, suddenly alert. A.

She touches her dry lips.

Whiskey, I say.

In the kitchen, I pour whiskey into a glass with 3 ice cubes.

I bring it to her in the bedroom.

Naked, sitting on the edge of the bed, she drinks it in little sips, using both hands to hold the glass, which seems heavy as a lump of lead to her.

The shutters are open, the windows, too. Beneath the yellow sky, the sea, too, is yellow.

In the bedroom whose walls are bathed in yellow light, I take the empty glass from her hands and place it on the bureau. I put her to bed, my aunt.

I get into bed fully clothed, beside my aunt, who is naked, and watch the ceiling turn orange, and slowly smell her smell, the smell of roses and whiskey, as the darkness of night makes it all disappear.

That night she speaks into my ear, waking Me:
Good-bye.
And after a wave crashes in the sea, 1 floor beneath us:
Good luck.
I wonder if there's a great beyond.
I wonder if there's a grape bee yonder.
And then after another huge wave crashes:
I'll be in touch if I can.
Or send you a sign.
And if I can't, well, then I won't.

Her breathing suddenly grows deeper, and outside the sea thunders again, and when the wave spreads across the sand with a sssssssssssssssssssssssssssss, I think I hear, where my aunt's heart is, a click.

19

In the morning when I wake up I touch her under the sheets. She's cold.

I get out of bed and uncover her, throw the white sheets to 1 side, and look down at my aunt lying on the white bedspread. Skinny, her rib cage sticking out from under her skin, motionless.

The green grass in the garden is full of little pink crabs that morning. My boots clump down first on 1, then on another 1, and another 1, crunch, crunch, crunch, as I walk, carrying my naked, dead aunt to my mother's grave. A black marble gravestone at the edge of the yard where the garden begins.

A black marble gravestone with the letters of her name cut into it and painted white.

LORENA NIETO

A gravestone with no date of birth or death or cross or star of David or anything. The Nieto family has had no religion since the 19th century.

But then I remember that my aunt and her sister didn't speak. I don't even know when they stopped speaking, because my aunt never even talked to Me about my mother. So it occurs to Me that if they didn't speak when they were alive, it might make them uncomfortable to be buried side by side now, underground, where they'll stay there like that for as long as the Earth exists.

So I retrace my steps, crushing crabs beneath my boots, crunch, crunch, crunch, and I deposit my aunt on the dewy grass, at the edge of the yard where the sand begins. The gardener's shovel is resting against the trunk of a lemon tree.

I dig. And dig. And I excavate a rectangular hole, piling up the dirt beside it. My naked aunt sunbathes in the grass, her 2 legs off to the left and her face to the sun, her green eyes open. I'll never be like her: even dead, she looks elegant in that pose.

Soaked with sweat, I pick her up once more. I jump down into the hole and place her on the ground. I climb out of the hole and look at my dirty white jeans and dirty hands. I pick up the shovel, fill it with dirt from the pile I've made, and toss it over my aunt.

The first shovelful of black dirt falls onto her white face, the white face of my elegant aunt, and that is when I can't take it anymore. I stab the shovel into the grass, lean my forehead against the handle, and stand there, not moving.

I don't know for how long.

Until I see a shadow pass over the round tip of my work boots. I look up, and it's a black buzzard, its wings taut, soaring in the wind.

I shovel the pile of earth back into the grave until it's filled.

My aunt asked Me to bury her in the ground with no coffin and no grave marker.

So you don't get your hopes up, thinking I'm there, she breathed into my face, which she held in both her hands.

And then she added, in another breath:

So you don't feel tied to some silly clump of dirt.

I disobey. Around the border of the quadrangle of earth covering my aunt, I place little white stones, so I won't forget the spot.

Zero, 0, was, for Max the parrot, the hardest number to comprehend, to apprehend.

Look, 3 apples, Max. How many?

3, he squawks in his old-fashioned phonograph voice.

Now I take away 1 apple, Max. And now how many are there?

2, Max says, opening and closing his pearl gray wings.

Ketchup! he adds.

Wait, Max. I'll give you ketchup later. Now I take away 2 apples of the 2 that were there. How many are left?

Max fixes his gaze on the table where now there is nothing.

30 seconds go by and he still has his gaze fixed on the table where there is nothing.

Zero, I say. There are zero apples. Zero.

Zero! Max finally caws.

I hold out a peanut and with his beak he snatches it from my fingers.

3 years to comprehend—to apprehend—the number 0 is how long it took Max.

0: the impossible number.

I, too, take time to comprehend that if I bury my aunt Isabelle, that means she is no longer on the balcony or in bed or in the dining room, and that it no longer makes any difference if I keep changing clothes every day or keep bathing or answering the house phone or my cell phone, that it makes no sense to turn on the computer or read the newspaper or talk to myself or even think: for whom?

So 1 afternoon, sitting out on the balcony, staring at the sea, I vanish. Where there was Me, now there is 0.

1 day the telephone wakes Me up. I find myself sitting on a black square of the marble checkerboard living room floor.

In the air filled with golden light, 29 butterflies flutter in a slow line and knock into the gray walls between which the windows are shattered and I realize that there is not a single piece of furniture in the living room and even in the kitchen there is no table and there on the counter the old black telephone is still ringing and then I disappear once more.

Another day the phone wakes Me up again and I'm sitting rocking on the wooden floor in my bedroom, a line of ants marching beside Me. I follow the line of ants.

The mouth of the anthill, where 15 lines come together in a swirl, is on the beach.

I'm hungry. So hungry. I take a fistful of sand and suck on it. It's salty. I remember the chauffeur when I was a girl used to kick my fist to make Me drop the sand. But I'm alone now and I don't drop it. I chew it. I think about Gorda, who has disappeared, left the house. And I think I'll have enough food: the entire beach is edible, all for Me, the hungry animal who is Me.

Another day the phone calls Me back to awareness. I pick up the receiver in the kitchen. It's Gould.

Karen, he says. Sit down.

What for?

Because this is going to be a blow.

I perk up and realize that I'm sitting on the blue tile floor in the empty kitchen, the receiver on my shoulder. So I say:

Okay, I'm sitting.

They blew up the fisheries, Gould says.

Where?

What do you mean, where? Where they were! Karen, pay attention! All 7 tuna fisheries have been bombed. They all exploded the same night.

I don't know what to say, I say.

Interpol is investigating, he continues. You, keep calm. They're insured but we'll have to rebuild them all from the ground up.

Oh. From the. So you mean. What about the tuna?

What *about* the tuna? I have no idea about the tuna, Karen.

The tuna are in the water, in their paradise, I say. I don't think they'll have gotten hurt.

I'm telling you I didn't ask about the tuna, Karen.

What month is it? I ask.

January, says the voice over the telephone.

January, I repeat, not fully understanding what it means.

I say:

That means I've been here several months.

Karen, call me tomorrow. We have a lot to do.

I hang up.

But this time I don't disappear. The tuna keep Me present. I think about them again—the tuna. And again and again: the tuna, the tuna.

I think: I have to take a bath so I can go see what happened to the tuna.

I can't figure out how it got into the tub, this thing. I'm about to turn on the water to run my bath and I lean over to pick it up out of the white, porcelain bathtub. A little toy fish, hollow plastic. It's a tuna, a bluefin, silvery, with an open mouth where you can see its pointy little teeth and red insides.

I turn it over and see on 1 side 3 tiny letters written in red ink:

ARM

The bathroom door opens slowly. I expect something awful.

But no, nobody comes in.

I step out but there's nobody on the stairs. The door just opened by itself.

In the library I get on the computer and go to the ARM Web site. I'm unsurprised to find a message on the homepage, in English, for the press and for Karen Nieto, president and founder of True Blue Tuna, engineer in humane slaughter.

Congratulations, Karen Nieto!

7 colorful celebrations rocked 7 coasts on the bluefin tuna migration route last night, lighting up the night sky in succession.

First, deafening explosions blew up the installations; then came the fires, the beautiful crackling flames, the sound of rafters falling, the tumult of walls collapsing; and at dawn, columns of gray smoke rising . . .

You were warned; we are deadly serious. We fight to win and we fight for the innocent. We've crossed the line of nonviolence and we will not be stopped.

Terror begets terror. Murder begets murder. Here is our

reckoning: 12 animal killers will be killed so that humanity sees their crimes won't go unpunished: 3 vivisectionists, 3 "scientific" torturers, 3 large fur traders, and 3 engineers in murder.

Karen Nieto, it is your turn to die.

Onward toward victory, for the animals forever.

ARM

20

The way Yasuko told it to Me, their plane touched down on the only runway of the tiny airport in Porto de Caeiro as a sliver of sun was just beginning to peek out over the horizon.

Gould walked down the steps in khaki Bermudas and his ever-present huaraches with the trailer-tire soles and a red baseball cap, followed by her, Yasuko, who was very formal in her gray tailored suit, the strap of her attaché case over 1 shoulder.

They stepped out of the taxi in the place where the fishery buildings had been and where now there was a grove of olive and lemon trees, shining in the silvery dawn sun.

Where the boats had been docked now there was a white stone walkway, but before that, under the last line of lemon trees, stood Me, awaiting them beside a wooden table in T-shirt, jeans and white sandals, the calm sea behind Me, flat.

I held out my hand and they both realized that something important had changed within Me since the last time we'd met, because I'd never offered my hand before.

Gould took my hand in his, I squeezed it carefully, using my thumb to feel the 5 bones that began in his wrist, and Yasuko hesitated before giving Me her hand. I squeezed it, too, very carefully, and with my thumb touched each of the 5 bones that began at her wrist.

In the 2 weeks I'd been in Porto de Caiero, I'd been practicing taking strangers' hands. I shook the hand of the doorman dressed as admiral who stands at the hotel entrance, just for a second, and felt a gag reflex and ran to the lobby bathroom where I vomited.

I shook the hands of the 4 hotel receptionists behind the white marble counter 1 after the other, holding my breath so I could stand the revulsion of holding something so naked and so intimate. The hand of an erect biped mammal, it was like holding a person's clammy, wobbling kidney.

The hand of the maid who came to clean my room was slightly less disgusting to shake, and I held it, using my thumb to verify that all of the finger bones were in place, 5 in total. This was a discovery: by counting finger bones with my thumb I was able to endure physical contact for over 10 seconds.

Each morning for 1 week, I shook hands with each of the workers who came to carry off the remains of the bombed tuna fishery. And the following week, I shook hands with every worker who came to sod the grass and plant the lemon trees.

Hello, I'd say, holding out my hand.

And I always had to overcome the first impulse, which was fear, and then the second 1, which was revulsion, as I counted the 5 finger bones of the alien hand with my thumb.

When did you plant the trees? Gould began the conversation, his blue eyes twinkling.

And finally I let go of Yasuko's hand and the 3 of us sat at the wooden table.

A week ago, I informed him. After they took away the ruins I ordered lemon trees and had them planted. They were already that big when we planted them, I specified.

You don't say, Gould replied. He was in a good mood. Now tell us about you. How many people went to your aunt's funeral?

Just Me.

Did you invite anyone? inquired Yasuko, who always asked perceptive questions.

No, I said. My aunt was the social 1. And she was already dead.

Aha, Gould said. How are you holding up, Karen?

I'm sitting down.

So you are, he smiled. So you are.

I got married, he informed Me and took off his baseball cap and something seemed odd to Me.

I married the head of my Shanghai office, you remember her, a tall, thin Chinese woman; you met last time you were in the China office.

I don't remember her, I said.

Sure you do, Gould went on. Tall, thin, black hair in a bun. Beautiful woman.

I don't remember her, I repeated.

That's impossible, Gould insisted. She took you to lunch, Karen.

Yasuko mediated:

Let's move forward.

Of course, yes, let's, concurred Gould, who went straight back to telling Me about the Chinese woman:

The thing is, she got pregnant, you see, and we got married. I bought a house near San Francisco, right on the beach, and now I work from home. Every day I run on the beach and I set up a gym in the house. I've got to get in shape if I want to raise this unexpected kid. I mean, I need to live at least another 25 years.

Until you're 104? I asked, adding 25 to his current age.

Why not? Gould asked. My mother is 96 and lucid as they come, still making plans.

Then I realized what seemed odd about Gould.

There's hair on your head.

He laughed:

Daily sex, I tell you. Made my hair start growing again.

It did? I asked.

No. I got surgical implants.

He said it and far out at sea all at once 3 dolphins leaped high into the air.

What was that? Yasuko asked.

3 dolphins, I said. I enlarged their paradise by 100 metres and let dolphins in, too.

So when do we start construction on the fishery? Gould wanted to know.

Someone with a bit more diplomacy would have phrased it differently, but my neurological connections don't work like that so I said:

Never.

Gould put on a Worried Face ☺. Yasuko, a Surprised Face ☺. I didn't put on any particular face but I explained:

In my whole life, I've had 1 original idea, I began. An idea that took 13 years to conceive. And in fact I didn't even think it all in my head but in collaboration with others. I'll enumerate the phases as they occurred to us.

I love how ordered your mind is, Gould said. Carry on.

I did:

1. 13 years ago I thought about catching tuna with no violence and no freezing. A humane yellowfin tuna catch.

2. 11 years ago Gould turned up at my house in Mazatlán and changed several things about the idea. He changed the yellowfin tuna to bluefin, changed the Pacific Ocean where we fished to the Atlantic, and changed our market by conceiving of how to sell in Asia, Europe, Australia and America.

That's right, Gould intervened.

3. Then, 4 years ago, thanks to a suggestion from the tuna, it occurred to Me that we should build paradises for our tuna, to fatten them and flavor their meat.

4. 3 years ago, the tuna themselves collaborated by spawning in their paradises and fertilizing the eggs.

That's right, Gould said again. We must applaud the tuna for their cooperation.

I continued:

5. And this year ARM collaborated by destroying the industrial phase of the process.

Yasuko opened her mouth wide, and then asked:

ARM collaborated?

That's correct, I said.

Don't you say a word, Gould ordered her.

Then he asked Me amiably:

You say the terrorists cooperated with us ... how exactly?

By destroying the industrial phase of the slaughter, I repeated.

Gould rubbed his hands together, irritated, and said:

And you see that as collaboration?

Correct, I confirmed. Thanks to them, we're now enlarging the paradises at our 7 fisheries and allowing dolphins to enter, too. In Nogocor turtles have entered as well, which is a good idea because they eat jellyfish.

In the distance, out at sea, 4 tuna jumped out of the water near the coral island and then with a splash reentered the sea, as if they'd been listening to us talk about them.

Where are the fishing boats? Yasuko suddenly asked, her eyes scanning the empty sea.

They're no longer necessary, I said. I sent them to Mazatlán where some potential buyers are coming to look at them.

Gould turned his head to the right and began kneading his

neck in an attempt to relax. Then he looked into my eyes and I, naturally, looked away.

Karen, he said firmly. I don't understand what it is you're proposing.

What the sixth and final phase of my great idea is?

Exactly. So, what is it, Karen?

I responded:

To stop catching tuna.

Yasuko:

We're in the tuna industry.

I continued:

But it's no longer necessary to catch them. Each year the tuna population in our paradises is going to quadruple, and by my calculations every 2 years they'll increase in size by ⅓.

Aha, Gould said, I see. Yes, yes, I see. So the number and size of tuna in the paradises will increase, and therefore it won't be necessary to catch them anymore.

Correct, I nodded.

Aha, this is making more and more sense. So we're going to reach those numbers exactly as the tuna in the open sea are shrinking and going up in cost.

That's right, I said.

Gould kept making calculations:

Which means that whether all the tuna in the sea die in 2

years, as your crazy friends at ARM predict, or in 10 years, as ICCAT predicts, we'll still have the only live tuna preserve on the planet.

That's correct, I concurred.

He clapped happily.

Karen, darling, you're a genius. This will be worth a fortune. It already would at today's prices—180,000 euros for a 200-kilo tuna—but by the time they disappear completely from the open sea, ours will go for 10 or 20, even 30 times that.

Jesus Christ! he yelled, slapping his thigh with his open hand several times, his blue eyes glinting. Jesus Christ, Karen! We could be talking about 6 million euros for a 300-kilo tuna!

Oh, Karen, dear, he said softly, it'll be like having 300-kilo gold ingots in the bank, except our ingots will have fins.

He cackled, delighted.

Then he asked:

So then, when do we kill them?

Again, a diplomatic person would have found a more indirect way to respond than I did:

Never.

Aha, he said.

He took a cigar out of his shirt pocket. Then asked curiously:

And if there's no slaughter then where's the profit?

The profit, I said somewhat exasperated, lies in multiplying the number of tuna, and in increasing their weight. Isn't that obvious?

No. No, it's not obvious, Gould responded.

He bit his cigar, held a lighter to the tip, inhaled, and then exhaled a stream of vanilla-smelling smoke and insisted:

Let me ask the same question another way. Where is the operational surplus? The difference between investment and return? Am I speaking Aramaic here, Karen? Where's the fucking profit for True Blue Tuna?

Now he was exasperated, too.

I raised my voice:

There is no profit for True Blue Tuna, there's only profit for the actual tuna. For True Blue Tuna, in fact, there will be only costs, the cost of maintaining the paradises.

Yasuko covered her face with 1 hand.

Aha, Gould said. He shifted in his chair.

Aha, he repeated. He wrapped his arms around his body as if to protect himself from a blow I might give him.

What exactly is it that you don't understand? I demanded. It's a very simple idea.

No, Karen, he said, hugging himself tighter, it's not. It's an extraordinarily difficult idea to understand. In fact, just trying to understand it is making my head hurt. You're saying we're going to increase the number of tuna just to increase the number of tuna?

That is correct, I confirmed.

Then it's not possible, Gould responded.

Of course it's possible!

Gould raised his voice even more than I had:

No, Karen, it's not!!! True Blue Tuna is a profit-seeking enterprise. Its partners and employees work out of self-interest. Self-interest is what makes the world go round. As Darwin taught us 150 years ago, the species all move out of self-interest. They decide to fight or cooperate out of self-interest.

I have no God, he suddenly confessed out of nowhere.

And then he unhugged himself and, furious, hurled his cigar into the sea.

He continued:

My only gauge for whether what I do is good or bad is whether or not it works in my self-interest. So, Karen dear, I veto this plan, at least until we can manage to come up with a way for it to benefit you, Me and True Blue Tuna employees, and not just the tuna.

He took a deep breath to compose himself and added:

Now, that won't be difficult if you take into account the fact that we'll have a reserve full of gold with fins.

SABINA BERMAN

He smiled.

And I screamed:

That's enough, Gould!

Surprised, he asked softly:

What's enough, Gould?

And so I told him:

Here are the facts: you already have plenty of other businesses and you're going to die soon anyway, even if you do have new hair, and I'm going to die soon, too.

With that Gould lost his temper:

Don't you tell me when I'm going to die! And don't you tell me that my money is going to be used to pay for 7 massive tuna sanctuaries whether I like it or not! Read my lips, Karen!

I fixed my gaze on his lips, ready to read them. And this is what they said:

I reject your plan. That's my right as majority shareholder.

No, I contested him calmly, staring at the sky, which had clouded over. My aunt left Me her shares in her will. So in fact I'm the majority shareholder of True Blue Tuna.

A drop fell on my nose.

I glanced at Gould out of the corner of my eye. His beady blue eyes darted uneasily, scanning the tabletop over and over. Technically, it's called escape-seeking behavior.

A drop fell on the table.

Tell me something, he said, turning toward the sea, his little eyes still seeking escape. When did this fantastic little idea come to you?

After I buried my aunt Isabelle. After the fisheries were bombed, I went diving on the high sea. And when my head was half out of the water, phase 6 of my great idea came to Me.

So it just came to you, just like that?

No, actually it came very slowly; it took Me 3 days and 3 nights to finish formulating it.

Aha, Gould said.

And his beady eyes locked on mine. Technically, it's called a predatory expression.

I'm going to kill you, he whispered.

I jumped up and took 3 steps back.

I'll set an army of lawyers on you! Gould threatened, standing in turn. I'm sure there's a legal term for this kind of abuse!

From which I gathered that the death threat had been a metaphor and that Gould was still cloistered in his human bubble, so I sat back down in my chair and he sat back down in his chair and said:

And when my lawyers are finished with you, you won't

have a penny in the bank and you'll probably be in jail. But for now, let me just say this: you're an idiot.

I thought about it and replied:

That's correct.

But Gould was still full of rage.

Only an idiot would think of investing money in something that would benefit only the tuna.

Again I said:

Correct.

No, idiot, you're not listening to me. Listen to me, you idiot!

I put on my Listening Face ☺.

Before I signed the True Blue Tuna contract with your aunt Isabelle, she warned me. I want you to know, she said, that my niece is a very peculiar person: an idiot with flashes of genius. And just in case I didn't believe her, she showed me your psychological test results, which classify you somewhere between imbecile and idiot—with a few areas of superior intelligence. I don't know why I always doubted it, why I never really believed you were an idiot. Well, Karen, now I know for certain: you're a complete and total idiot and I must have a little idiot in me, too, for having believed that such an idiot wouldn't go and do something so profoundly idiotic.

Even an idiot like Me could see Gould was making an effort to hurt my feelings, and I said to him:

Do Me a favor, Gould. Don't use the word *idiot* again.

To which he replied:

Imbecile.

And 9 drops fell on us, 1 after the other.

I got up from my chair. Fearing the worst, Gould, too, got up from his chair and took 2 steps back, thus doing his part to ensure that the worst in fact did happen: I put my arm around his waist, heaved him over my shoulder, kicking, and carried him to the water at end of the walkway.

Don't do it, Karen! Yasuko shouted. He's 79!

And I dropped old man Gould into the water, its surface pointy with raindrops.

It rained all morning in Porto de Caeiro.

And all afternoon it rained. And all night. And it kept raining in the days and nights that followed.

You could hear the raindrops hitting the red-tile roofs of the houses and you could hear them hitting the leaves of the trees and the asphalt of the streets, and in the channels throughout town the rain went ploosh ploosh ploosh.

The rain climbed the steps of the cathedral in the main square and from my hotel room I watched it open the doors and enter the temple.

On day 3 of the torrential rain, it hailed.

The whole town echoed under a bombardment of hail. Dogs barked, frightened, behind closed doors and a man with an umbrella came out of his house across the street and the hail punctured it and he ran, terrified, back to his front door.

And after that it was just rain—heavy, dense rain blocking out the sky and the world and coming in through the roof. They brought Me pans and buckets to position all over the floor and the rain filled them and I had to empty them into the tub again and again and again.

The rain came up through the toilet, gurgling and brown.

Dogs paced, stir-crazy and dispirited, locked up indoors. In the second-floor window of the house across the street a man spent hours smoking, his palms pressed to the windowpane. Sometimes his wife came and pulled him away by the shoulder and he'd leave the window and then the 2 of them circled like hostile animals. Sometimes they slapped and kicked each other and sometimes they kicked their kids and their dog and I saw them open their mouths wide to shout—or at least that's what it looked like, because nothing could be heard except for the sound of rain.

I thought of Nunutsi, whose white fur stood on end right before lightning struck. I thought of my aunt, buried beneath the dry Mazatlán sun. I thought of the tuna in their paradise in Porto de Caeiro, safe in their refuge 2 ocean layers down, swimming in the green, watching the surface of the sea, pointy with raindrops for so long now.

Phone lines went down, the power went out.

In the hotel lobby, where the furniture was covered with thick plastic and you couldn't walk without tripping over pails and buckets, someone standing in candlelight said this was a result of climate change and therefore developed nations were to blame and someone else said from the darkness that no, it was the flood that had come and was the fault of humans, who had angered God with their bigamy and their alcoholism and because they don't love their children or their parents and it was time to build Noah's Ark, and I left them arguing over whether what lies at the center of all things in the Universe is man and only man, or if it's man and God, obsessed with what man does or does not do.

That night I had a memory or a terrible fantasy. Me, who almost never has fantasies or memories.

It was raining in some part of my memory, or my fantasy, and I was running down stairs like the ones in the house in Mazatlán and a horrible woman with matted black hair was chasing Me, a cigarette between her lips. I was a little girl, naked and filthy, and the woman was wearing a pink silk nightgown and smelled of sour perfume and she held it to my chest—the lit cigarette—and I screamed but the rain drowned out my cries and she threw Me against a glass windowpane and I fell 2 storeys down into the mud and a triangle of glass fell on top of Me and stuck into my back where my crooked scar is now, blood flowing from the gash and rain washing away the blood at the same time.

I opened the window and stuck my head out into the rain and then I didn't think anything, the rain left no room for the sound of any thought.

Then inside the house across the street I saw a boy in a T-shirt and shorts pretending to be his father. Smoking, his palms pressed to the window. Then he moved and I couldn't see him anymore and the front door opened and the boy in T-shirt and shorts came out into the rain with a little fishing pole.

Hello, autistic boy, I waved at him but he couldn't hear Me through the rain.

I called the pilot on my cell phone to tell him to prepare for an afternoon departure but he responded from San Francisco saying that Gould had ordered him to forget about Me and that the plane was no longer mine, so I took a taxi in the rain to the airport and got on the first plane that dared to take off in the rain.

As we flew through the lead-grey clouds, I made a few projections about my life as lightning flashed.

In 1 week I turn 42. By the time I finish overhauling the fisheries to turn them into paradises suitable for the tuna to give birth I'll be 45. Nieto women have brain hemorrhages at 67. So when the renovations are done I'll have 22 years left. And several million dollars in the bank. I can afford the upkeep of the paradises until I'm 66.

Then in January of that far-off year, I'll open the gates of each paradise and all the dolphins and tuna will swim out into the open sea, exhilarated at the immensity of their new home, and they'll promptly begin their journey: a migration route thousands of kilometres long that's been imprinted onto their DNA like a map.

Or not. Maybe their migration route isn't imprinted into their DNA. Maybe only the oldest tuna in the school will remember, those who are almost 30 years old, and the young tuna will huddle near the open gate in fear until the older ones take the lead and hesitantly swim forth, guiding them, trying to recognize signposts on the journey.

Or not. The route from the frozen North to the warm South may have been forgotten by even the oldest tuna, may not be imprinted anywhere at all, as is the case with the majority of events occurring on the planet Earth. In which case we'll have to escort the multitude of tuna in the hesitant tribe with 2 ships, accompanying them during their first year of newfound freedom. Defend them from the sharks and killer whales that might approach, if indeed there are any sharks and killer whales by that time. Scatter anchovies and shrimp in the sea on days they don't find any food. Travel beside them slowly when storms burst in the sky and rock the sea's surface for days and nights. And consult compasses and satellite information regularly to redirect them toward the warmth if they get off course.

In short, be patient with them, as if they were slow learners, that is, as if they were Me, while they're relearning to move quickly and confidently in the first year of their new freedom.

After that I don't know what their fate will be. I can't take charge of what happens after my death, I suppose.

As soon as I got to Mazatlán I began carrying out the wishes my aunt Isabelle had expressed in her will.

I took Gorda a cheque. She turned out to be living in the slums in a house with cement walls and a corrugated tin roof and 2 daughters, 8 grandkids and 10 tiger cats. They all came to meet Me outside the house on a little dirt patio bordered with cacti, their faces blank. I handed Gorda the cheque and waited for her to say thank you or something like it, but all she did was look at the cheque as if she'd never seen 1 before or couldn't make sense of it or something, so I started to walk off and then heard a commotion and when I turned around I saw she'd fainted into her family's arms.

I went to the old office to give Peña the deed to Consolation Tuna Ltd. I thought the damned idiot would have said thank you but what he said was:

I'll be right back, and he walked out of the office with the deed and slammed the door.

Through the dusty window I gazed out at the 4 parallel docks with 20 boats. 20 boats, the way it had been when I first saw it. After selling off 15 of them my aunt had reinvested her True Blue Tuna profits to get them back for her grandfather's fishery and now she was giving it all to her general manager.

Peña returned with his face all red and the deed in 1 hand and took a seat at his desk.

Again I waited for him to say thank you or something along those lines, but what he did was anxiously begin arranging 10 pencils on his desk, first separating them into groups of 5, then into groups of 3, this entire feverish graphite procedure being enacted as he explained to Me why it was that what my aunt Isabelle had left him was, in fact, an unworkable problem.

The U.S. embargo on Mexican tuna had finally been lifted, he told Me. Lobbyists were paid a fortune to get American congressmen to admit that the dolphins were no longer being killed in Mexican catches but what happened after that, nobody had predicted. Cans of Mexican tuna crossed the border and Clean Seas—predictably—once again refused to grant them the dolphin-safe label, standing by the old argument that even if the Mexican catch wasn't hurting dolphins, there were dolphins present and they were being traumatized for life, but the incomprehensible part was that owners of large supermarket chains chose the Clean Seas ruling over that of their own Congress and their shelves remained full of Chicken of the Sea and other brands of white tuna and our cans were accepted only by small supermarkets in areas with high concentrations of Mexican immigrants, who preferred them because they reminded them of home, and then the Mexican shopkeepers had to fend off attacks by eco-warriors.

Fend off attacks? I asked. I don't understand.

Heroically fend off attacks, Peña confirmed, inserting a fresh, unsharpened pencil into his very old, electric pencil sharpener. Gringo ecologists turn up at the supermarkets to steal all the cans of Mexican tuna and the shopkeepers have to chase them out with brooms. And that's why I cannot accept 2 of the clauses in the Consolation Tuna Ltd. cession.

1st unacceptable clause: why should Consolation Tuna pay to renovate the Mazatlán Museum of Natural Science?

With that, he finally removed what had been a brand-new pencil and was now ½ a pencil from the pencil sharpener and placed it into a jar full of very pointy ½ pencils with a self-satisfied look.

More moron every year, I thought, and replied:

To make it the Planet Earth Museum of Natural Science.

2nd unacceptable clause, he continued, ignoring Me: why should Consolation Tuna finance the soup kitchen for the destitute for the rest of time?

To which I responded:

Because if not then give Me back the deed.

I held out my hand and took the deed but Peña snatched it from Me and slipped it into 1 of his desk drawers, and then slammed it shut.

And that is why Mazatlán has a respectable museum of natural science and a free soup kitchen where every day approximately 1,200 bowls of tuna soup are served.

After that I deposited money into my aunt's lovers'

accounts. What Baldy did with his money I never knew, which is hardly surprising given that I knew nothing about him for all the years he, my aunt Isabelle and I lived together. The doctor sent Me an 8-page letter which I lost without having read. But I was interested in what the painter did with his money.

He bought the ruins of a cathedral in his hometown of Nopaltepec, in Veracruz, as well as the neighboring convent, both of which sit on the top of a hill. He emptied them of all the crucifixes, saints and confessionals and on the floor he planted a cactus garden and a rock garden populated by lizards, iguanas and chameleons. He disconnected the electricity and lined the roofs with solar panels to use energy from the sun, pulled the crosses off of the 3 cupolas, and in place of the crosses he put up Y-shaped turbines to turn the wind into electricity. He used 1 nun's cell as a bedroom and 1 nun's cell to store his canvases and the roof to paint, and the rest of the space is open to reptiles and people, who stroll around the botanical gardens as if it was theirs.

A Darwinist temple, I call it.

Some nights the solar panels and the turbines don't generate enough electricity and everything is dark and still and the only sound is the cicadas chirping. The painter wrote that to Me and also told Me his ingenious solution for surviving those long, dark nights.

Go to bed and sleep.

Around that time 4 men were arrested in London. All 4 swore they didn't know what ARM was and definitely didn't know what True Blue Tuna was, but in the apartment they were sharing Interpol found 3 kilos of dynamite and more than 100 hits on their computer to the Web site build-yourownbomb.com

Detective Iñaki Belloso wrote to Me requesting a drawing of each of the 4 men who had kidnapped Me in Paris. I sent him drawings of the 4 men, though I doubted they could be of any use, because the sunglasses the 4 men wore during the kidnapping covered ½ of their faces.

I was wrong. Interpol had also captured their sunglasses, which they found in their apartment. All 4 men were photographed wearing each of the 4 pairs of sunglasses. The photos were placed beside my drawings. 4 of the photographs were identical to my 4 drawings, Belloso wrote. So my drawings were taken as sufficient proof to send them to prison.

The 4 are now in jail awaiting trial, none have admitted their guilt or confessed the names of the accomplices who blew up my fisheries, and they've gone on a hunger strike, because they see eating the greasy chicken broth and sausages fed to the prisoners as a violation of their human rights and even more of a violation of the chickens' and pigs' rights, and in the meantime the ARM Web site is asking for donations to be sent to their account to cover the cost of having a group bring in vegetarian food for them every day.

I donated 2 British pounds.

And back in Porto de Caeiro, it was raining again.

I asked and they told Me that no, it wasn't the same rain as 10 days ago; that had cleared up and everyone had gone to the beach or sailing and then—now—the rain had returned.

So in my hotel room I began writing this book.

This book, typed to the rhythm of the rainfall.

When I finish, I'll spend my time on the bluefin tuna paradises and when I finish those, I'll have 22 years left to live but that doesn't trouble Me. Leaving the tuna alone in their paradises and letting them grow and multiply will be quite simple, basically just a matter of leaving them in peace, and what to do with the rest of my time, my body will decide.

In the same way birds sing at dawn from an excess of energy, in the same way a branch uses excess sap to form a stem and then a lemon, I, too, will have something to offer the planet Earth.

And, at some point, in the same way the ripe lemon becomes too heavy and falls from the branch to the ground, I will fall to the ground from a brain haemorrhage.

As I was writing this book I went through several possible titles.

1. *Me and the Tuna*, since we're the protagonists.

2. *Me and the Tuna and My Aunt*, since I'd like to invite my aunt into the title.

3. *I Am, Therefore (and with Difficulty) I Think*, which describes my condition and my advantage over standard humans.

4. *Me*.

5. And finally, *Me Who Dived*, a title that presents a few problems.

a. It sounds odd, I think. It's grammatically incorrect or something, I don't know.

b. It's not that relevant to what I've written up to this point and in fact refers specifically to 1 afternoon on the high sea when, with my head ½ out of the water, I finally thought up phase 6, the final phase of the only original idea I've ever had in my life, an experience that I decided not to recount out of modesty.

Nevertheless, it's still raining in Porto de Caeiro, so now I will write about that afternoon. And as far as the book title goes, I'll let some title expert, which I'm sure exists, make that decision.

21

The communiqué ARM had sent Me said:

Here is our reckoning: 12 animal killers will be killed so that humanity sees their crimes won't go unpunished: 3 vivisectionists, 3 "scientific" torturers, 3 large fur traders, and 3 engineers in murder.

Karen Nieto, it is your turn to die.

The truth is, I found ARM's plan convincing.

Convincing: capable of persuading someone to do something.

I thought: maybe this is the best thing I can do for the tuna and other large fish in the sea.

I knelt before the rectangle of white stones that was my aunt's grave and asked her what she thought. But she offered no opinion other than silence.

So I decided to comply with the sentence ARM had given Me. After all, now that my aunt was dead I could think of no reason to live.

Dressed in my wetsuit I climbed into the boat, turned on the motor, and headed for the horizon.

On the high sea, I heaved the orange tank onto my back, pulled on my mask, bit the mouthpiece, and checked my instruments: the depth timer, the alarm and the oxygen tank's pressure gauge.

I was about to set the alarm on the tank to alert Me when there were 5 minutes' worth of air left so I could reach the surface but then I remembered that the plan was to kill myself so I didn't set the alarm.

I sat on the edge of the boat and dropped backward into the water.

I descended through the 1st turquoise layer.

I kept going through the 2nd green layer.

And once in the deep blue layer I swam, looking for a flat rock.

As always, I deposited my head on the rock and waited for my body to slowly descend onto the sand. I inhaled deeply and exhaled deeply and silver effervescent bubbles enveloped my head as I left the realm of thought behind.

I was gone, merged with the sea, just another blue stone in the blue ocean.

Now comes the part I'm embarrassed to tell.

I was brought back by a sentence:

Death doesn't do any good.

I heard it like a tiny voice inside Me. A voice coming from my chest, not my head. A voice that soon fused with the sound of my heart beating.

I touched my chest and even though it was hidden inside my neoprene wetsuit, I felt it pounding arrhythmically. And that was how I realized 2 things at once.

1. I'd just decided not to die.

2. Technically, I was in the midst of a heart attack.

As if to confirm that this was the case, pain seared my chest and gripped my whole body. I sucked in through the mouthpiece but very little air came through: the tank was almost empty.

And again I heard myself think from my heart:

Shit, I need help. I have to call an ambulance. Or at least take 2 aspirin. But I'm at the bottom of the sea. Oh, shit.

With great difficulty I lifted my head from the flat stone and held it up and swam, sucking in tiny streams of air through the mouthpiece, but my body had no strength and would not rise off the ocean floor, and suddenly the strangest thing happened.

Floating slowly, a cloud of light moved toward Me. Or rather, a thing that was approximately 40 centimetres and radiated light.

The thing had a halo of light that grew larger and smaller around a calm, illuminated face.

An angel, I thought, and the pain left Me completely.

The sailors' angel that Ricardo told Me about, I thought again.

Oh fuck, I'm dead, I thought.

And, slowly, the angel held out 1 of its luminous extremities to Me.

And I held up my left arm and with 2 fingers I touched the tip of the hand of the luminous angel, who encircled my 2 fingers and then my whole hand and then suddenly an electrical current surged through Me.

Then everything became light.

The angel of light lifted Me effortlessly through the deep blue layer and through the sky blue layer and kept lifting Me through a tunnel of light to the green layer.

Then my heart began pounding again, out of rhythm again, and the pain took hold of Me again and I thought:

Lack of oxygen causes hallucination. When people are asphyxiating, what they see are hallucinations. Even the tuna, out of water and before the air gun kills them, open their mouths and move their blinded eyes because they're hallucinating. Which means that I'm asphyxiating and this is a hallucination.

And realizing this, little by little, everything went back to its proper place.

No, it wasn't a tunnel I was traveling through, guided by the little angel's hand; it was a column of bright light piercing the water through which I ascended. And no, it wasn't an angel that led Me to the surface of the sea; it was a jellyfish with a pulsating head—luminous and possibly poisonous— that had resuscitated Me with an electric shock. And in no way had it led Me; if anything it was fleeing from Me as best it could and I swam after it.

I let the poor jellyfish go and, once freed, it darted into the deep in 1 go, and with the last of my strength I kicked and my head came up through the water's surface.

I spat out the mouthpiece, yanked off the mask, and what I saw then must be the biggest miracle anyone has ever seen.

360 degrees of turquoise blue sea, white clouds breaking leisurely in the sky above and leaving more room for the

sun, that ball of fire from which came not a tunnel but a cone of light that painted the sea around Me a golden color.

Miracle: something that exists without cause.

What's odd, I thought, is that Me of all people should think of something supernatural, an angel.

I inhaled.

What's odd, I thought, is that anyone should need to imagine an angel or anything else supernatural, when everywhere reality itself is overflowing.

When each and every thing is where it is, and each and every thing is what it seems to be.

The sea, I thought, is the sea. The sun is the sun. And I am Me.

And there's nothing more to add.

That's the miracle and there's nothing more to add.

I am Me, but what's new is that I am thinking from my heart. Not from my head. And for the first time I'm thinking from my heart without blocking out reality and without reality blocking out Me.

Or rather, reality is thinking through Me.

And what it's thinking doesn't separate Me from reality.

Feeling myself speak from my heart muscle, I said:

Meeeee.

The trick, reality thought again through Me, seems to be not to kill.

Not to kill reality nor to let reality kill Me.

I thought:

Could I exist like this?

Exist. Me, in with everything else.

This is the trick, reality thought through my heart in the center of the 360 degrees of sea and sun:

Not to kill.

I saw my boat, a little red dot on the horizon, and felt the poison from the jellyfish start to sting inside my wetsuit.

On the shore, in the white mansion in Mazatlán, in my bedroom with light blue walls, hanging in my harness, 1 metre above the bed, naked, with welts from my scalp to the bottoms of my feet, I spent 3 days and 3 nights sweating out the damn poison from that angelic jellyfish.

Here is the instruction manual I created:

1. Always be centred in my chest.

2. Listen, there, to the way the real world thinks in Me.

3. When the real world lets go of Me and I let go of the real world, grab it back. Grab onto it with every sense. Which means, grab hold of whatever is close with both hands—the

chains on my harness, for example. Smell carefully and listen carefully to whatever is nearby. For example, the sea through my window. And watch the real world patiently. For example, the sea, sky, horizon, or whatever is there. Which means, plug back in to the real world with every sense.

1 morning I awoke welt-free and ravenous. I took the safety catch off of the pulley and fell onto the mattress with a thud, climbed down from the bed, and put on my clothes.

I put my change of T-shirt and white jeans, my clippers, razor, cell phone, toothbrush and computer—that is, the indispensables—into my briefcase and went to the hospital.

The emergency room doctor handed 2 black-and-white photos of my heart across the desk.

Compare them, he said. 1 is from 10 years ago, the other from today.

As you can see, he continued, you have an enlarged right atrium. It must be, as you said, that you had an acute myocardial infarction, a heart attack brought on by extreme stress that obstructed the superior vena cava. Your right atrium bulged out severely and, luckily, managed to unblock the superior vena cava so blood flow to the auricle was reestablished, but the effort, as I say, has left you with an enlarged heart.

The doctor was a man with a round, puffy face and round glasses. I said to him:

It wasn't luck. It was the electric shock from the jellyfish.

First his face turned red and then it turned into an Angry Face ☻. He snatched the 2 photos of my heart from my fingers and stood up. Then he gave Me an order.

Follow Me. We're going to carry out a few strength and stamina tests to see what kind of physical shape you're in and then we'll make a diagnosis.

We walked out of the office and into a long, white hallway down which the doctor strode purposefully while I, being careful not to make any noise, turned around on the rubber soles of my yellow boots and walked to the elevator, which took Me down to the hospital's ground floor.

I am my physical shape. Why would I need a test to ascertain my physical shape?

I was fine, with an enlarged heart behind my rib cage, that's all.

At the airport cafeteria I had 8 plain yogurts with honey for breakfast. And there, spoonful after spoonful, with my right atrium enlarged, the plan hatched itself within Me, the plan I would offer my partner Gould and trusted that he would like very much.

And that was how the great idea that took all of my adult life to conceive was finally finished.

*

It's stopped raining in Porto de Caeiro.

The morning sun is the yellowiest sun ever to be seen and shines brightly on the layer of water still covering the streets. Humans come out of their houses to engage in the activity they find most essential: speaking to each other, which they do very loudly while hugging or shaking hands or patting each other on the back, as if they wanted to make sure nobody had disappeared during the days and nights of the flood.

Children splash through the water in the streets, splash, splash, splash, with backpacks on their backs, splash, splash, splash, and there among them goes the autist with his fishing rod over his shoulder, splash, splash, splash, and the black swallows swoop down off of the red tile roofs to the square where they compete with the pigeons pecking for grain, insects, whatever they can, frenzied in their hunger because they haven't eaten properly throughout all the days and nights of rain.

The first boats move through the channel, headed for the market, and beneath the water's surface the first red carp swim in the opposite direction, headed for the sea's entrance.

Off in the distance, the sea is a silver streak, in the turquoise layer, in the True Blue Tuna paradise, the tuna are having yellow bonitos for breakfast, and a red bird with black wings comes to perch on my windowsill.

And cheeps.

Cheep, cheep, cheep, cheeps.

And now I'm done with the book.

If you'll excuse Me, I'm going to go get a glass of water.